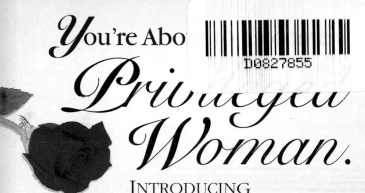

You're Abo...

Privileged Woman.

INTRODUCING
PAGES & PRIVILEGES™.

It's our way of thanking you for buying
our books at your favorite retail store.

GET ALL THIS FREE
WITH JUST ONE PROOF OF PURCHASE:

◆ **Hotel Discounts** up
to 60% at home and
abroad ◆ **Travel Service**
- Guaranteed lowest
published airfares
plus 5% cash back

$50 VALUE

on tickets ◆ **$25 Travel Voucher**
◆ **Sensuous Petite Parfumerie** collection

◆ **Insider Tips Letter**
with sneak previews
of upcoming books

*You'll get a FREE personal card, too.
It's your passport to all these benefits– and to
even more great gifts & benefits to come!*

There's no club to join. No purchase commitment. No obligation.

Enrollment Form

☐ *Yes!* I WANT TO BE A *Privileged Woman.*

Enclosed is one *PAGES & PRIVILEGES™* Proof of Purchase from any Harlequin or Silhouette book currently for sale in stores (Proofs of Purchase are found on the back pages of books) and the store cash register receipt. Please enroll me in *PAGES & PRIVILEGES™*. Send my Welcome Kit and FREE Gifts -- and activate my FREE benefits -- immediately.

More great gifts and benefits to come like these luxurious Truly Lace and L'Effleur gift baskets.

NAME (please print)

ADDRESS   APT. NO

CITY   STATE   ZIP/POSTAL CODE

PROOF OF PURCHASE
SAMPLE ONLY

Please allow 6-8 weeks for delivery. Quantities are limited. We reserve the right to substitute items. Enroll before October 31, 1995 and receive one full year of benefits.

NO CLUB!
NO COMMITMENT!
Just one purchase brings you great Free Gifts and Benefits!
(More details in back of this book.)

Name of store where this book was purchased_____

Date of purchase_____

Type of store:

☐ Bookstore   ☐ Supermarket   ☐ Drugstore

☐ Dept. or discount store (e.g. K-Mart or Walmart)

☐ Other (specify)_____

Which Harlequin or Silhouette series do you usually read?

_____

Complete and mail with one Proof of Purchase and store receipt to:

U.S.: *PAGES & PRIVILEGES™*, P.O. Box 1960, Danbury, CT 06813-1960

Canada: *PAGES & PRIVILEGES™*, 49-6A The Donway West, P.O. 813, North York, ON M3C 2E8   **PRINTED IN U.S.A**

"Don't tease me,"

Elizabeth warned Steve. "Or I'll leave you out here in the cold, without a kiss."

Fat chance, twittered her libido. Elizabeth craved that kiss. Wanted it more than anything in the world.

But, on again, off again, desire warred with parental anxiety.

On again. She'd wanted Steve's kiss—badly— every day after school, as they met to collect their unrepentant teenage feuders. Wanted it at Saturday detention, as they waited for their unreconstructed rebels to be released. She'd waited a long time for that kiss. And she intended to have it. Right now.

Off again. But what if this kiss she wanted so much drove her to throw all caution—and both their kids—to the winds?

On again. Off again.

Promised ecstasy. Certain agony.

Dear Reader,

Special Edition's lineup for the month of July is sure to set off some fireworks in your heart! Romance always seems that much more wonderful and exciting in the hot days of summer, and our six books for July are sure to prove that! We begin with bestselling author Gina Ferris Wilkins and *A Match for Celia.* July's THAT SPECIAL WOMAN! goes looking for summertime romance and gets more than she bargained for in book two of Gina's series, THE FAMILY WAY.

Continuing the new trilogy MAN, WOMAN AND CHILD this month is Robin Elliott's *Mother at Heart.* Raising her sister's son as her own had been a joy for this single mother, but her little family seems threatened when the boy's real father surfaces... until she finds herself undeniably drawn to the man. Be sure to look for the third book in the series next month, *Nobody's Child,* by Pat Warren.

Father in Training by Susan Mallery brings you another irresistible hunk who can only be one of those HOMETOWN HEARTBREAKERS. Also continuing in July is Victoria Pade's A RANCHING FAMILY series. Meet Jackson Heller, of the ranching Heller clan, in *Cowboy's Kiss.* A man who's lost his memory needs tenderness and love to find his way in Kate Freiman's *Here To Stay.* And rounding out the month is a sexy and lighthearted story by Jane Gentry. In *No Kids or Dogs Allowed,* falling in love is easy for a single mom and divorced dad—until they find out their feuding daughters may just put a snag in their upcoming wedding plans!

A whole summer of love and romance has just begun from **Special Edition!** I hope you enjoy each and every story to come!

Sincerely,

Tara Gavin
Senior Editor

Please address questions and book requests to:
Silhouette Reader Service
U.S.: 3010 Walden Ave., P.O. Box 1325, Buffalo, NY 14269
Canadian: P.O. Box 609, Fort Erie, Ont. L2A 5X3

JANE GENTRY

NO KIDS OR DOGS ALLOWED

Published by Silhouette Books
America's Publisher of Contemporary Romance

To all the Airedales we have loved:
witty Snooker and goofy Daniel, darling Maggie I and
clever Patrick, charming Dillinger the Thief and our rescued
Maggie II, the best and sweetest of them all.
Almost all breeds have rescue committees for purebred dogs who
need new homes. Call the American Kennel Club headquarters in
New York City and ask for adoption and rescue information.

 SILHOUETTE BOOKS

ISBN 0-373-09972-X

NO KIDS OR DOGS ALLOWED

Copyright © 1995 by Jane Malcolm

Printed in U.S.A.

Books by Jane Gentry

Silhouette Special Edition

No Kids or Dogs Allowed #972

Silhouette Desire

Lightning Strikes Twice #400
A Taste of Honey #449

JANE GENTRY

is married to a corporate gypsy. She has lived in twenty-two different cities, which she uses as settings for her writing. She is fascinated by the cadences of voices, the differences in regional accents and dialects, and the changes in climate and opinion, terrain and history, from place to place. At present, she lives in Scottsdale, Arizona, where she and her husband are managed by their Airedale, Patrick, a chair tester, food taster and general bon vivant.

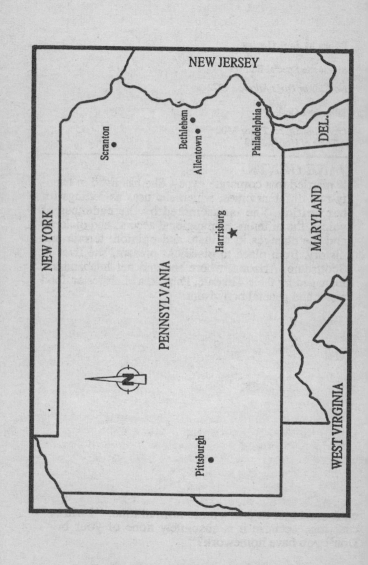

Chapter One

Elizabeth Fairchild gave her daughter an exasperated look and tried to remain calm.

"It is too damned hot for this," she said.

It was the first of October, and Philadelphia sweltered in unaccustomed heat. Elizabeth twisted her heavy black hair into a bun and skewered it with a pencil. Damp tendrils escaped and tickled her nape. City traffic rumbled outside, and her daughter, Cara, rumbled inside, and that was the trouble with being a CPA with an office at home: there were no secretarial buffers to shield you from the intrusions of the real world.

She bent her head over her papers, hoping to discourage Cara's attention. "I am trying to work, Cara. Go away."

"You always have a reason not to discuss it," said Cara, who was thirteen and knew everything. "Why won't you admit it? You need a man."

"I do not need . . ." began Elizabeth, and heard her voice scaling up toward the E above high C. Then she stopped and regrouped and said in a more normal tone, "I will not discuss this, because it is absolutely none of your business. Don't you have homework?"

"You don't even date," said Cara, perching on the edge of Elizabeth's desk. "It's not normal."

"Go away, Cara."

"Well, you need sex," said Cara. "Everybody does."

Oh, God! thought Elizabeth frantically. *How would she know about that?* Then she stifled her panic. Cara attended the Harkness School for Girls in Philadelphia. The only boys she saw were in strictly supervised environments, unseductively clad in flannel slacks and school ties and sedate, blue wool blazers. There was no cause for hysteria. Yet.

Cara continued relentlessly. "Vonnie Chrysler's mother said so."

"Vonnie Chrysler's mother has been married five times," said Elizabeth, "which I think indicates a nearly fatal capacity for self-delusion." She tried to close the subject by turning back to her work.

Cara thought about this. "You talk funny sometimes." Then she begged, "Won't you even *look* at him?" She was pleading on behalf of her history teacher, over whom her entire class was swooning.

"Certainly not," said Elizabeth. "Really, Cara. *Look* at him? You make poor Mr. Salvini sound as if he's in a shop window, up for sale." She recalled last year's history teacher. Cara had been enamored of him, too. She was too young to realize that interesting men were very rare. Last year's teacher had hair like James Dean—Elizabeth remembered wondering if it had been artfully arranged not to look artfully arranged. No real human male had hair like that.

"You have to at least talk to him," Cara said. "I told him we had swords and letters and stuff from the Civil War, and we could show them in class. Is that okay?"

Surely Cara's attention was diverted by this new topic. Elizabeth relaxed a little. "Sure," she said, determined to keep the wind blowing in this direction. "We'll get them out after dinner."

"And after you just *talk* to him, you could maybe go out," said Cara earnestly. "Dad wouldn't care if you just *dated* somebody. I mean he does sometimes."

"What I do, except with respect to you, is none of your father's business anymore," said Elizabeth. "Just as what he does isn't any of my concern. We've been divorced a long time, Cara."

"That's what I mean," said Cara earnestly. "I mean, even if you and Dad did decide to get back together, he wouldn't care if you went out with Mr. Salvini."

"We are not ever getting back together, darling. What gave you that idea?"

"I know you're not. You told me. That's why I want you to just *talk* to Mr. Salvini. Okay?"

Cara continued her impassioned appeal until the phone rang. Elizabeth sighed and lifted the receiver to her ear.

The caller was Miss Edwarda Westcott, headmistress of the Harkness School.

Cara quietly and rapidly disappeared.

A few minutes later Elizabeth, much annoyed, concluded her conversation with Miss Westcott. Miss Westcott had done all the talking and had requested, in a voice which brooked no refusal, a conference at 8:00 a.m.

Elizabeth went to the head of the stairs to summon the transgressor.

"Cara!"

No answer.

"Cara!"

Still no answer.

She went downstairs and out into the yard. Cara was industriously weeding a flower bed.

"Cara," said Elizabeth. "Who is Melody Riker, and why is Miss Westcott calling me about her?"

"She's this stupid girl at school," said Cara sullenly. "I hate her."

"I understand she's new this year. It's only October. How could you learn to hate her in four short weeks?"

"She's a total dweeb," said Cara. She leaned on the trowel and looked glum.

"Why's she a dweeb?" asked Elizabeth patiently.

"She feels like she's just going to die if she doesn't answer every single question in class, all day," Cara said, insulted by the mere idea. "It's so gross. All the teachers just lo-o-ve her. She thinks she's so cool, and she's not."

"What are you doing that would make Miss Westcott want me to have a conference with her parents?"

"Nothing." Cara saw the look on Elizabeth's face and said it again, earnestly. "Nothing. Honest, Mom. I don't even talk to her."

Cara, unsettled by her mother's suspicious scrutiny, scooted on her bottom until she was hidden by some shrubs and began to chop at a new set of weeds.

Elizabeth returned to her desk and reached for the school directory. Riker. Riker. The name sounded familiar. Maybe they'd been introduced at the first PTO meeting. She shook her head. She couldn't put any faces to the name.

Well, they were new, after all, and she could hardly be expected to remember everybody. She thumbed through the pages to the *R*s and found the Riker entry. Melody's father had a local address. Her mother had a different name and lived in New York.

Elizabeth slapped the book onto the desk and stared at it thoughtfully for a few seconds. She'd only have to deal with the father; at least she wouldn't be outnumbered. She leaned back in her desk chair and gazed out her open window at the maples in the front yard. They were beautifully red and gold—except for the two sturdy saplings that had sprung up of their own accord a few years ago. Those were still green. Obviously adolescent, thought Elizabeth, since they were deliberately stubborn and out of step. How in the world, she wondered, could Cara possibly be...

...How in the world could Melody possibly be in trouble for fighting? Steve wondered, astonished by Miss Westcott's call. Not that he hadn't done enough fighting in his own youth, at that Dickensian boarding school he'd attended while his parents were living it up at the embassy in Riyadh. But Melody, who got teary-eyed at the idea of a mousetrap and thought Disney's *Peter Pan* was violent?

She wasn't available for interrogation. She was across the street at her friend Caroline's, squealing about whatever it is thirteen-year-old girls squeal about.

Which, he considered, picking up a stack of unread mail, was everything.

Another day in the life of a single father. Melody was turning him gray. It wouldn't be long until there wasn't a single strand of blond left in his thick hair, if all of her adolescence was as stressful as the beginning.

He propped his feet on his kitchen table and shuffled through the mail. There was the daily letter to Melody from her mother, which augmented the daily phone call at bedtime. Marian might be a long-distance mother, but she made every effort to be involved in Melody's life. Steve wondered what Marian knew about Cara Fairchild—Melody told Marian nearly everything. He tucked the envelope behind the others.

Next up, A Chance to Win Ten Million Dollars! He'd had about one a week of those in the last year, thanks to magazines he'd bought from Melody's Scout troop. Hadn't won ten million yet. A package from his publisher, containing fan mail; letter from his agent, asking if he wanted to be the keynote speaker at a science fiction convention; a letter from the IRS. Damn it, they kept sending the same letter over and over and over and he was tired of responding to it.

He tossed it into the trash, along with the chance to win ten million, and went to his office to work on the book he was writing, last of a series of five. The book was due in three weeks, and he was behind schedule. And thanks to Melody, tomorrow morning would be lost to labor, since he had to spend a long unpleasant stretch of time consulting with the Fairchild kid's parents.

In addition to his more important concerns, in two hours he had to come up with something for dinner. Melody was tired of pizza, Chinese, Tex-Mex and fast-food hamburgers. And to tell the truth, so was he; they'd been ordering out nearly every night for a month. For a man who'd lived alone for much of his life, he was unreasonably inept in the kitchen. Maybe he'd buy a cookbook and a couple of decent pots and pans. He'd never much liked to cook, but he liked to eat. And so did Melody. Definitely time to learn something about that alien technology looming menacingly from the wall labeled Oven.

Spaghetti. He could cook spaghetti with reasonable Oscar Madison-like facility. After he looked up the Fairchild entry in the school directory, he'd to go to the store. He stuffed the mail he hadn't thrown away into one of his many junk drawers and made a list: spaghetti, sauce, hamburger. And as an afterthought: wine, ice cream and get a check cashed so Melody would have lunch money. He hoped, with a niggling feeling of guilt, that the Harkness kitchen cooked better than he did.

Oh, well. She seemed to be growing nicely on what he'd been feeding her. Unless her present unpleasant change of personality was due to some kind of malnutrition.

Miss Westcott had been headmistress of the Harkness School for twenty-five years. She looked deceptively pliable, with her matronly figure and her curly gray hair, because she had the self-confidence of a neurosurgeon and the command presence of Julius Caesar. Her laser glare had been known to reduce senators, combat generals and captains of industry to mumbling incoherence in twenty seconds flat.

Elizabeth had passed under the stern Westcott jurisdiction, herself. Consequently, she hesitated outside the closed office door for a few seconds, stifling a feeling of schoolgirl panic.

No conversation came from behind the old oak door. Great. Melody's father hadn't yet answered the summons, and Elizabeth would have to face the dragon alone.

She tapped on a dark wood panel, opened the door and stepped inside.

A tall man stood as she entered. Steel gray eyes met her green ones and locked there for a short, electric second. Then his lids narrowed and his thick blond brows lifted slightly to acknowledge an instant, undeniable and mutual attraction.

Now there, she thought, *is an interesting man.* He had a long, straight Yankee nose and a long, straight flexible mouth and a long, lean tan face which made his hair seem even blonder than it really was. His hair did not look artfully arranged. It looked as if he had toweled it dry, combed it into place and commanded it to stay put.

Her back was turned for an instant as she moved past him to an empty chair. She felt a delicious prickling at the back of her neck: he was indulging in the kind of frank male inspection which had indicated aroused interest since Adam had first caught sight of Eve.

Elizabeth tossed her head like a flirtatious girl and sent a froth of black curls skimming across her shoulders. It was an automatic reaction to his attention, as unplanned as blinking. She was astonished at herself. With an effort she collected her wits, sat down in one of the burgundy leather wing chairs that faced Miss Westcott's desk and turned to speak to him.

"You must be Steve Riker," she said.

"And you're Elizabeth." He smiled and stepped forward and took her hand.

Afterward Steve could hardly recall the ritual politeness or the smile. But he remembered, with uncanny clarity, the sight of her, the sound of her husky voice, the small soft hand which was so warm in his own. The slight enchanting apricot flush, which heated her cheeks as he touched her, freed an essence of autumn air and sweet, late-summer flowers. She wore a dress the color of a Southern sea, which reflected luminously in her dark-lashed green eyes.

And no wedding ring.

God bless Melody, he thought, *for being an intractable adolescent twit.* He returned the hand to its bemused owner and said, "I understand we have a problem."

"I *am* sorry about that," said Elizabeth, looking into the penetrating gray eyes and liking what she saw. Liked the entire package, basically. Liked the eyes and lean brown face and the long legs. Liked the tweed jacket and the broad shoulders in it and—yum—liked the unseductive, straightforward, no-nonsense smell of the after-shave which she caught as he leaned forward to take her hand. Well, she mustn't act hypnotized.

"I gather that Melody has given your daughter quite a bit of trouble," said Steve.

"Miss W̶e̶s̶t̶c̶o̶t̶t̶ told me it was the other way around," Elizabeth said. "As a matter of fact, I got the idea that their little feud was upsetting the entire school."

The door behind them swung open and Miss Westcott came in, breathing fire.

"As a matter of fact," she said, "it is. And something has to be done about it. They have somehow managed between them to force every child in the Lower School into one faction or the other. I had two eight-year-olds fistfighting on the lacrosse field yesterday. Fistfighting. At my school."

Elizabeth took a deep breath and moved nervously in the big, uncomfortable chair. "But Cara told me that she and Melody don't even speak to each other."

"They don't," said Miss Westcott grimly. "But everybody else does, with insults and catcalls too various to relate. I have assigned so many detentions that the Lower School is beginning to resemble a juvenile incarceration facility."

"Has the school counselor talked to them?" asked Elizabeth tentatively.

"Yes," stated Miss Westcott, "and I commend her efforts. The girls merely reiterate that they don't like each other and give vague, specious, undeterminable reasons for their rancor. Why they do not like each other is not at issue. This is a matter of plain bad manners, which we, as of this minute, will refuse to tolerate."

She leaned forward and punctuated her words by tapping on the desk with a cut-glass paperweight, which she held in her hand.

"As of today they will be assigned together in everything. In the dining room, in the classroom, on the playing fields and in the chapel. Every sport, every project, every social occasion. They will succeed together or they will fail together. For every unkind word that is uttered or uncivil act that is committed on the behalf of either girl, by any party whatsoever, Melody and Cara will receive a detention. I am going to do away with this idiocy before it infects the Upper School, too."

Steve cleared his throat. "Uh. I can see the justice in trying to force them to bridge a chasm that they've created, but what if it doesn't work?"

Miss Westcott speared him with an icy, slivered glare. "It simply does not matter what they think of each other. What matters is that each girl learns to exhibit common courtesy and intelligent self-control upon every occasion. It is our job to enforce good manners, and we intend to offer every opportunity for them to be displayed. It is your job to teach good manners, and how you do it is your own affair."

She stood. "It is Tuesday. Next Tuesday is Parents' Night. We will discuss our progress then. The girls will be waiting for you on the Upper School steps this afternoon after their detention. You may pick them up there."

She set the paperweight down with a thump and left the room.

There was a turgid silence. Finally Steve said, "I haven't had an interview like that since I was in the Army and two of my men got drunk and tore up a whorehouse."

Elizabeth shook her head slowly. "I simply can't imagine Cara with the kind of personal magnetism that would mobilize half the school."

"Or Melody, either." Steve gathered his long legs underneath him and stood. "Why don't we go get some coffee and discuss our mutual confusion?"

She tilted her head to smile into his eyes and took his breath away. Her polished ebony hair curled enticingly around her face; her emerald silk dress clung discreetly to her alluring curves. Milk white pearls nestled against the shadowed hollow of her throat—a hollow just made for the touch of a man's lips, for the slight gentle flicking of his tongue.

He didn't particularly want the coffee. What he really wanted was a long, slow, deep, soul-stirring kiss. And after that he wanted—suddenly he felt short of oxygen. What he wanted didn't bear thinking about. Not in this light and on this occasion. With an effort he forced his wayward libido to behave itself and realized she'd been speaking.

"I'm sorry," he said. "What did you say?"

"Coffee," she told him. "There's coffee here. Do you want some?"

Steve looked across the big room and saw a mahogany sideboard bearing a plate of cookies and a silver coffee service. Crystal lamps burned softly on each end, and cups and saucers gleamed politely in the buttery glow.

"Huh," he said. He surveyed the dark, polished wood and oriental carpet and imagined the subdued click of the bone china cups against their saucers. There was the distinct odor of "old money." It made him want to sneeze.

"I'd be more relaxed sitting at the foot of the papal throne," he said, opening the door to the hall. "Wouldn't you like to go somewhere else?"

She didn't commit herself until they were standing on the wide stone porch that overlooked the green playing fields and the long, tree-lined avenue to the front gate.

"I really can't," she told him, with real regret. "I'm supposed to meet a client in five minutes." She went down the broad steps to her car. "See you later," she said over her shoulder. And smiled. An enchanting, bewitching, captivating smile, rising from the tender soft lips to shine in her eyes.

Her curls shimmered blue-black in the sun, and the emerald silk danced and swirled and floated joyously on the light warm breeze. The entire world seemed made for her beauty—the dark, cushioned grass and the high, clean sky and the great, shaggy trees with their red and gold leaves glowing like jewels in the sun.

For the third time in less than one hour, Steve found it hard to breathe.

The girls were waiting, as announced, on the Upper School steps. Cara sulked at the top, leaning against a potted tree. Melody scowled at the bottom, on the ground beside the granite banister, her face hidden in the shadow of the wall. They were silently raging and unrepentant. Every inch of each small form spoke of impassioned civil disobedience. Thoreau would have been proud to call them sister.

As soon as Cara saw her mother, she bolted down the stairs, hurled herself into the car and slammed the door.

"Let's go," she said.

"I have to wait for Melody's father," Elizabeth told her. "It's getting dark and cold. We can't just leave her standing out here alone."

"I don't see why not," said Cara heartlessly. She folded her arms and glared at her feet. "Who would want to kidnap *her?*"

Elizabeth sighed and opened her door. Steve had pulled to a stop behind her and was walking toward her car.

"Where are you going?" demanded Cara, as alert as a young wolf.

"It is polite," said Elizabeth, as she stood. "To say hello."

God help me, she thought, as he approached. He looked better to her than he had that morning, and the mere memory of the morning made her heart race. He wore a battered, old, brown leather flight jacket against the chilly evening breeze, and his sandy blond hair was tousled by the wind. His eyes crinkled around the corners as he greeted her, and his attention was on her alone, despite the hostile scrutiny of their offspring.

He moved so that he sheltered her from the worst of the wind. "How'd it go?" he asked.

His long, shadowed form swayed toward her with his words. She longed to put her hand to the soft leather and draw the zipper down. To slide it under the denim shirt and feel the warmth of his bare skin against her palm. She threaded her nervous fingers together to keep from touching him.

"I haven't seen any miracles," she said.

"A miracle sometimes takes a little preparation." He stuck his hands deep into his pockets and gave her a look that was mostly pure masculine speculation. His lips tightened and his eyes narrowed. "We'll give it a week, and then see if we can help it along a little."

His swift glance over her body paused for an instant on her breasts, which seemed to Elizabeth to swell burstingly against the silk of her dress. For the first time in years she felt a hot savage turgidity between her thighs. Not the usual amorphous dissatisfaction of deprivation, but the specific, focused, covetous hunger of her woman's body for one specific man.

Perhaps that was miracle enough itself.

Grateful for the lowering dusk, she folded her light coat around herself and got into her car.

"Perhaps we will," she said. And she didn't know whether she meant to bring together their feuding daughters or their own desiring flesh.

A detention every day and one on Saturday. Elizabeth knew that God had rested, but she wasn't sure Miss Westcott did; Sunday was a welcome respite. From Cara's attitude, Elizabeth felt certain that she was in for an endless winter of hauling herself out of a warm bed before dawn every single Saturday. John Milton would have loved it, or Dante.

Cara's opinion, which offered Elizabeth no hope for relief, was that as everything was Melody's fault, Melody should get twice the detentions, and Cara shouldn't get any. Every conversation they had turned inevitably either to Robert or to Mr. Salvini.

"I told Dad about Mr. Salvini," said Cara on Monday night, while she and Elizabeth washed the dinner dishes. "I said maybe you'd talk to my class about the Civil War, and he said you knew all about it."

"About what?"

"Civil War," said Cara, not understanding Robert's caustic imputation.

Maybe I shouldn't have divorced him, Elizabeth thought. *Maybe I just should have put out a contract on him.* Cara saw Robert twice a year when he had business in Philadelphia, and he always agreed to whatever she wanted whenever he talked to her on the phone. He said yes to everything—and left Elizabeth to clean up the mess. It was terribly unfair to Cara and so like Robert to cause that trouble.

"So could we get the Civil War stuff out?"

Elizabeth obligingly went up the back stairs to the cedar chest in the guest room. The pictures and letters were in a box at the bottom, the sword wrapped in an old army blan-

ket against the back edge. Cara sat cross-legged on the bed
and took the lid off the box. She picked up the document on
top and puzzled over it.

"'My dear wife,'" she read. "'Rec'd.' *R-e-c-d?* What's
that?"

"Abbreviation for *received*," said Elizabeth.

"Oh," Cara said, and continued reading:

"Received the package you sent in July. It was most
timely, though it has been a-wandering these many
months. The woolen stockings and the blanket are most
needed now, with such terrible wind and rain as we have
had. We are cold all the time. But the most welcome—
he spells it wellcom—of all was the little lock of dear
Baby's hair. How I wish I could kiss his sweet face and
yours. I have heard from Capt. Trilling of a new kind
of daguerreotype. If you could find such there, please
have a likeness of you and my little son made as soon
as such is possible, and send it to me. I would like to
have a remembrance of him while he is still in skirts, as
it now seems likely that I shall not see him until after
the little baby things are put away and he is a great
grown boy. Tomorrow our company moves away from
Md. to be attached perhaps to a new command. Thus
are the rumors. That we are decamping, we know.
Whither, we know not. I will write when I know the
truth. I pray God to bless and keep you and our precious child and keep you under his constant sheltering
wing. Your loving husband, Elijah Thomas."

Cara looked up from the faded letter. "What does he
mean, 'in skirts'?"

"Babies used to wear dresses until they were about two."
Elizabeth lifted the rest of the letters gently and set them on
the bed beside her. "Long ones, down to their ankles, and
they had little ruffled petticoats under them."

"Even the boys?"

Elizabeth nodded. "Even the boys. I think they looked
very sweet."

"Do you think she made the picture?" asked Cara, rooting through the box.

"Yes, here it is." Elizabeth handed Cara the stiff old photograph, and they looked at it with a new comprehension, having read the tender letter of the father. The baby boy, about eighteen months old, stood solemnly beside his mother, his eyes wide and his fingers clutching at his mother's sleeve. His embroidered white dress fell from a yoke to his ankles. He had one little bare foot placed slightly over the other, and its small toes curled like a fist. His young mother was hardly more than a baby herself, with her wide eyes like the child's and her curly hair, which refused to be permanently captured in its snood.

"What was her name?" asked Cara. "Is she related to us? She looks like us."

Elizabeth looked at her daughter, whose face so resembled the one in the picture, and whispered a prayer: might Cara never be at home with a baby, waiting out a war, wondering where her soldier-husband was and whether he were safe.

"Her name was Elizabeth," she said. "Like me."

They gathered up their treasure to take downstairs. Cara, for once, was subdued.

"Mom?"

"What, honey?"

"Do you know if her husband got home okay?" Cara was worried about that small vulnerable family. "It would be terrible if she loved him a lot, and they never got to be together anymore."

Yes, it certainly would. Unthinkable. Elizabeth sighed. The letter and small picture had touched her heart.

Cara came clattering up the stairs. "Don't forget tonight."

"I won't," said Elizabeth patiently. Cara had reminded her four times that it was Parents' Night.

"Don't forget I want you to meet Mr. Salvini."

"I won't," said Elizabeth. "Please don't cling to the hope that I'll be fascinated."

"Oh, Mom!" Cara squirmed onto the edge of the desk and leaned her face into Elizabeth's. "Aren't you through *yet?*"

"No. Please move your head. I can't see the computer screen."

Cara, who was unable to sit still more than fifteen minutes at a time, jumped to her feet and started a football cheer routine, leaping and swinging her arms. "Can I go to a public school next year?"

"No," said Elizabeth, trying to concentrate on a spreadsheet. "And it's *may I.*"

"Nobody says *may*. Not even my English teacher."

"She's young. Perhaps grammar will overtake her yet."

"Why can't I? Dad says I can."

"Your father is two thousand miles away," said Elizabeth. "He is hardly in a position to make informed decisions. Go away, Cara. I have to finish this before we can leave."

This time Elizabeth put enough exasperation and impatience in her voice to propel Cara from the room. She left leaping and spinning.

"Damn Robert," Elizabeth muttered. "Always promising her things he can't deliver."

There was five minutes' peace. Elizabeth leaned back into her desk chair and sighed. Cara adored her father.

Well, Elizabeth couldn't blame her. She had loved him once herself. He was beguiling, handsome and terminally irresponsible, and Elizabeth had married too young to be able to tell the difference between character and charm. If she hadn't been experienced enough to understand at twenty, how could she expect Cara to do it at thirteen?

The one positive result of the union had been Cara, who was as normal an eighth-grader as any parent could desire, with a mouthful of braces, which she hourly deplored, a drawerful of makeup, which she was not allowed to wear, and a Born to Cruise bumper sticker taped to the door of her room. She was by turns exasperating and endearing and often unconsciously funny in her quest for adulthood. Elizabeth cherished her.

Elizabeth simply couldn't bring herself to shatter Cara's belief in Robert's interest and concern. Robert cared about Cara only in the abstract—as long as Cara didn't cause him any personal effort, he was perfectly happy to have a daughter. Cara was only a child; she needed to believe in a loving father, and Elizabeth wasn't about to let her find out that all her perceptions of Robert were false. That would wait until Cara was grown, if Elizabeth could manage it, until Cara was old enough to be philosophically tolerant of Robert's faults.

Cara bounded into the room again, waving her arms with geometric precision. She spun through an airborne maneuver Elizabeth recognized from her own cheerleading days and landed with a thump in front of Elizabeth's desk.

"I hate the way I look," complained Cara, who was a young duplicate of her mother. "I am absolutely gross. I have yucky black hair and a stupid short nose and my lips are fat."

"Oh, you're not so bad," said Elizabeth mildly.

"I love Vonnie Chrysler's hair," said Cara. "All the boys are crazy about it."

"How do you know?" Elizabeth privately considered Vonnie Chrysler's hair to be improbably red.

"Vonnie said so. She said they like to run their fingers through it." Another spin; the thud of sneakers. "Can I get my hair dyed?"

"*May* I," said Elizabeth automatically. "No."

"I've got these horrible gross green eyes," said Cara mournfully. "At least red hair goes with green eyes. Please?"

The horrible gross green eyes were wide open, enormous in Cara's small anxious face. Elizabeth suppressed a smile— it was so hard to be newly thirteen and convinced that everything in the world was wrong with you.

"No," she said firmly, emphasizing her words with a gimlet look from her own green eyes. "Cara, if you want to eat next month, you will have to go away so that I can finish with these audits."

"It's *my* hair," said Cara. "I can do anything I want to with it."

"Fine," said Elizabeth, who was a battle-hardened veteran. "Go ahead. You'll have plenty of time to admire it in the mirror, because you'll be grounded until it grows out."

"I knew you'd say that," Cara told her glumly. "You always say that."

Elizabeth looked at Cara and considered surrender.

"Darling, *please* find something else to do!" she said. "Just for thirty minutes, then I'll come downstairs and we can argue to your heart's content."

Apparently a spark of empathy somehow glowed in Cara's still-flat adolescent breast, because she grinned and bounced around the desk, her good humor miraculously restored.

"Okay," she said. "We have to be at the school at seven, don't forget." Then off she went, to rattle and thump down to the kitchen from Elizabeth's second-floor office.

Elizabeth bent over her work again, trying to block out the noise from the TV and the two radios that were playing downstairs. Since she both needed to make a living and wanted to be a stay-at-home mother, she had started an accounting business with her office in the house. CPAs always had plenty of work, even the bad ones, and Elizabeth knew she was very, very good.

The only thing she lacked, she thought, was the ability to ignore the outside world. Noise rammed its way up the stairs and bounced off her office walls. China shattered; she heard Cara moan, "Oh, God!" Glass tinkled. Cara said, "Oh, God," again.

Elizabeth knew when she was beat. With a sigh she shut down her computer and went to the kitchen.

"What broke?" she asked her daughter.

"Only a glass," said Cara. Then she added, "That's the good news."

"What's the bad news?"

"It had grape juice in it."

I will not, Elizabeth told herself, *ask how it happened.*

"I cleaned it up." Cara adroitly changed the subject. "I have to be at school by seven so I can help with the name tags. *May* we," she said carefully, "go get pizza first?"

By seven-fifteen Elizabeth had been provided with a name tag, by Cara, and a cup of coffee, by Melody. Then she was rushed through a truncated version of Cara's daily schedule, from the Pledge of Allegiance to the final subject of the afternoon.

There was no sign of Steve.

At eight forty-five she sat in Cara's history class and tried to pay close attention to the charms of Joe Salvini, figuring that Cara would give her the third degree once they were in the car and on the way home.

He certainly was attractive, she thought. No wonder all the Form II girls were swooning. Very dark—dark hair, dark eyes. His hair was wonderful—hers should look so good. If the man hadn't been so frankly masculine, she'd have thought he spent a lot of time on it. His nose was wonderful, too. It was large and hooked and Roman, and it made him look different and interesting. Yet there was something—something vaguely familiar about him. She looked at him more carefully and realized what it was.

Except for the nose and the eyes, which were brown instead of blue, Joe Salvini looked very much like Robert.

That explained why Cara was so taken with him.

"This is a two-semester class of the history of the United States," said Mr. Salvini. "And it's a subject I love. I hope to get the girls to love it, too, although the anonymous survey I took at the beginning of school indicated that most of your daughters would rather take penicillin than history."

Every parent in the room brightened up—a good speaker; maybe they'd listen with both ears.

"My name," said the teacher, "is actually Guiseppe Salvini. My dad changed it to Joe as soon as we emigrated to the U.S. thirty years ago, when I was six. That accounts for the slight but fascinating touch of Italian underlying my Philadelphian accent."

He continued to speak and was witty and funny. Several times there were bursts of laughter and applause.

"Since I am an immigrant," he said, "I am very interested in the United States and the way it developed from families like all of ours. This year, all the girls are going to do a personal history telling about the immigrants in their own families. Even—" he grinned "—if they got here in 1621."

Elizabeth glanced around the room. No Steve. She considered having her feelings hurt—he'd acted so interested. They'd spoken every day when they collected the girls from school. But he hadn't called her, even once.

She'd acted interested, too. Maybe she'd acted *too* interested.

Impossible. She and Steve were both too old to play silly adolescent games. So why hadn't he called?

There was another eruption of laughter. Elizabeth wrenched her attention back to the front of the room.

"Before we wrap this up," Joe concluded, "I have to tell you that when we study nineteenth-century immigration to the United States—probably early next semester—we'll make a trip to the Italian Market and buy all the ingredients for a real Italian dinner. Then we'll go to my family's restaurant, where my father and mother will show the kids how to cook the food they've bought. We will need chaperones. I made the mistake of telling the girls, and you have all been volunteered. Please go and initial your name on the sign-up sheet if you're willing to go, and then I'll see you in the cafeteria for cake and coffee."

There was a mad rush for the sign-up sheet. Elizabeth hesitated, then decided that no teacher needed more chaperones than students. She didn't want to go, anyway; it didn't sound appealing. Nothing appealed to her—except Steve. And he obviously didn't want to see her. Now she had to go make small talk and drink bad coffee and eat tasteless cookies in the cafeteria with two hundred other parents who would all tell her how brilliant and popular their daughters were.

You are being idiotic, she said, scolding herself. It didn't do any good. She sighed and made her lone, melancholy way out into the hall.

Steve Riker was waiting for her. He stepped forward as she approached and held out his hand. She took it eagerly—too eagerly; held it, she knew, too long. And to her embarrassment and chagrin, she saw sympathetic understanding in his smiling eyes.

Chapter Two

"Have you enjoyed Melody's classes?" she asked. She spoke too quickly, ran the words together like a sprint for the finish. Drop his hand. Talk about acting stupid. What was she, anyway? A schoolgirl? Geez. Get a life. Anybody'd think he was the only man she'd ever seen.

Well, he *was* the only one she'd seen that she liked, since Robert.

That was certainly an unsettling thought. Her attraction to Steve was primal instinct. And so had her attraction to Robert been. Obviously her instinctive mechanism wasn't working in her best interest. Definitely a good reason to back off this time.

So she did, literally, and folded her hands behind her back.

A slight shadow crossed Steve's face, covered by a quick wash of stubbornness. He stepped forward. She stepped back. He stepped forward, tacitly daring her to move again.

She wouldn't.

"Melody's classes," she repeated, and clipped the words. She could imagine the scene: she moving backward, Steve moving forward, all the way across the room, in some sort of silent, determined two-step. The thought made her grin, and Steve's determined jaw relaxed.

"Haven't been to any classes," he said. "I've been consulting with General Westcott, instead. She tells me that the open warfare has decreased, but the combatants show no signs of a lasting truce."

"Oh, dear," said Elizabeth absently, distracted by her thoughts, two-step, instincts and all.

What was the matter with her? She knew he'd been attracted to her when they'd met. So what? She had been attracted to him. *And how!* said her libido, stomping on her logic. People are attracted to each other every day. That didn't mean they intended to do anything about it.

"Miss Westcott said," Steve continued, "that the junior varsity lacrosse team is losing games because Melody and Cara won't pass to each other. They are in danger of being benched for the season."

That bit of information got Elizabeth's attention. Cara's major ambition in life was to be the starring center on an internationally televised championship lacrosse game. Making the Harkness varsity was a cherished interim goal. To think that Cara had deliberately sabotaged her own success to snub Melody was bewildering.

"That's the strangest thing I've ever heard," she said, as they followed the crowd of parents out of the classroom building into the cafeteria. "Cara is a lacrosse fanatic. I simply can't understand it." She took a cup of tea and a piece of poppyseed cake from a tray being carried around by one of the students.

Steve eyed the tea. "Don't they serve coffee here?"

He was acting perfectly naturally. Either he was the best actor she had ever seen, or he really hadn't noticed her unguarded greeting. Elizabeth began to relax a little. Perhaps she'd have a chance to redeem her self-respect, after all. She would act just as he acted. Polite. Calm. And kind. Combined with a little attractive indifference.

Or maybe not. He made her salivate.

Maybe she'd just work a little on piquing his interest. The two-step certainly implied that he had at least noticed her as a woman. Even instincts deserved another chance. Practice made perfect, didn't it? There simply couldn't be two men like Robert. And Steve did, after all, have custody of his daughter. Surely that indicated an inclination toward commitment and the ability to love someone besides himself.

"Patience," she said, taking a cue from his attitude and tone. The idea was to show interest, but not desperation. "Someone will be around with it shortly." She held out her saucer. "Here. Have some cake while you wait."

Steve put a bite in his mouth and chewed thoughtfully. "Has Cara told you why she doesn't like Melody?" he asked, after a minute's rumination.

Elizabeth shook her head. "Says she's a dweeb, and that's the end of it."

"Well, at least they speak the same language," said Steve dryly. "That's what Melody says about Cara."

"Bad chemistry," said Elizabeth.

"Even the most explosive mixtures can be stabilized," Steve told her.

"Are you a chemist?" *His* chemistry certainly was explosive, Elizabeth thought. Every woman in the room had glanced their way, even old Mrs. Ridley, who had graduated from Harkness in 1929 and who showed up every year for Parents' Day to see if the quality of the clientele had deteriorated.

"No. I write science fiction."

His voice was marvelously deep and just a little gravelly. It vibrated through her the way a sea wind shook a racing sloop, making a sail swell tight and surge forward at command.

"Really?" she said. "That sounds exciting." The science fiction and he the wind and she the fulfilled sail.

"It is, but the excitement's all in your head. Physically, it's pretty dull work. You never get to go outside in the daytime. That's why I have this prison pallor."

"Dracula never gets to go outside in the daytime, either," said Elizabeth, trying to look suspicious.

And trying not to look lascivious.

"I used to hang around with him," said Steve. "But then he said my teeth were too short, and all his friends made fun of me, and I got tired of the liquid diet, so I split."

"Is that when you started writing science fiction?" If he wanted to try another nip to reestablish his technique, she was willing to offer her throat to the experiment.

"Yup. A lot of it's real-life experience," he said.

I cannot continue this way, she scolded herself, thinking about getting him to bite my neck. I have *got* to pay some attention to this conversation. I've let myself get out of hand.

"Thought you said you never got to go outside," she said, forcing her mind off her baser desires.

There. That was better. A good hard mental shake does everybody good. Even sex-starved suburban mothers.

"Experience from my Dracula days," said Steve. "I live and work on memories."

"Do you talk about your books?" She turned just slightly away from him. So she couldn't see the strong, white teeth and imagine the feel of them just grazing her throat as he kissed and teased her into passion.

"Only after they're finished. I rather like to let them speak for themselves." There was more gravel in his voice than ever. He cleared his throat and let a deep breath out slowly.

"I've never read much science fiction," said Elizabeth, taking a deep breath of her own. "But I'd like to. Everybody I know who reads it likes it so much."

"Why haven't you?"

She shrugged. "I keep intending to, but I don't know where to start, and every time I go into a bookstore, there are so many science fiction books that I get confused, so I just buy a mystery or romance writer I've heard of and go home." She smiled. "Maybe I could start with one of yours. I'd like that."

"I'd like it, too," said Steve. "I'll bring you one."

"Deal." She pushed her torrid imaginings out of her head and scanned him thoughtfully: the rough tweed, the polished wing tips, the civilized urbanity. "You look like you write mysteries, not science fiction."

"What do science fiction writers look like?"

"Their hair is longer and they wear tennis shoes with their suits. No ties."

The description was so apt that he laughed. "I have half a dozen friends who fit the image perfectly," he said.

"Actually, I always think they're very sensible. About the tennis shoes, I mean. You've just moved here, haven't you? Why'd you pick Philadelphia?"

"Close enough to New York for Melody to see her mother and far, far away from twenty-seven degrees below zero and the squall winds off the Atlantic. We were living on the coast of Maine."

"I wouldn't mind a squall wind and twenty-seven degrees right now," said Elizabeth. "My office is like a sauna."

"Is the air-conditioning broken?" The answer didn't matter, he thought. What mattered was to keep her talking—she had a voice like dark chocolate, rich and sweet and unexpectedly deep. It matched the rest of her: she was the subtly elegant result of good breeding and good schools and good manners.

"There isn't any. I work out of my house, and indoor plumbing was a novel concept when it was built. Besides, this daytime heat can't last more than another week or so—it's cool at night."

She sounded so hopeful that Steve laughed. "Can you live a week in a sauna?"

"What doesn't kill me makes me stronger," she said. "My grandmother used to tell me that."

"Is it true?" He couldn't get enough of her. A burgundy silk blouse peeped demurely from under her white wool suit and deepened the natural rose of her cheeks, and the pearls that nestled sweetly just above her breasts had the same satin sheen as her skin. He could almost feel the smooth shell buttons against his fingers; could see the blouse falling open at his touch; could imagine his palms gently rounding the soft curves of her body. "Does it make you stronger?"

"I suppose." She grinned, and the perfect oval of her face took on an unexpected elfin quality which made her seem as young as the children around them. "I don't have to like it, though."

"What kind of work do you do in this sauna?"

"I'm a CPA."

"You don't look like a CPA," he said, automatically mimicking her remark about his writing. *It is sexist of me,* he told himself, *to wonder what she would look like without her clothes.* The thought of any man having the same reaction to Melody made Steve squirm. Double standard, he thought to himself uncomfortably, and tried to control his unruly imagination.

"And what does a CPA look like?" Her lips rounded softly, sweetly, deliciously around the words.

Steve spoke through a sigh. "Ink-stained fingers and wire-rimmed glasses and sensible shoes," he said.

Elizabeth glanced at her narrow feet. "These are sensible shoes."

"So they are," acknowledged Steve, but he was eyeing the long beautiful legs above the low-heeled pumps.

"I have the wire-rimmed glasses at home," she told him. "I wear contact lenses for state occasions."

"What about the ink-stained fingers?" he asked, reluctantly withdrawing his attention from her legs to smile into her big green eyes.

Elizabeth held out her hands for his inspection. "Bleach," she said. "Does wonders for ink stains."

"Certainly does," he said, but he didn't look at her hands. His gaze wandered from her eyes to her lips and back again. He took a deep, controlling breath, which he let out carefully, so she wouldn't notice and be troubled by his frank and growing desire to take her hands and fold them into his own and pull her into his arms and kiss her thoroughly, there, in the sedate school, with people milling all about them.

He swept his gaze around the room to distract himself before he did anything irrevocably stupid. And caught Cara's implacable eye.

"Here comes your daughter," said Steve. He was certainly distracted, he thought wryly. Cara's fierce and determined countenance was enough to dampen any ardor.

Elizabeth glanced over her shoulder and saw Cara marching toward them with indignation evident in every line.

"She looks just like you," said Steve. "Except for the scowl."

"I thought you were going to talk to Mr. Salvini," said Cara in a tone a police interrogator might have envied.

Elizabeth caught Cara's eye and glared. "Cara," she said, with emphasis. "You remember Mr. Riker."

"Yes," said Cara. The *yes* sounded flat and ominous.

"And here comes Melody," said Steve, anticipating the worst.

Melody, like Cara, was all angles and elbows and glinting braces. She was blond like her father, but with blue eyes and a sweet, round, rosy-cheeked face that could have graced a soap commercial. She walked toward them eagerly, smiling at Steve, smiling at Elizabeth. Then her eyes lit on Cara. The walk slowed; the smile faded; suspicion grew and blossomed on her face.

Uh-oh, thought Elizabeth.

The two girls stared at each other. The hostility rose between them like heat waves off a highway.

"This is Cara's mother," said Steve to Melody. "You've only seen her from the car."

Melody turned long enough to give Elizabeth a shy smile. Then she ducked her head and stared at the floor.

Cara took uncompromising possession of her mother's arm and deepened the unremitting scowl. There was a short, uncomfortable silence.

Finally Melody said, "Would you come meet my friends, Daddy?"

Steve gave Elizabeth a rueful smile as Melody tugged at his sleeve. He shook his head and shrugged.

Elizabeth relieved the embarrassment by saying, "Do please excuse us. We really ought to circulate a bit ourselves. I'll see you at the next PTO meeting."

You'll see me a lot sooner than that, Steve vowed. Then he yielded to Melody's pressure and let her lead him to another part of the room. And watched, with an unaccustomed turmoil in his chest, as Elizabeth was approached by Joe Salvini.

Melody introduced him to Vonnie Chrysler and her mother, Merle. Steve tried to seem interested. He smiled and nodded and mouthed pleasantries and maneuvered himself so that he could see Elizabeth talking to that damned history teacher.

He knew what Salvini was after. Steve had watched through the door of that classroom, and Salvini's focus had clearly centered on Elizabeth.

Sane reason warred with wrath. Why shouldn't Salvini be interested in Elizabeth? He was a normal man. Why shouldn't Elizabeth respond to Salvini's attention? Steve had established no claim on her. She was mildly interested, perhaps, but that was all. So what if Steve had been flooded with an unexpected surge of adolescent passion? That hardly gave him the right to dispose of any possible suitors with ham-fisted passion.

All this lucid argument came to nothing. He watched as Salvini laid his hand lightly on Elizabeth's arm, and a primitive rage sent adrenaline rushing into a brain that he knew had already abandoned logic and wit.

Merle was laughing. Good God—what had she said? Obviously some response was needed. Melody and Vonnie were laughing. Everybody was laughing. The entire room rang with hilarious good humor.

Steve, as camouflage, lowered his head and forced a chuckle.

He should be laughing, too, he thought bleakly. Laughing at himself. At his lack of self-command. At his unreasonable emotion. At the thick dark jealousy that rose like black bile in his throat.

All Elizabeth wanted to do was leave, but she let herself be accosted by several parents, all of whom wanted volunteers for various projects. They all volunteered themselves and—Elizabeth noted unkindly—they all had fat trust funds which enabled them to work for no pay. "Can you work in the tuck shop on Tuesdays?" "Can you chair the silent auction?" "Will you help with the art fair?"

Maybe she could manage the art fair, if all she had to do was sell things. Several families bought enough original art that they could always induce their pet artists to contribute paintings and sculptures and such. Then they all went to the fair and bought all the donated art themselves. Sort of incestuous, but who cared? The art fair always brought in huge amounts to augment the scholarship fund.

She tried to sight Cara before she was cornered and pressured by anybody else. But Mrs. Ridley caught her eye and beckoned imperiously. Elizabeth sighed and obeyed.

"New beau, dear?" Mrs. Ridley could get away with questions like that, because she was as old as Mrs. Noah and as insensitive as an armor-plated tank.

"Who?" said Elizabeth, though she knew very well to whom the dreadful old termagant referred.

"That young fellow over there," said Mrs. Ridley. "The one Merle Chrysler's looking to buy."

"No," said Elizabeth, speaking in quick monosyllables and hoping to escape before Mrs. Ridley said something really horrible. "New this year. Just met him."

"Oh-h-h?" said Mrs. Ridley, her old voice shrilling like a police whistle. "Thought ye knew him better'n that. He was lookin' down your shirt for half an hour."

"Really, Mrs. Ridley," said Elizabeth with indignation, but the terrible old woman only heard what she chose to hear.

"Here comes another one," she said, pointing with her mottled witch's finger. "Better button that shirt, miss."

Involuntarily Elizabeth put her hand to her throat. Her blouse was opened a scant three inches. She turned to face Joe Salvini, as Mrs. Ridley watched with bright, malicious old eyes.

"You didn't initial the field trip sheet," said Salvini. "Don't you want to go?"

"I thought you had enough parents already," said Elizabeth, holding out her hand. "I'm Cara's mother."

"I know," he said. "The sheet's over there." He took her arm and pulled her out of danger.

"Thanks," she said. "I was on the verge of homicide."

"Can't say that I blame you," he told her. "Can she see me staring down your shirt from here?"

"She sees everything," said Elizabeth, with resignation. "She's like the God of Moses, only not as nice."

"Well, there's no point in trying to be discreet, is there, Cara's mother?" He grinned. "Does Cara's mother have a name of her own?"

"Elizabeth Fairchild." He really was quite as charming outside the classroom as in. If she hadn't been brooding over Steve, Cara and Mrs. Ridley, she'd have found him very appealing. "I suppose," she said, seeking refuge in tradition, "that Cara's told you all about me."

"Yes," he said. "She certainly has."

He inspected her with such an odd mixture of interest and amusement on his face that Elizabeth, with a pang of anxiety, wondered what Cara had told him. Cara's words echoed in her head. *You need sex. Everybody does.*

Oh, no. She surely couldn't have said that to him. Could she?

Elizabeth, who never blushed, blushed.

Cara, who had appeared when Salvini had, quickly attached herself to a passing group of girls and began an animated conversation.

"Before I tell you whether I'll go," Elizabeth demanded, recovering her composure, "suppose you tell me what Cara said about me."

Joe Salvini laid his big hand lightly on her arm.

"Nothing too horrible. Only that she figured you were ready for a new romance, and I was just the kind of man you had in mind."

"Oh, God!" groaned Elizabeth, who seldom audibly swore. "How could she?"

"She meant well," said Joe kindly. "They're all so indiscreet at this age."

"Cara, I fear, has been indiscreet at every age," Elizabeth informed him. "She says whatever pops into her head."

"Don't be too hard on her," he advised. "Personally, I hope she's right. At least sign up for the field trip. You can listen to my mother and Cara compare matchmaking techniques."

Behind her, from across the room, came Steve's deep chuckle and Merle Chrysler's sultry laugh. Elizabeth maneuvered so that she could see and felt unaccountably annoyed.

Merle Chrysler's head was as red as Vonnie's. She had on an ice-green dress. She looked spectacular.

She had more curves and higher heels and fewer inhibitions than Elizabeth. She didn't dress herself in dull Main Line habiliments like burgundy silk and her grandmother's pearls. There was no denying Merle appealed to men.

Melody and Vonnie discoursed amiably beside their parents; no antagonism there. Merle touched her daughter's curls with two well-manicured fingertips and made a smiling comment. Steve bent his head forward to catch her words. Definitely interested. Damn.

"While I've got you here," said Joe, "I want to talk to you about the Civil War artifacts Cara said you'd let us use. Is it true?"

"Be glad to."

Merle was certainly a rotten end to the day. She looked thoroughly toothsome. With Steve's Dracular experience, he was certain to be interested.

"Think you'd have time to come talk to the class yourself?"

"Why not?" said Elizabeth, eyeing Merle with malevolence. "Just tell me when."

"February, probably," said Joe.

He sounded puzzled. She didn't blame him. He couldn't see what she saw, and even if he did, it wouldn't make sense to him. Men were pretty stupid that way. She wished she could think of a way to spike Merle's cannon or hoist her petard or whatever the term was.

"You're new here," said Elizabeth, with sudden malicious inspiration. "Let me introduce you to some of the other parents."

Joe was a very masculine and good-looking man. Perhaps Vonnie had designs on him, herself, on behalf of Merle. Not the nicest thing to do, pushing poor Joe into the web, but on the other hand, he was a grown man. Surely he could take care of himself.

Joe Salvini glanced once at Merle Chrysler and adjusted his tie.

Merle watched them approach and smoothed her skirt over her hips with both hands—a clear signal she'd shifted her attention to Joe. Good.

"I have to go," Elizabeth announced, after she had effected the introductions. "And I didn't want to leave poor Mr. Salvini standing over there with no company. He's new this year."

With that, she fluttered her fingers at the little group, collected Cara and started toward the door.

Behind her, she heard Joe Salvini exclaim, "Riker. Steve Riker. But you're famous."

She stopped in her tracks.

"Hardly that," said Steve. A modest disclaimer.

Merle cooed.

Elizabeth turned and looked at Steve's rapt listeners. The surrounding crowd, now fascinated, drifted closer to hear him speak.

Famous for what? she wondered. Should she drift along with the captivated, or pretend uninterest and take her lone self home?

She drifted for a second, long enough to hear him say, "Well, I'm a little superstitious. I don't really like to talk about works in progress. I'll talk your ear off about the rest of them, though."

She had to listen to Cara chatter about Joe Salvini on the way home, when with all of her heart and all of her body, she yearned for Steve Riker.

Elizabeth's penance for the subterfuge was to spend the next few weeks trying to drive thoughts of Steve out of her head. Not all of him at once; just isolated images which appeared whenever she let her guard down. The steel of his eyes, piercing her own. The width of his shoulders when he'd had his back to her, as she watched him from across the room. His voice. His laugh. And once, God help her, she was nearly overcome and reduced to gibbering by the clean smell of his after-shave wafting from a sample bottle as she passed the cosmetics counter in the drugstore.

"This is ridiculous," she muttered, after one particularly trying period when his face kept popping up between her and her computer screen with such persistence that she couldn't concentrate at all.

She was acting like a love-struck seventeen-year-old girl mooning over a rock star, instead of a mature, settled, thirty-three-year-old woman who had no intention of succumbing to an imaginary romance.

She didn't even know the man; she'd seen him for a total of perhaps twenty minutes a day, counting their initial meeting, Parents' Night and three weeks of quick, evening and Saturday-morning stops to pick up the girls. That was enough, apparently, to generate thick-coming fancies—if you were completely unbalanced and needed psychiatric care. And the fantasies were even worse on the rare days when Cara and Melody managed to escape detention.

She needed romance.

And Cara was right, damn it. She needed sex. It had been six extremely long years. That was the one good thing about Robert: the sex was really great. She had tried for six long years not to think about it. She missed the sex—really missed it—but she wouldn't touch Robert again with two ten-foot poles tied end to end, even if she knew no man would ever hold her in his arms again.

That was the really horrible thing about being divorced. No sex. Not that she hadn't had opportunities—men abounded who were perfectly willing to sleep with her. But mere appetite wasn't good enough for her. She required mutual caring and commitment. That dismissed the great majority of men who wanted to take her out—caring and commitment weren't words in their vocabularies. The few who had begun to fall in love with her were gently discouraged. They hadn't been able to create that answering spark in her own heart and body.

Until Steve Riker, who hadn't been impressed enough to call, and who had obviously decided that the daily attraction wasn't great enough to overcome the flamboyant lure of Merle Chrysler.

She was still musing over this depressing thought when Cara came in from school. Elizabeth could divine Cara's mood by the sounds from below. The door slammed. The book bag hit the floor with a sullen thud. She skipped the refrigerator—usually her first stop—and came directly up to Elizabeth's office. Her shoes stomped on every stair.

"I hate Melody Riker," Cara announced, without preamble.

"Is there a reason for this rancor?" Elizabeth asked.

"She's a complete glophf." Cara supported herself against the wall and looked glum.

"A glophf, huh?" said Elizabeth. That was a new one.

"She chews with her mouth open like this." Cara made exaggerated chewing motions. "She does it on purpose to make me sick to my stomach."

"You might try being polite, Cara."

"I would, if she would," said Cara. "But she won't."

"You could start first. Think about the Golden Rule."

"She'd say I was just trying to get her to be nice to me," said Cara. "And she'd tell all her friends I was brownnosing, and they'd all laugh at me, and I won't."

The syntax was a little garbled, but the message was clear. Elizabeth, recognizing defeat but unwilling yet to surrender, delivered a last pitiful attack on prejudice. "Once you get to know her, you might like her."

Cara gave that idea exactly the attention it deserved. She ignored it.

"She talks about her dumb stupid dog all the time, Sammy this and Sammy that. And her stupid aunt. *My Aunt Lin has a farm. My Aunt Lin has horses,*" Cara said, in a scathing falsetto. "Like anybody wants to know about her stupid Aunt Lin or her stupid dog or her stupid horses. And," she continued, in a normal voice, "she flirts with boys and everything. It's so gross."

Oh-ho, thought Elizabeth, so that's the crux of the problem. "How do you know she flirts with boys?"

"*Mom!* She's on my same *train* every single *day!*" Cara slid to the floor with a despairing thump. "She talks about lacrosse with them, just like she knows all about it, and football and everything."

"It isn't necessarily flirting to talk to a boy about lacrosse," said Elizabeth sympathetically, remembering her own adolescent embarrassment and her envy of girls who could converse easily with the mysterious Opposite Sex. She gave Cara the same useless advice her mother had given her. "You could do that, too, honey. Just act natural and talk about normal things, like you would with a girl. School and sports and things."

"You just don't understand," said Cara.

Oh, yes she did. Cara should have witnessed the Parents' Night conversation with Steve. She'd never ask Elizabeth for advice to the lovelorn again.

"Cara, she really seems like a nice girl," said Elizabeth, hearing her own mother's voice echo in her ears and knowing exactly the reception her words would be given. "She's new here. You ought to try to make her feel comfortable."

"She has more friends than I do," said Cara gloomily, getting to her feet. She left the office and started down the stairs. Her doleful voice wafted back to Elizabeth's ears. "You don't need to worry about stupid Melody Riker. You ought to worry about me."

It was just as well that Steve wasn't interested. The overt animosity of the two girls would derail even a casual friendship, let alone a developing romance. Elizabeth turned back to the financial spreadsheet displayed on her computer screen and worked despondently until it was time to fix supper.

By nine that night, Cara was tucked up in her room with her friend, Allison, who was sleeping over. The girls had appeared once, to ask if they could have a pizza, then disappeared, giggling, back up the stairs to phone in the order. Elizabeth turned on the porch lights for the pizza delivery and settled back in her chair to stare, unseeing, at the evening news.

Too bad she couldn't take her own advice, she thought. Just act natural and talk about normal things. She supposed she was acting naturally—it was surely natural, this sexual desire. And it was natural for the memory of his presence to fire a fantasy so strong that she could almost feel his body under her hands.

Unfortunately, she could almost feel her body under his hands, too. Could imagine the weight of him covering her, could smell him and feel him and taste him. The unwitting illusion of his presence was bad enough during the day, when she had her work to occupy her mind. But it was unbearable at night, when she was alone in the big bed, half asleep and half dreaming. She dreamed at night of hunger, that she was starving and there was no food to be had, and she woke each morning feeling edgy and tense and incomplete.

She heard the delivery truck stop. When she opened the door, the truck was driving away and Steve stood on the steps, holding the pizza, with a couple of books balanced on its flat box.

He had on Saturday-morning jeans—old, soft and form-fitting—and a denim work shirt that had two buttons open at the neck. No jewelry but a University of Wyoming class ring. No tacky nouveau-riche gold necklace adorned his ego: there was a military stainless steel chain around his neck, the kind that carried dog tags or medical information.

"Surprise," he said.

She took the pizza from him, and he curved his hand around her small wrist as he let go of the box.

The sight of him recalled a host of midnight fantasies. She could have dealt with those, could have sternly put them out of her mind, but the touch of his hand kindled in her longing body a physical desire so great that she knew it showed as hunger in her eyes.

Her lips parted. His grip on her wrist tightened, and he pulled her gently toward him.

How could she ever have thought he wasn't interested? His body was as tense as hers; the desire in his eyes was frank—and growing. She had made a nearly unconscious decision to step forward into his arms, when Cara came clattering down the stairs.

"Is that the pizza?" Cara said. Then she saw him. "What's *he* doing here?"

Elizabeth shifted her attention slowly, like a sleeper disturbed by a hornet's buzz. She stared at Cara for a long, uncomfortable second.

"Apologize to Mr. Riker," she said. Her inflection was perfectly even and brittle as ice.

Cara, defeated in open aggression, did. The apology was perfect, pronounced in a voice as cold as a February night.

"Take this pizza," said Elizabeth, "and go upstairs."

There was a swift, silent clash of wills. Cara gave Steve a toxic look, handed Elizabeth the books, took the pizza and stomped back to her room.

Elizabeth gave a little impatient hiss.

"I'm sorry," she said. "It's not you. She's decided that I'm going to date Joe Salvini and doesn't want me to talk to anyone else with a Y chromosome."

"Ah," said Steve. "Well, I can understand that. I'd just as soon you stayed away from other Y chromosomes, myself."

"Please don't complicate matters," said Elizabeth. Why was everything so difficult? Cara was difficult. Business was difficult. And romance was difficult at thirty-three, even without Cara, Merle and Melody as complications.

Life, damn it, was difficult. Her grandmother had told her that, too. And the stout-hearted old lady had been 101 percent right. Elizabeth wanted a good fairy to set everything straight.

"I hate to echo Cara," she said, feeling embattled. "But what *are* you doing here, anyway?"

Steve smiled down at her. "I finished my book. I came to celebrate. Do you have any wine?"

"What book?"

"The one I've been working on eighteen hours a day." He looked at her shrewdly. "That's why I haven't called."

"Did you think I wondered?" Oh, God. Her face must be as readable as a kindergarten primer.

"If you haven't wondered," he said, "tell me, and I'll leave. I'm wasting my time."

Like he didn't know already, she thought, trying to keep her expression pleasantly neutral. She'd never been told she had a poker face, but surely age and increasing sophistication could conspire to protect her from the most embarrassing of her thoughts. She held the books to her chest, as a sort of psychic shield.

Books... Suddenly she made the connection between his name and his occupation. She'd read a *Time* book review about a year ago. Skimmed it only superficially, at the time, but her efficient mind had filed the information: seminal fiction, archetypes, new era in science fiction.

"Books!" she said. "Joe was right. You're famous."

"Oh, so you heard him, then? I was a little disappointed that you didn't come back to find out what he was talking about."

"Had to get home," she said speciously. "You've had two bestsellers in three years. I read about you in *Time*."

"You haven't actually read the books, themselves, I hope."

"Why do you hope?" she asked.

"Because if you have, and you can't remember their names, my name or the plots, I am in significant trouble and need to reconsider the way I'm writing."

She laughed and relaxed. "But how rude I'm being. These are yours, I take it?" She looked at the covers of the books he'd brought: *Fire in the Hole* and *The Hail Mary Margin*.

"You said you wanted to read one," he said diffidently.

"Yes, absolutely, I do. And I honestly mean that. I'm not just being polite," she said, leading him into the kitchen. "I was about to have some wine. Come and join me. Where's Melody?"

"Spending the night at my sister's."

He was close behind her, close enough for her to feel the heat of his body. Just his shadow on her shoulder seemed to have a weight and presence of its own.

"Aunt Lin," said Elizabeth. "Horses and a farm."

"Seems the girls have been communicating, after all."

"In a primitive, unsatisfactory way." She shoved at a solid door and led him into a vast, elderly kitchen.

Its one concession to the late twentieth century was an ugly fluorescent light dangling from the high, old ceiling. Steve, seeing the ancient, slate flagstone floor and granite cabinet tops, wasn't sure that good light was an improvement.

"Good Lord," he said.

"It was last remodeled about 1890," said Elizabeth, grinning. "Except for the stove and refrigerator, which my grandmother forced herself to buy in 1952." She got a decanter from the shelf above her and picked up an open wine bottle which sat beside the sink. "I have to pour this off— it's full of sediment."

Steve, who knew something about wine, read the label and whistled.

"I didn't buy it," said Elizabeth. "I inherited it, along with the house, from my grandmother. She built a nice wine cellar."

"I'll say. How much of it do you have left?"

"Quite a bit of this. And some others which are twice as old. There are some nice whites down there, too, but mostly I give them as presents. Except for the Graves. I don't have the palate my grandmother did."

"How do I get on your gift list?" he asked, trying to imagine inheriting a cellar full of vintage wine. Unobtainable wine. Like the ruby treasure flowing smoothly into the decanter on the granite slab.

"I can open one of the whites for you," she said carelessly. "It isn't chilled, but it doesn't have to breathe."

"That would be the wildest, most reckless extravagance," he said, with real shock in his voice.

Her laugh blended exotically with the trickle of the wine. "Hardly that. Shall I?"

"No. Oh, no, indeed," he said hastily. "This Bordeaux's been famous for fifty years. I never thought I'd ever have a chance to taste it."

Elizabeth expertly twisted her wrist and stopped the flow of wine into the ancient decanter just as the first scant brown sediment appeared on the bottle's green lip.

"Pretty slick," said Steve approvingly. He shut the kitchen door behind him and leaned against it.

"Ought to be. I learned it at my mother's knee." She half filled two claret stems and handed one to Steve.

"What about your parents?" He found it hard to divide his attention between the legendary wine and a woman so enchanting that she must surely disappear if he blinked his eyes.

"My father was killed in Viet Nam when I was five, so I don't really remember him. My mother remarried when I was twenty and lives in France with her husband. He's a very nice man, who wistfully reviews the cellar every time he visits."

"I can't blame him."

The heady bouquet of the wine enveloped him magically as he watched Elizabeth lift her glass. Crimson wine touched crimson lips, and green eyes, shot with sparks of gold, glowed at him above the deep, clear crystal.

Two sips were all he could manage. His open hand rose irresistibly, and like a man moving slowly through a wonderful dream, he saw himself lay his palm against her cheek.

Chapter Three

The warmth of his hand traveled like a river from his fingertips, straight to her heart. Jumbled notions tumbled in her head like small shells in a foaming sea. They surfaced and sank and resurfaced, churning so quickly that she hadn't time to think about them: I want this kiss, Cara may come down, it's too soon, kiss me, I'm too involved, I have to think about it, I need more time, kiss me.

Steve watched this rapid advance and retreat cloud her eyes and switched his attentions immediately. He drew back a little, and she relaxed.

"Too many distractions, aren't there?" he said, smiling.

She nodded gratefully. "Even when they're out of sight, they're not out of mind."

"That's the nature of children, I think." He tapped her cheek with two fingers and said, "Incoming."

Elizabeth let reason seep from her cerebral cortex and wash against her consciousness.

"Cara," she said, listening. She took a sip of her wine.

Cara and Allison pushed through the kitchen door in search of soft drinks. Allison smiled. Cara didn't, but she didn't scowl, either. Elizabeth supposed that was progress.

Steve had moved away from her. He and the rich Bordeaux were framed in her narrow, focused vision: a vineyard of pleasure which seemed forever out of her reach. The giddy passion which had possessed them just seconds before had moderated. She couldn't decide whether to be disappointed or relieved.

But, oh—how she had wanted that kiss. She had seen Steve nearly every day for six entire weeks and she had wanted a kiss for all of that time. Coveting by day, dreaming by night, wanting, wanting, wanting.

She just wanted it under different circumstances, is all. She wanted peace in her home and freedom to fall in love, if that's what she decided to do.

Melody and Cara made peace and freedom very difficult. And while the unpleasant company of their two scowling daughters did not exactly constitute the fertile earth of love, it created absolutely the garden of desire, to be able to look, but not touch. To hear his deep voice uttering daily pleasantries and imagine love words coming from his lips. To have him shake her hand and cling to her fingers a fraction longer than necessary under the cold disapproving eyes of their sour-faced chaperones.

She gave a wistful little sigh.

Steve stood motionless with his hand flat against the cold granite. He could feel her under his hand, the velvet softness of her skin, the pulse at her throat throbbing its manic beat, to heat his blood and fire his imagination. He set his teeth against the storm in his body. The heat and the imagination still raged.

He could not touch her, not now. He reached instead for the wine bottle in front of him. As Elizabeth watched, he laid his palm lightly against the gentle curve of its side and smoothed his fingers up its long elegant neck. Wine clung to its lip, one drop of sweet wine, and it glistened and trembled as it sensed his coming. That same wine slicked Elizabeth's lips, wine red like her lips, trembling like her lips, waiting for his touch. The one long finger of his hand grazed the lip of the wine, circling it, stroking it, dipping lightly into it as he spread the droplets around the entrance to its dark and dewy cloister.

His eyes never left her face.

Elizabeth held her breath, transfixed. His hand seemed to move across her naked skin as his supple fingers moved across the dark glass. A fantasy touch caressed her, her throat, her breasts, her belly and her seeking thighs; it reached and tickled into her and fed the small electric flutter, which was a sure herald of pleasure yet to come.

I can't stand any more, she thought to herself, and on legs like water, she sequestered herself safely behind her thick, wooden kitchen table. It had been pounded, scratched and dented by generations of naughty children, and it definitely looked its age. No one could possibly look at it and think of romance.

"Is this where I squeal 'No, no, no'?" she asked. "And you twirl your mustache?" She wanted to squeal "Yes, yes, yes."

"Never fear, fair maiden," he said, carrying the wine to the table. "I can't seduce you. My mustache is too short. And—" and she could hear the truth in his tone "—I want you willing and clearheaded, unencumbered by doubt, unfuddled by drink and uncompromised by imported chocolates. No seduction. It's dishonest." His eyes glinted like battleship steel, cutting into her heart and into her soul. "My own appeal will have to suffice."

It suffices, she thought.

"Besides," he continued, sitting across from her. "This Bordeaux is far too civilized for seduction. You have to have very young wine for seduction, a wine made by lusty, energetic, purple-footed peasants."

He greatly desired to remove the glass and taste the dark wine on her lips. Instead, he stifled a sigh and said, "For seduction you need an uncomplicated wine, one that depends on nothing but youth and raw power."

"And a loaf of bread?" She was wrong. She *could* look at the table and think of romance. Of sex. *Romance* was the wrong word, entirely.

"No bread. A blanket and a secluded spot," he told her.

"With satyrs and dryads lurking in the glade," she said.

"As long as they stay out of the way, they're welcome to lurk," he said. "How about a picnic on Saturday, with a playful young wine? We could wrap up in the blanket and sit with our backs to the wind.''

"That sounds wonderful, particularly the blanket part," she said. "But we might just as well take a serious old wine, because we will also have to take the girls."

"Eris instead of Eros," said Steve. "A perfect occasion for the Graves."

Elizabeth giggled. "There's one of the few witty puns I've ever heard anybody make," she said.

"Well?"

"An interesting thought. We can go down to Valley Forge Park and watch Melody and Cara radiate enough hostility to melt sand into glass." That was a way to banish libidinous ideas from her head—think of Cara and Melody seething like fulminate of mercury merely one blanket over, unstable and ready to explode.

"The Feds would get us for destroying a national treasure," said Steve. "How about a nice noisy fast-food pizza place, with a huge video arcade? It'll give those two little grumps something to do."

"You mean play those shoot-'em-up games?" Two could be alone in a crowd, if two disagreeable little somebody-elses could be successfully diverted. The future looked a little brighter.

"We'll give the kids two sacks of quarters to go away and play the games, and during that romantic interlude we'll pick all the pepperoni out of the cheese and feed it to each other," he said, and his voice was lower and huskier than he meant it to be.

"Do you know a place like that?" The scratched and scarred old table was an ineffective barrier.

"Yes." He wanted to take her in his arms and pull her close. *I am all hormones,* he thought. *And no sense.* He was very heavily in lust. He looked at the big green eyes. Well, he thought philosophically, the love would probably come, if he didn't do something to stop it. If neither of them wanted to do something to stop it.

"Is the food any good?"

"You're so innocent and adorable," he said. "So Main Line. So *very* upper class. People don't go there for the food."

The wine might not have been young enough for lust, but Elizabeth was, and she definitely lusted. Undignified. Dangerous. And absolutely luscious.

"What do they go there for, if the food's no good?" she asked. Strange how her demeanor hid the secret workings of her mind.

"Star Attack," said Steve. "The latest in virtual reality shoot-'em-up games. There was a line around the block to play it, until the owner put in a take-a-number system. He had to. Nobody was buying pizza. They were all standing in line."

She looked at him doubtfully. "Are you kidding?"

"No, indeed. I've stood in it myself, I'm embarrassed to say." He sat down opposite her. "It's so popular that the manager of the restaurant has limited the play to six minutes a person. That's two turns. There's a sign posted. But—" he said, with a devilish, delighted, heart-stopping grin "—he can be bribed."

"Virtual reality, like on Star Trek?" she asked, imagining a holodeck, populated by a complete, invented universe, full of invented people as real as life itself.

"Sorry, no," said Steve. "Nothing so elaborate. I think you'll like it, though."

She picked up one of the books he'd brought. There was an explosive sun on the cover, with a swirling vortex at its center. Steve's name was written in huge incandescent letters across the top of the cover, and the title of the book, *Fire in the Hole,* twisted down the center, getting smaller as the vortex narrowed.

"Is that what you write about?" she asked.

"Sometimes. I write about ideas that interest me," he said, with the look of a man who is satisfied with his work. "Science fiction is suited to that—you can stretch your world to include infinite possibilities. You can pull in or invent anything you need."

She traced her fingers across the letters of his glowing name. "Is this the first one you wrote?"

"Yes, why?"

"I want to read them first to last. Things make more sense that way."

"That's the accountant in you," he told her. "First thing you do, when you pick up a sci-fi book, is look to see if it's part of a series. You read 'em in order, even if other books by the author were written in between. This is the first book in the *Fireman* series."

"Are all your books written by the 'several'?" Interesting. Everything he said was interesting. She'd found something besides Cara and Melody to distract her.

"Pretty much."

"How come? Can't you write just one book?"

"Depends on what you're trying to do." He squinted at her. "Do you mean to tell me that you haven't even read *Foundation*?"

"Shameful ignorance, I know. But I did read *Don Quixote*."

"Did you like it?"

"As a matter of fact, I did."

"You ought to like science fiction then. The good stuff turns on themes like Cervantes's."

She looked at the back cover of *Fire in the Hole*. A much younger Steve smiled out from the page. His face had that raw-boned youngster look, full of himself and all cocky self-confidence. Very young. Very endearing.

Steve knew what she was going to ask. "I was twenty and thought I knew everything."

She smiled across the table. "And did you?"

"Surprisingly enough, I knew a great deal more then than I seem to know now." He shook his head. "My world now is much more confusing than it was then. All I had to think about was the next page, the next bar and the next brawl. The more complicated my life gets, the less confident I am that I'm making the right decisions." He shrugged. "Life's like that."

"Sounds like a theme for a book."

"I expect it will be. I've been thinking a lot about it, lately." He cocked a brushy eyebrow at her. "Tell me what you've been thinking about, Lady Greeneyes."

As if he didn't know. Elizabeth looked at him: he was intelligent, sexy and full of fun. Unconsciously she listed the virtues she'd discovered in him in the past few weeks—his commitment to Melody, his dedication to his work, his honesty and ethical behavior. For the first time since her divorce from Robert, she thought, *I could fall in love here, if I'm not careful.*

And if she did, how would she reconcile Cara, the Immovable Object, to Steve, the Irresistible Force? Elizabeth had read the statistics about how easily disapproving children could destroy a relationship between a man and a woman. She sighed.

Steve reached across the table and tapped her hand with a gentle finger. "What are you thinking?"

"I'm thinking I'm sorry Cara was so rude to you tonight." That was close enough to the truth.

"It's not me she doesn't like. It's Melody. I'm just caught in the fallout."

"I hope that's all," said Elizabeth. "I'm afraid she's hoping that her father and I will eventually see reason and reunite. I'm sure that's why she wants me to date Joe Salvini—except for the nose, he could be Robert's brother. Not as good-looking, but there's a definite resemblance. So she'll take Joe as a temporary substitute, until I'm sensible enough to invite Robert to come back."

"Pretty normal, I think, for her to want her father and mother to be together," he said, wondering if Elizabeth also harbored that hope. She'd been divorced for six years and hadn't had a serious relationship since. Could she still be committed to Robert and yearning for him despite his faults?

"Yeah, it's normal." She propped her chin on one hand and stared into her empty glass as if she looked for wisdom in its crystal depth. "She thinks he's wonderful, and I've encouraged her. Maybe I've overdone it."

Steve split the last of the wine between them. "It's not a bad thing for a girl to admire her father."

"I know. That's why I did it." She regarded the wine pensively. "She's too young for perspective. Robert's her father—if she hated him, she'd have to hate herself. So I emphasize his good points."

"What are they?" he asked, and watched her carefully to see if he could tell how she really felt about Robert.

"Damned if I know," said Elizabeth, and grinned. "Well, okay. I'll be honest. He does have good points—two of them. He's very charming and incredibly handsome. Sort of like a Ken doll who's been to a personality-plus seminar. But that's all there is to him."

"How does he manage with these terrible handicaps?" he asked.

"I only said he's shallow. I didn't say he wasn't smart. He negotiates contracts for professional athletes, and he's very good at it. I can't imagine why—he tells everybody exactly what they want to hear, whether it's true or not. It's a very poor way to conduct your affairs."

"Does he do that with Cara, too?" he asked.

"Of course. I told you. He does it with everybody."

Was she bitter and hurt, he wondered, or just annoyed with Robert and worried about Cara? Testing the waters, Steve said, "That's bound to cause trouble later."

"Oh, absolutely," said Elizabeth gloomily. "I suppose I haven't been telling her the truth, either. I let her think he's something he's not. But I mean well. And he does love her. He's just irresponsible, that's all."

"That's all?" said Steve, sounding irritated despite himself. How could she defend a jerk who wouldn't take any of the emotional responsibility for his own daughter? Cara was stubborn and determined, a feisty and resilient fighter. Those were invaluable traits. If she learned to use them properly, she'd be a world-beater. Any father ought to be proud to have a hand in raising a kid like that.

Of course, he wasn't under any illusion about whom the feisty and resilient Cara was fighting, and there was no use pretending that thirteen-year-olds of either sex could be motivated by logic and justice. It just wasn't in them.

The thought of Cara scowling and facing him down like a scrappy little alley cat made him smile. Elizabeth, seeing this, scowled herself.

"You couldn't possibly think this is funny," she said, with some heat. "So what are you smiling about?"

"Cara."

"How could you smile about Cara? She's been perfectly horrible."

"Oh, not perfectly," he told her. "I'll admit I wish she'd warm up to me, but there's a lot to be said for anyone who fights as hard as she does for what she believes, even if it's wrong."

"Good Lord," Elizabeth said. "You've been addled by the wine."

"I'm addled, all right," he said. "But not by the wine." He gathered his long legs under him and got to his feet. "Come out from behind that oak plank barrier you've got between us and walk me to the door. I wouldn't want Melody to be late for a Saturday detention because I overslept."

"I'd forgotten about the damned detention," said Elizabeth.

Steve walked around the table and pulled her to her feet. Hand in hand, they walked to the front door.

"Want to kiss me good-night in here or out there?" he asked, gesturing with his head toward the porch. "Cara's in here, the neighbors are out there."

"The neighbors pay absolutely no attention to anything I do," said Elizabeth, avid with anticipation. "Cara's the problem."

"Cara will come around," he said. "I'll see to it."

She opened the door and stepped outside into the frosty November night. Steve reached a long arm around the door frame and switched off the porch light. The cold dark shadows of the trees and houses closed in around them, and the stars were far away and very dim.

"Well," he said, putting his hands to her waist. "Shielded enough?"

She murmured assent.

"Still want the kiss?"

"Don't tease," she said. "Or I'll go back in the house and nurse a grudge, and you'll still be out here in the cold, sans kiss."

Fat chance, twittered her libido, which knew beyond doubt that she craved that kiss. Wanted it more than anything in the world just then.

On again, off again, as desire warred with anxiety.

On again. Worry about it later. She'd wanted that kiss, wanted it badly, every day after school as she and Steve met in front of Harkness to collect their unrepentant feuders. Wanted it on Saturday mornings, when they talked after they delivered the girls to the reforming dicta of Miss Westcott. Wanted it as they lingered after Saturday detention, waiting for their unreconstructed little rebels to be released.

She *deserved* that kiss, she'd waited a long time for it, she intended to have it.

And worried about it, briefly, as he touched her cheek. What if this one kiss she wanted so much drove her to throw all reason to the wind? Off again. On again.

He raised her chin with one finger and she closed her eyes. He was too close to see, to close for her to breathe. He kissed her firmly and gently, his lips tasting hers for far too short a time: a get-acquainted kiss, a let's-see-what-comes-of-this kiss. An invitation to a beginning. Then he hugged her hard and drew away.

It was not enough to satisfy her physical desire, but certainly, emotionally, quite enough for now.

Elizabeth stupidly padded around her bedroom barefoot with her feet freezing, until she was ready for bed. Then she snuggled under a wool blanket and a down comforter and wondered how cold feet could make her whole body miserable. Since the barefoot padding was an unbreakable habit, every winter night brought the same chill and the same annoyed philosophizing. She tucked her feet into the tail of her flannel nightgown and for the thousandth time, she thought, *I need a hot-water bottle.*

For the first time she thought, *No, I don't. I need a man.* A man like Steve. The thought warmed more than her feet. She imagined what it would be like to have him share the big bed, to wrap her closely to his naked body, to grow hot against him under the protective weight of the soft, white wool and silk-covered down.

Intruding into this seductive fantasy was Cara, who opposed Steve with the mindless ardor of a fanatic. Cara had no real reason to dislike Melody and Steve. That fact made the situation worse, not better. It was almost impossible to alter prejudice with reason. What would happen to all of them, Elizabeth wondered, if she let herself fall in love with Steve and found that she couldn't manage Cara, who became more stubborn and less tractable with every passing day?

Steve. She groaned and rolled over in bed. The sexual fantasy had made her body burn, and worrying about Cara made her head ache, and anxiety made her mouth dry, and the combination made her irritable.

I can't think about this now, she said to herself, and recalled Scarlett O'Hara. *I'll think about it tomorrow.*

She tossed. She turned. She yearned.

Damn.

Finally she went to find the books Steve had brought her. She was terribly tired. If she read, she'd relax, and the reading would put her to sleep. A good way to get to sleep, she thought, but not too flattering to the author. She wouldn't tell Steve that his baby had grown up to be a soporific.

She piled pillows against the headboard and climbed back into bed with the book. She snuggled down until her head was supported and the light hit the page just right, and opened the cover of *Fire in the Hole*.

"He had always been afraid of fire," read the first line. "So afraid that as a child he dreamed at night of licking flames and scarring heat, which made his infant face melt into his outstretched hands."

And Elizabeth was hooked.

Fire in the Hole was an exhilarating fantastic romp through accidental universes. It braided, looped and spun like a flight of acrobats, across three hundred pages that shimmered with wit and charm. It was a remarkable piece of work for a boy just twenty years old. Jord Varic was the hero, and obviously the young and fearless hero was Steve's imaginary alter ego.

To Elizabeth's great astonishment, she liked it very much, just for herself and not because Steve had written it.

Jord Varic, the Fireman, was in charge of a problem-shooting team of astrophysicists who roved through these universes eliminating anything which threatened to destroy the balance of our own. The Fireman was cocky, sure of himself, felt physically invincible and was irresistible to beautiful women. He was very James Bond-y, full of hope for the future and the unshakable belief that good would always conquer evil.

However dazzling the writing, thematically it was so exactly what a twenty-year-old boy would write that it made her smile with tenderness for his youth and innocence.

Though it touched metaphorically on the problems of the world, it focused more on the problems of the studly protagonist, who might get horribly trapped in an alternate universe—except that the youngster, who brandished his hero like a vindicating sword, harbored the very endearing and completely specious idea that nothing horrible could possibly happen to him. The Fireman, like the writer, knew that he controlled his life and his future and refused to be misguided by any notion to the contrary.

The thoughts, the ideas, the thrust of the plot all revealed a great deal of what Steve must have been like as a very young man. She lay back on the pillows, musing. Whatever she had expected from reading his books first to last, she hadn't thought she'd have such a mirror on his mind. Drowsily she wondered what the other books would tell about him.

Did Steve, like the Fireman, at twenty, believe implicitly that he could wrestle destiny and by his own strength defeat it?

Did he still believe it, the older Fireman who struggled on the cover of *The Hail Mary Margin?*

She was too sleepy to find out. She sank deeply into a wonderful dreamless sleep which lasted exactly fifty-seven minutes. Then her alarm heartlessly sawed its way into her brain and used no anesthetic.

After a few exhausted moments of groggy resentment, she forced herself out of bed and went to waken Cara.

"Detention time," she said, switching on the light.

Cara opened her eyes and glared at her mother. "I hate Miss Westcott," she announced.

"It's a waste of time to hate Miss Westcott for your own transgressions," said Elizabeth, whose head ached from lack of sleep. "If you would give up this idiotic feud, we could both sleep late on Saturdays."

"I'm not feuding," said Cara. "Melody is."

"Takes two to tango," Elizabeth said, leaving Cara's room to go and dress. "Get out of bed."

Back in her bedroom she drew the curtain and peered into the dark morning. Dawn had yet to come, though the horizon was lightening in the east. One thick, icy, well-muscled cloud plated the sky gray-black, and a heavy drizzle was beginning to turn to sleet. She stood on the edges of her bare feet to minimize their contact with the wooden floor; it made her ankles hurt, and her feet stayed cold, anyway.

The weather worsened by the second.

Her bed, still warm, invited her to crawl back under the covers, and the comforter waited, curled protectively around the hollow she'd made for herself during the night. With enormous strength of will and considerable rancor for Cara and Melody, she turned to the old wardrobe that held her clothes and began to root in the top drawer for wool socks and a silk undershirt. Heavy jeans. A red plaid flannel shirt. Duck shoes.

Her jeans were cold against her legs. Her feet were cold, under the argyles. Her hands were cold; her nose was cold. And by now, the bed was cold. The wind rose with the sun, and the sleet clicked decisively against the glass.

It was a long time till summer. Hard to believe that a few weeks ago she'd been sweltering in her office... that she hadn't met Steve. Had not wanted a man. Had not seen one who caused thick-coming fantasies so seductive that they engendered a passion she could still feel in her body and taste upon her lips.

She wandered, bemused, down the hall and found Cara still in bed.

"Damn it," she said.

Cara took one look at her mother's face and bounded to the floor. "I'm up, I'm up," she said.

"If you are not downstairs, fully dressed, in ten minutes..." Elizabeth began.

But Cara had fled to the bathroom and was out of earshot.

Elizabeth went downstairs and put on the coffee and a pot of water for oatmeal. The thermometer in the kitchen read fifty degrees. She muttered at the thermostat and turned it to eighty. It was a symbolic gesture; she and Cara would be out of the house long before the kitchen was warm enough to be comfortable. The furnace had to make a considerable and lengthy effort to take the chill off the granite and flagstones.

She stirred the oatmeal and looked around the room, musing. Like a cave in this kitchen, in bad weather. Ought to do something about it. Needs a rug, a nice braided rug with some bright color in it, instead of that tatty grayish thing that's under the table now. Yellow curtains, get rid of that wretched Philadelphia-conservative navy-and-gold print. Better lights, so shadows didn't squat in all the corners. Wallpaper, maybe. White paint, cover up that dark woodwork. New clock. Bigger, so she could see it without squinting at it from across the room.

And squinting, she saw that it was six thirty-five and she yelled up the stairs for Cara to come to breakfast.

On the way to school, fortified by the oatmeal and the coffee, she said to Cara, "We're going out for pizza next Saturday." Perhaps in seven days, Cara would be used to the idea.

"Great," said Cara, unsuspecting. "Can I bring a friend?"

"May I," said Elizabeth, pulling up to the Harkness front door. "Actually—" she took a deep breath "—Melody and her father are going to pick us up."

Cara stiffened.

"Well, I won't go," she announced. She slammed out of the car and stomped up the stairs to the detention hall.

Melody was just in front of her and let the door slam in her face. With an expression of sheer vitriol, Cara yanked it open and stalked inside.

Elizabeth watched anxiously.

Steve tapped on her window. She lowered it and looked at him. The wind tousled his sandy hair and lifted the collar of his scuffed, old, leather bomber jacket. He looked like an adventurer.

"I hope you realize that this pizza venture is doomed," she said, feeling as certain to be thwarted as Juliet Capulet.

"Let's talk about it over coffee. Is the Humpty Dumpty's Diner over by the Bryn Mawr station all right with you?"

She nodded, and he slid into the front seat beside her.

"You do know this thing with Melody and Cara isn't as bad as it looks, don't you?" he said, laying his arm across the back of the seat.

"*Steve,*" she said. "You've been writing too much fiction. This is reality. It is exactly as bad as it looks. Maybe worse. You can't move those two girls around like you can move the characters in the books you write."

"You can't move the characters in a book around, either," he said. "They have minds of their own. But that's beside the point."

"Just what is the point?" She started the car with a jerk and rolled down the driveway.

"The point is that they're two children, malleable and flexible. We're the parents. If we're firm and confident, they'll see that their opposition is useless, and they'll give it up."

She glanced at him. He was the picture of firm confidence. His eyes smiled at her from across the seat.

"Oh, yeah, right," she said. "Cara says she won't go next weekend."

"So does Melody. But she will."

"Interesting picture," said Elizabeth, after a pause. "Both of them bound and gagged and propped into a booth."

"An appealing picture, sometimes," said Steve. "We'd get some relief."

"Relief? What happened to being firm and they'll come around?"

"Oh, I'm convinced they'll come around," he said. "But that doesn't mean they aren't wearing on me. Here's the diner, right here."

They could smell bacon as soon as they got out of the car. Elizabeth, who had not intended to eat, began to reconsider. A rasher of bacon, two eggs, cottage fries and two cups of coffee later, she said, "I read *Fire in the Hole.*"

"Did you like it?" he asked. And couldn't believe how much he cared about her answer.

"I loved it," she said honestly. She tilted her head and smiled across the table at him. "Is that what you were like, at twenty?"

"I wish." He shook his head, remembering the boy he had been. "That's what I wanted to be at twenty. Savior of the world."

"Do you still want to save it?"

"Oh, yes. The difference is, now I know I can't."

"When did you decide that?"

"Somewhere along the way," he said. "Keep reading."

"Could I have all of them? The Fireman books?" she asked. "All right now, I mean. I don't want to have to wait after I finish the next one. I want the third one right there at hand. What's it called?"

"*The Lion's Whelp.*"

"Then?"

"*Kalik the Destroyer.* The end of innocence." He didn't say whether it was his innocence that ended, but the look on his face hinted at it. "Then *Fields of Gomorrah.*"

Were the subsequent four as psychologically autobiographical as the first? She couldn't ask.

"When may I get them?" she said.

"This morning, if you want to," he said. "I have to go by the house to pick up Sammy so I can take him to Lin's, and if you'll come with me, you can take home all the books I have."

"Good offer," she said. "I accept. When do you have to leave?"

"Ten-thirty or so. Want to kill some time in between?"

"If you don't mind running an errand with me. I'm going to remodel my kitchen. I decided this morning." She sipped at her coffee, then added more cream. "Only the Penitentes could feel comfortable in there."

Steve reached for her hand. "Great idea," he said. "I never saw a kitchen in such dire need of improvement. What are you going to do?"

"New curtains. Paint the woodwork and cabinets white, I guess. Wallpaper. And a new rug. I hate that gray thing I've got now." Her green eyes looked past him, far away, as if she could already see the transformation.

He could see it, too—Elizabeth in a red shirt and tight jeans, standing at the counter in a blaze of bright light, sipping at wine as red as her lips.

His fingers curled around hers and his thumb massaged gently at the center of her palm. He loved tight jeans.

If we were alone, he thought, *I'd put a kiss right there—* looking at the dimple beside her mouth. *And then I'd unbutton that shirt.*

"Why'd you keep it so long?" he asked, feeling a hunger that no amount of breakfast could ever assuage. He cupped his hand around her fist and squeezed gently.

"Inertia, I suppose," she said, sounding a bit short of breath. She pulled her hand away and toyed with the last of her toast. "I thought I'd go to a carpet store this morning while I wait for Cara to get out of detention."

"I promise not to offer any advice."

"You're welcome to offer advice if you please." She really didn't know what she was likely to do, she thought, if she managed to get him alone anywhere. It was so unsettling to look at a man and want to tear all your clothes off, and all his, too.

Steve reached for the check and Elizabeth said, "Let me pay for mine."

"Absolutely not. I drank about forty dollars' worth of wine last night. I owe you at least twenty more breakfasts, at that rate."

She tossed three dollars on the table. "I'll get the tip, then."

As soon as they were in the car, Steve said, "That was thirty percent, that tip. You left thirty percent."

"So?" said Elizabeth. She wrapped both hands tightly around the steering wheel, trying to forget the erotic pressure of his stroking thumb. She backed out of the parking space and crept into the southbound traffic.

"Mad extravagance," he said. "And from an accountant, too. It's shocking."

"Why are all men such bad tippers?" She turned the heater fan to high. Cold air swirled around their feet and ankles.

"I'm not a bad tipper. Thirty percent's too much."

"These people depend on tips for a living."

"I only get six and a half percent. I depend on that for a living."

"Six and a half? Are you kidding?" Sleet had built up at the edges of the street. Elizabeth turned cautiously onto Montgomery. The tires slipped a little before they caught. She *had* to quit thinking about sex and concentrate on her driving. Maybe the frigid air blowing out of the heater would have the same effect as a cold shower.

"One and a half on overseas sales," said Steve.

"Good God," said Elizabeth, marveling. "I thought writing was easy money. How do you manage?"

"I write fast."

"You must...you're eating." She shivered. "Is there anything you can do about that heater? I'm freezing."

Freezing. But only on the outside. New discovery: it was not possible to quit thinking about sex with the object of your desire less than three feet away, with his hand lying across the back of the seat and his fingers playing with your hair.

"Not until the engine's hot. How far is it to the carpet place?"

"Ardmore Square. Right there."

Steve pointed. "On the corner? They don't look open."

"That," she said, sliding the car neatly into a small space by the curb, "is why there's a place to park."

He laughed. "You're so pragmatic. The perfect accountant. What shall we do while we wait?"

"You think of something," she said. "You're the one with all the imagination, which makes you the perfect writer." She sighed. She almost wished he could read her mind. But if he could, there wouldn't be time to buy a napkin, let alone a carpet.

"The perfect writer for the perfect accountant," said Steve. "A natural fit, my sweet. You'll see." His words were light, but his voice had dropped and slowed.

"Will I?" she said, trying not to sound breathless. Maybe he *could* read her mind.

"Oh, yes." He tugged at her hair. "Look here at me."

There was a dangerous glint in his eyes. All Elizabeth's Main Line inhibitions ran gibbering about in her brain. *Broad daylight, it's broad daylight. There are people walking down the street, and they can see in the car and what would my mother think?*

She reached for the door latch.

"Wait," said Steve, smiling. "Don't get out yet."

There was laughter, damn it, in his voice.

"Why not?" She knew why not.

"I'm waiting for the windows to fog over."

"They won't fog," she told him. "The car's still cold."

He cupped his hand around her shoulder.

"They'll fog. We'll see to it." He turned her gently toward him. "Come here."

"It's broad daylight," she objected, but she moved across the seat and into his arms.

"I'll kiss you twice tonight, to compensate for the trauma of public exposure." He brushed the curly hair away from her face and looked deeply into her clear green eyes. "Put your arms around my neck."

She did. "All those people outside can see us."

"Won't they be jealous, though," he murmured, and he put his lips to hers.

She didn't know any of those people on the sidewalk. Who cared what they thought, anyway?

Chapter Four

When Elizabeth finally opened her eyes, the windows were definitely fogged. The people passing outside were no more than shadows falling on frosted glass.

"The world looks out of focus," she murmured.

"Ignore the world. Focus on me," said Steve, snuggling her head under his chin.

A few minutes later she reluctantly pushed herself away from him. "You don't think I should focus on a rug for the kitchen?"

"Oh, yeah. The rug. I forgot." He tapped her chin with his forefinger and smiled. "You look like you've just been kissed, did you know that?"

She tilted the rearview mirror and took a look for herself. She did, indeed, look kissed. Her lips were red and full and moist; her cheeks and chin were scratched a little from his beard.

She loved it. "Can I go shopping like this?"

"If you get out of the car really, really fast, you can," said Steve. "Otherwise, we aren't going to buy a rug today."

"We have to buy a rug. We've done all we can do in this car."

"Oh, no, we haven't," Steve told her. He leaned toward her and beckoned. "Come here and I'll show you a few of the other things that are possible." His grin was positively devilish and his intent was clear.

"I think not," said Elizabeth regretfully.

"Better go look at rugs, then," said Steve.

A rush of cold air enveloped them as they stepped onto the sidewalk. The sleet had turned to soggy snow, and big wet flakes lumped over the ice pellets to make a slippery slush underfoot. They picked their way to the carpet showroom and hauled the door open against the wind.

The quiet inside the building was a pleasant contrast to the turbulence outside.

"Maybe we should just stay here until spring," said Elizabeth. "Roll up in a rug and hibernate."

"Sounds good to me," said Steve. "Make sure there's room for two." He looked at the confusing mounds of oriental carpets on the floor, the racks of Berbers on swinging arms, the tables of carpet samples. "How are you going to pick one out of all these?"

Elizabeth examined an off-white Berber carpet with an intricate weave. "I thought I wanted a braided rug, but now I don't know. This one's pretty."

"Spaghetti sauce," said Steve. "Ketchup. Mustard. Red wine. Grape juice."

Grape juice? Elizabeth jerked her fingers from the carpet as if she'd been burned.

"Could I see something with brown in it?" she asked a saleswoman. "And green. Dark green."

The saleswoman pulled out a mottled shag which looked exactly like a forest floor—decaying leaves, pine needles, toadstools and all.

Elizabeth viewed it with great distaste. "That's not exactly what I had in mind," she said. The understatement of the year. "We'll just look around for a while, if that's all right."

"Get something with red in it," said Steve.

"Cheerful in the mornings, these dark days," the saleswoman agreed.

Steve touched the glossy hair streaming over the collar of Elizabeth's coat. Red would be a wonderful color for her, he thought. He could see her at the breakfast table, in a red wadded-silk robe, with her coffee and a pen and the crossword puzzle. Could see himself, sitting across from her, looking at her hair, still tousled from sleeping in his arms, and her lips, still red from his early-morning kisses.

Could see the girls slopping cornflakes onto the oak, glaring at each other across the table.

He had to woo and win Cara as well as Elizabeth. He wondered with a sigh how he would ever be able to do it. Cara was the least woo-able little character he'd ever seen. He didn't think she was in the least susceptible to either blandishment or honest admiration. His lips twitched upward—he certainly could provide honest admiration. Cara reminded him of a feisty little terrier, all fuss and fluff, with that terrier conviction that she could fight the world and the world would give up and let her have what she wanted.

Steve enjoyed being a father. He'd loved the baby smell of Melody, the feel of having her scrunch her drowsy little body up in his arms and snuffle into his neck while she slept. Loved having her cling to his forefinger as she took her first steps. Loved the baby babble and the spate of clear speech which followed. Loved the guiding and the teaching and the confident unthinking trust in his love and support which would give Melody the confidence to conquer any world she chose. It would be so easy for his heart to expand enough to tuck Cara in beside Melody.

If she'd let him.

A few minutes later, when he and Elizabeth were sifting through a pile of the braided rugs she'd come in to see, she asked, "What kind of mind could design that green horror, do you think?"

"A cave dweller," said Steve, still somewhat melancholy from contemplating his problems with Cara. "Who dines on insects. That carpet probably comes with its own supply of beetles." He slipped a rug from the stack. "Here's one. It'll look great on that gray slate floor."

It was an oval braided wool, in narrow-banded shades of red, cream, dark green and navy.

"It's beautiful," said Elizabeth. She looked at the tag. "A thousand dollars! I can't afford a thousand dollars."

"You can get the beetle one for $400," Steve told her.

"Oh, very funny." The rug was perfect. Except for the price, which ran about $100 a linear foot.

"Says on the wall there you can try it out for a few days."

"You really think I ought to buy this thing," Elizabeth marveled. "Aren't you the man who caviled at a three-dollar tip?"

"I was wrong. You should always indulge your whims," said Steve. He beckoned to the saleswoman. "May we bring this back if it doesn't fit our kitchen?"

"Whose whim are we indulging now?" Elizabeth asked, liking the rug better with every look. She took a charge card out of her wallet and handed it to the clerk. "Okay. I hope you're satisfied. That's a tenth of Cara's tuition."

"So get a second job," he said. He began to roll the rug like a sausage. "Here. Take one end."

The rug had looked normal on the floor. Rolled, it looked a block long and as big around as a submarine.

"Pick it up? I don't think so," protested Elizabeth. "Let's have it delivered."

"Nonsense," said Steve. "Don't wimp out on me." He maneuvered the carpet onto one broad shoulder. "We can manage this. Let's take it now. Pick up the other end."

"It's started raining. My rug will get wet," she said, trying again.

"Oh, no," said the clerk cheerfully. "It's been treated— sheds water like a duck."

"Thanks a lot," muttered Elizabeth. She struggled to heft the short end of the roll. The weight of it made her knees buckle. She hauled it onto her left shoulder. It was only slightly less heavy than a barge full of gravel.

"Why are we doing this?" she gasped. "Do you just hate delivery vans or what?"

Steve started for the door, with Elizabeth staggering after him, panting and clutching her burden. "I want to see what it looks like on the floor right now. I don't want to wait for three days."

"This is stupid. My piano weighs less than this," she said. "It's giving me spots in front of my eyes. I'm sure it can't be good for me."

"What doesn't kill you makes you stronger, remember?" He shifted the rug forward so that he bore most of its weight. "Your grandmother told you that. Don't you believe it?"

She laughed in spite of herself. "Only in the abstract."

Steve maneuvered the rug so that he could open the door of the car, then squashed its mighty bulk into submission in the back seat.

"Now," he said, with the air of a man who has settled things to his satisfaction. "We get to go home and do it all again, in reverse."

The words *our kitchen* echoed in Elizabeth's head all the way home. The heft and savor of them as she formed them with her silent tongue were deep and weighty and delicious. *Our kitchen* meant much more than mere joint possession. She was just beginning to learn what it was like to have a man for a companion. The day-to-day confidences and sharing of concerns magically increased her comfort and decreased an isolation she hadn't realized, until lately, that she felt.

Thus she said, "Our kitchen?", after they'd wrestled the rug into the house and had it in place under the table.

"Just trying out the idea," said Steve imperturbably. "To see how it sounds."

It sounded wonderful. *Our kitchen, our kitchen, our kitchen* sang in Elizabeth's head like a symphonic melody. She could hear the tinkling of china, the clear ring of wineglasses, the huffing of boiling stew, hum of conversation—all the noise and commotion and laughter which composed a normal family life.

And throbbing inexorably beneath the theme was an ominous discord orchestrated by Cara and Melody. She managed to put that out of her mind by backing against the far wall of the kitchen to view the full effect of her new purchase. The kitchen was transformed. The rich colors of the braids glowed against the old gray slate. Even the dark cabinets and woodwork seemed to take on a new energy, shining with a fresh luster under the peacock spell of the rug.

"I'm in love," said Elizabeth. "It's the most gorgeous rug I ever saw. I adore it." She gazed around the vast old room. "I'm definitely going to have the woodwork painted."

"Good," said Steve. "I know a painter. Now, drive me to my car so we can poke Sammy out of his chair and take him to Lin's."

"We can go in mine."

"You probably wouldn't like that. I keep washing his feet, but they seem to stay muddy."

"I wish it would quit raining," she said, gazing out the window at the gloomy sky and soggy landscape. "And snow instead."

She definitely needed Christmas.

Elizabeth had seen a couple of Airedale terriers, neatly and sleekly trimmed, except for their legs and mutton chop whiskers. Very elegant looking dogs, with their black saddles and red-tan curls. Big dogs, but not gigantic. More Cary Grant than Arnold Schwarzenegger.

This memory served her well until they started up the front steps of Steve's house, and Sammy's basso-profundo bark shook the foundations of buildings half a block away.

He sounded like an earthquake.

Steve emptied his mailbox and opened the door.

"Sit," he said to the bouncing dog inside. He tossed the mail onto his couch and reached to pat the dog's huge muzzle.

Sammy sat, and sitting, his nose touched Elizabeth's belt. He was mammoth and as furry and curly as a Scots Highland ram. His eyes twinkled up at her from his enormous head, and his tongue, which looked as long as a table runner, lolled good-naturedly out of the side of his mouth.

"He's sort of a cross between a sheepskin coat and a Shetland pony," said Steve.

"Mrrmpph," Sammy said, looking winsome. He held up his right paw, decided that was all wrong, and switched to the left one.

"He's irresistible," announced Elizabeth, by now completely captivated by the big dog's charm. She reached out a hand to scratch behind a fuzzy ear, which was the approximate size and shape of a shovel blade. "No wonder Melody talks about him all the time."

Sammy pushed his head against Elizabeth's fingers and groaned with ecstasy. Elizabeth, thus encouraged, plunged both hands into his curly pate and kept scratching. He leaned his head against her hip and relaxed against her, bit by bit, until his weight pushed her off-balance. She stepped backward and Sammy folded, boneless, to the floor. His wounded expression of disappointment, when he opened his eyes to see what had become of her, was comical.

"Grin, Sammy," said Steve.

Sammy grinned. His lips stretched happily open to reveal two rows of gleaming white teeth.

Steve took Sammy's cheek and pinched it like a doting aunt. "Good dog," he said.

Sammy knew he was a good dog. He wriggled onto his back. His paws flopped. "Aowrrr," he said, suggesting that someone scratch his tummy.

"I'm in love," said Elizabeth, dropping to her knees.

"I thought you were in love with the rug," said Steve.

"A bagatelle. This is real love." She leaned forward so Sammy could lick her chin. "Where in the world did you ever find a dog like this? Did you have to fight fifty families to get him for yourself?"

"Actually, no. I got him from one of the Airedale Rescue people."

Elizabeth looked up. "What do you mean, rescue?"

"I mean that some Samaritan found him on the road and picked him up and called a vet who called the rescue people."

"Arrmph," Sammy complained. Steve squatted and resumed scratching where Elizabeth had left off.

"You should have seen him," Steve continued. "His hair was all matted, and he had on a collar he'd outgrown, skinny as he was, with a piece of rope still tied to it. He could hardly breathe and had a hard time swallowing. I've spent a lot of time hoping that the people who hurt him came to no good end.''

Elizabeth couldn't believe it. ''But why would anybody give him up?''

''Some people just aren't willing to give Airedales the time they need to make good pets.'' Steve shrugged. ''And they're big dogs. They act like puppies nearly forever—at least three years. Sometimes they never outgrow it, like this big doof. Most of 'em are really smart, and they're notorious hardheads. They can be a lot of trouble—too much trouble for people who just want a dog that snores by the fire. Especially when they're young.''

''So he acts like a puppy. So what?'' Elizabeth crooned to Sammy, speaking in baby talk. Sammy had found a champion.

''The *so what* is,'' said Steve, standing up, ''if they're bored, they find some way to entertain themselves. Mostly you won't like what they find. Sammy, for instance, goes through the house opening drawers and cabinets until he locates something interesting, then he takes it and drops it down the stairs.''

''He can open drawers?''

''He can open anything. That's why I have dead bolts. He can open doors. He turns the knobs with his teeth.'' Everybody had quit scratching his tummy. Sammy wheedled; no response. He whined; no response. He lumbered to his feet and stuck his nose in Elizabeth's face. She kissed him.

Steve grinned. ''Get away from her,'' he said to Sammy. ''She's mine.''

Sammy wouldn't.

''Want a bagel?'' said Steve.

Sammy ran to the kitchen. When Elizabeth and Steve arrived, he was barking at the refrigerator. Steve got a frozen bagel and defrosted it in the microwave.

''This is the flop side to the 'lot of trouble.' They're natural comedians and they like company.'' He fed the bagel to Sammy, who was slavering at his side. ''It's hot,'' he said to the dog.

Sammy dropped the bagel and poked at it with his nose.

"Let's get you those books and get out of here," said Steve, leading the way to his office. "You can pet him all the way to Lin's. Grab that mail for me, will you?"

Elizabeth picked up the scattered mail and arranged it as she walked behind him. A very official-looking envelope wound up on top. In small menacing capitals, it announced its origin: United States Treasury, Department of Internal Revenue.

"Steve," she said. "Here's something from the IRS."

"Toss it in the trash," he said. "They keep sending me the same letter over and over."

Elizabeth knew something about the IRS.

"They don't just go away, you know. You don't owe them money or anything, do you?"

"No. They only think I do." He saw her concern and explained. "Every couple of months, for the past few years, I've gotten this letter which tells me I owe the IRS $4800. For a while, I wrote back and explained why I don't owe them anything and proved it, and they sent me another letter saying they were sorry. I wrote six times, they replied six times. I'm still getting the letters, but now I just throw them away. I figured six times is enough."

"With any normal entity, you'd be right," said Elizabeth. "But with the IRS—you'd better keep writing."

"Bah," said Steve. He took the mail from her hand and threw the offending missive into the trash can beside his desk.

Elizabeth shook her head. "You never know," she said. "You really ought to open that."

"Bah," said Steve again. As he made his way across the cluttered room, he flapped a hand at the bookshelves. "Help yourself to anything you want."

Elizabeth looked about her. His office seemed made of books. Books poked into shelves, books stacked on chairs, books scattered on the floor, piled on the desk, balanced on the narrow windowsill. It looked chaotic, but he seemed able to put a finger on whatever he wanted. He dug about in a box and surfaced with the last three volumes in the *Fireman* series.

"There," he said, giving them to her. He dusted his hands over his hair. When she started to look at the one on top, he clapped one big hand across the cover. "We gotta go, toots. You can read them on the way." He left the room bellowing, "Ride in the car, Sammy."

Sammy met them at the door with his leash.

Elizabeth looked at her watch, once they were on their way to Lin's. Ten-thirty exactly. In a scant twenty minutes, Steve turned off the highway onto a narrow country road, and then into a narrower, meandering driveway. The rain had stopped and only mud remained.

"Here we are," he said.

The house was a big fieldstone edifice that looked about two hundred years old. The springhouse still squatted over a fast little brook, and an old well—with a cast iron grate bolted to the top—was cool with water.

The front door slammed open before Steve and Elizabeth could get out of the car. Four towheaded little boys shot out to welcome them, followed by an immaculate, white standard poodle who was almost as tall as Sammy. Kids and dogs capered about like mad things, until Lin appeared and restored order with a whistle that could stop an army in full flight.

"Hi!" she called. She was as towheaded as the kids and pregnant.

Steve hugged her and introduced Elizabeth. Then he pointed to her barely rounded maternity shirt and said, "Again?"

"I knew you'd say that. That's why I didn't tell you." She turned to Elizabeth. "He's really rude. Come on in—I'm dying for company."

"I never saw anybody with so much company," Steve teased. "Look, Lin. Don't you know what causes that?"

"If it's what I think it is," Lin said, "I'm not going to quit. Where's Charles?" she asked the biggest boy.

"Hiding," he said.

"Well, find him," she instructed. "And if you can't, then come get me. Okay?"

The child nodded solemnly. He had thick, blond lashes and eyes as dark as the blue in the American flag.

"That's good, then," said Lin, giving his blond thatch a pat. "You want to meet Uncle Steve's friend?"

No nods. Eight blue eyes stared at Elizabeth.

The boys clung to the hem of Lin's shirt. She identified them by size and age, starting with the tallest. "Zach, Dan, Sandy and John. Seven, five, nearly four and just barely two."

The baby looked sideways at Elizabeth and stuck two fingers in his mouth. Steve picked him up and sat him on his shoulders. Johnny squealed. His three brothers looked envious.

Lin grinned up at her brother. "Go find Tom, you itch. He's in his shop. And take these brats with you. Don't forget to look for Charles, Zach."

She led Elizabeth into a big, bright kitchen with a long refectory table down the middle. She poured them both some hot chocolate and sighed as she sat down. Elizabeth looked around curiously.

"I'm redoing my kitchen," she said. "I know it must be younger than yours, but it doesn't look half so good."

"Mine used to be horrible, too. Tom fixed it."

"Do you rent him out?"

"I'm sure something can be arranged." She waggled her head. "You look just like I thought you would."

"What has Steve told you?"

Lin reeled off a catalog of personal information: Cara, Melody, Robert, Elizabeth's kitchen, her grandmother's wine, her business.

"That about covers it," said Elizabeth, liking Lin immensely. She fit like an old shoe—maybe because she was so much like Steve. "Cara has brought home 'horses and a farm.' What kind of farm?"

"We raise dogs and kids."

"No crops?"

"God, no. Tom can't even keep paint green, let alone a crop. And I have other concerns, obviously." She refilled the cups. "Tom's an expert on antique restoration. He consults with museums and teaches at U. Penn. He did this table. You should have seen it when he brought it home. Looked like kindling."

A sturdy subterranean thumping began, and a faint voice called, "Hey! Hey! Zach! Let me out of here."

Lin looked annoyed. She rose and kicked the corner of the rug aside to reveal a trap door in the maple floor. She grabbed an iron ring and pulled. A dirty little boy emerged.

"Charles, what are you doing down there?" Lin demanded. She dropped the trap back into place and covered it with the rug.

"We were playing spy," said Charles. "Dan put me in." He went outside.

"I have to get a lock for that thing," said Lin. "Today. Want to walk out to the shop with me? I'll get Tom to do it now."

"Wait," said Elizabeth. "I want to see. Why's it there?"

Lin opened the trap door again. "This house was a stop on the Underground Railway. The main part of it was built in the 1700s, and the family just kept adding room after room as they needed space. So in 1830, when they added a kitchen and a still room, they dug a hole in the floor and put a trap door over it." She paused. "Gives me chills to look at it."

Elizabeth peered into the dark, dirt-walled hole. It was barely deep enough to stand in. There was no light at all. To be shut up in there in the dark, cold and wet, hungry and afraid for your life and the lives of your children—horrid, unthinkable, and yet people had been there, had feared and had survived. She shivered.

"It affects me the same way," said Lin. "I keep imagining me down there, trying to keep the baby quiet while people who want to kill me and my children walk around the room over my head." She stopped and looked very unhappy. "It's such a clear picture. Sometimes I dream about it at night. And I don't want the kids playing there. It's too solemn a place for play."

The two women were silent for a minute, then Lin said, "How are the girls getting along?"

"Like the Hatfields and the McCoys," Elizabeth told her. "Oh, Lin, they're awful. I don't know what we're going to do. You should see them."

"I should. Maybe I could help. I've been talking to Melody about it. You know, she really likes you."

"I like her, too." Elizabeth leaned back in her chair and sighed. "She's a lovely little girl. And so is Cara. But you'd never believe it when they're together."

"Steve's falling in love with you, you know."

"I know," said Elizabeth. "I can see it coming. But it's a mistake."

"I could say I don't want to pry," Lin said. "But I'd be lying. How about you?"

"Oh, I could love him, all right, if I let myself," Elizabeth said. "But I'm afraid to. Cara and Melody are so awful. And what if we do fall in love, and they keep hating each other until we're ninety? We'd be miserable forever."

Lin looked worried. "Is it as bad as all that? Steve said he thought it would work out just fine. He said you were making progress."

"Steve," said Elizabeth with exasperation, "is a man. What does he know? It was men who thought we could survive a nuclear war, if you'll recall."

They laughed together, a little.

"Why don't you bring the girls out here and leave them with me every once in a while?" said Lin. "They could keep the kids occupied. They'd have to cooperate, and maybe they'd learn a little about each other."

"I will if you're not afraid they'll mark the baby," said Elizabeth. "Or frighten the boys."

Lynn laughed. "Now, really. They can't be that bad."

"You think," said Elizabeth. "They're as intractable as a religious war."

The men rattled around the back door.

Lin rose to reheat the cocoa. "You guys bring them out anytime," she said. "If nothing else, it'll give you a break."

Elizabeth knew she meant it, and thought the experiment was worth a try. Lin was calm and cheerful and sensible, and really not involved except as an impartial counselor. Maybe she could do something with Cara and Melody. You never knew: miracles sprang from the most unlikely sources.

Tom and Steve had the menagerie in the mudroom, removing boots and hats and washing off anything that moved. In a few minutes they emerged, not exactly clean, but not tracking mud, either. The children charged up the stairs to the playroom, with Sammy gamboling behind like a spring lamb. The poodle came around the table and tried to get in Lin's lap.

"Poor little Miggy," said Lin. "Did those nasty rough boys give you a hard time?" She hauled the dog's forequarters onto a pair of clean jeans. "Give Mama a nice kiss. Isn't she a pretty girl?"

Miggy went to greet Elizabeth. "She's gorgeous," said Elizabeth truthfully, letting Miggy nuzzle her. *But she's no Sammy,* she added to herself.

"Miggy," said Lin, "is the kids' college fund. She's won every show she's entered. A few more points and she'll have her championship. And her puppies will sell for a fortune."

"Will they sell for enough to cover the vet bill?" Tom wanted to know. His blue eyes smiled at Elizabeth from above a Viking's red beard. He stuck out his hand and introduced himself. "Can you guys stay for lunch? It's my turn to cook."

"In that case, we can't stay," said Steve.

"But it's haggis," said Tom. "I made it especially, out of my own sheep."

"I'm not staying unless there's scrapple, tripe or chitlings."

"I'm going to throw up," said Lin.

"So am I," said Elizabeth. "And I'm not even pregnant. We can't stay for haggis," she told Tom. "Because we have to pick up our termagants at noon. But thank you for the offer. We really must leave now, before the haggis comes out of the stew pot."

"Lin's corrupted your taste," said Tom. "My haggis is wonderful."

Pandemonium reigned in the playroom. Sandy came downstairs crying, followed by Johnny who said proudly, "Me bite. Me bite."

Sandy held out his arm and exhibited a perfect imprint of John's small teeth.

"Everybody here bites," said Tom. "Except me." He popped Johnny into a high chair, and Lin carried Sandy off to the sink to wash his wound.

"Well, Libby," said Steve. "We'd best escape the haggis." He kissed his sister and the two little boys and high-fived Tom, who was busy putting peanut butter onto bread.

Elizabeth looked covetously around her. This was exactly what she wanted: a big cheerful kitchen full of dogs and babies and noise and love.

Outside, it had begun to rain again. And back in town Cara and Melody waited. Elizabeth hugged Lin, and Sandy held out his arms.

"Bye-bye, Aunt Steve," he said, turning his sweet round face up for a kiss.

I would love to hear him call me Aunt Libby, she thought wistfully, taking him into her arms and cuddling the warm little body to her. Then she shrugged into her coat and ran to the car through a pelting rain.

"I didn't want to leave," she said, as Steve turned onto the highway. "It's so lovely there, with all the kids and commotion."

He folded her hand into his. "It makes home seem awfully quiet, doesn't it?"

"Yeah." She watched the windshield wipers click from side to side. "Lin said to bring the girls out. She thinks they can learn to cooperate by baby-sitting."

"Stranger things have happened. We'll try it."

Ahead of them, brake lights flashed. Traffic slowed to a crawl.

"I'm going to be late to pick up Cara," said Elizabeth anxiously.

"They'll be all right until we get there."

"It's not them I'm worried about. It's me."

"Afraid we'll get caught?" asked Steve. There was a little steel in his tone.

"Well, I don't see any reason to look for trouble," said Elizabeth defensively. She watched the wipers for a while before she spoke again. "I mean, we're going to have enough of a trauma with the pizza trip, aren't we?"

"We'll see," said Steve. He was grimly thoughtful on the drive to Harkness, where Melody and Cara were waiting, on opposite ends of the broad porch.

"Great," Elizabeth muttered. "They're out already."

Steve pulled to a stop beside her car. "I won't kiss you, out of deference to your fear of your daughter," he said. "But I'm telling you, Elizabeth, we're in for some big trouble if we don't take control of this situation now. Think about it."

"If you have any concrete ideas about how to take control of it without destroying those two children," she said, "I'd be happy to hear them. But just steaming around making portentous male pronouncements is hardly helpful. And I am not afraid of Cara."

"I'll call you from New York tonight," said Steve. "We can fight some more then."

"I'm not fighting," she said.

"Good," he said, and gave her a smile that melted her heart. "Chin up, chickie. Think about what I said, even if it does make you mad."

She knew what she'd think about.

"Be careful driving to New York," she said. And she leaned across the seat to kiss him. She'd take the chance that the rain would obscure the girls' vision and that Cara would wait under the porch roof until Elizabeth got the car as close as possible to the bottom step.

Steve put his hand gently to her face. "Be of good heart," he said.

Elizabeth got out of the car with the uncomfortable feeling that she might, indeed, be afraid of Cara. Or at least, afraid of the trouble Cara would have caused if she'd seen that kiss.

Steve was right. They had to come out in the open.

Chapter Five

At ten that night, Elizabeth was in bed with *The Hail Mary Margin*. She liked it, but a good book was hardly what she wanted, she thought, as she opened its cover. She couldn't concentrate. Every minute she expected Steve to call, and she couldn't relax until he did.

Still, she couldn't help being captivated by the story Steve had written. The hero of *Fire in the Hole* had changed. Jord Varic had to destroy a flaming rogue star fragment, which threatened his home planet and the woman he loved.

Steve was no longer twenty and no longer wanted to be James Bond. He had just married Marian, and *Hail Mary* idealized women as men newly in love and newly committed tended to do. His face on the back cover had changed and matured. The cocky impudence had quieted into self-confidence, and there was a sexy twinkle in his eye that made her grin at the picture.

She was deeply into the book and jumped when the phone rang. Steve! Finally! She snatched the receiver off the hook like a drowning woman clutching at the very last straw in the ocean.

"Hi!" she said, breathless with anticipation.

"Cara just called," said Robert irritably, from the other end of the line. "You have to talk to her."

"Damn it, Robert," said Elizabeth. "What now?" Why, why, why did she have to be afflicted with Robert?

"She wants to come to California, and she can't," said Robert. "I want you to tell her that."

Oh, God. More trouble. Robert was always trouble. She'd rather have cockroaches than Robert.

"Why don't you tell her that, Robert?" asked Elizabeth, through her teeth.

"I tried," said Robert. "I told her how busy I am, and I told her I had lots of trips coming up."

Elizabeth pinioned the phone between her shoulder and her ear and curled all ten of her fingers into claws. "Did you actually say 'No, Cara, you can't come'?"

"Of course not," said Robert. "I couldn't make her understand."

"I don't see why not. It doesn't seem that hard to me," Elizabeth told him. "You both speak English. I'll tutor you. Just say, 'Cara, I don't want you to come.'"

Robert wouldn't answer that. "It's just not convenient for her to come," he said. "I'm too busy for her right now."

Elizabeth could hear noises in the background: music, the tinkling of glasses, the sound of a woman—one woman—singing along with the melody from an old show tune. She was off-key.

"You've been too busy for Cara since the day she was born," Elizabeth told him. "And if by some horrible celestial mistake you should find yourself with a free day, I wouldn't let her any closer to Los Angeles than the eighty-second meridian."

That was true. Cara was too innocent to know the truth about Robert. Robert's women got younger as he got older, so the one with the tin ear was probably just above the age of consent. Robert had the ego of a four-year-old and the sexual habits of a goat, and Cara's presence wouldn't inhibit his selfishness in the least. Elizabeth couldn't let Cara see that. She needed to believe in a loving father, and Elizabeth intended to see that she could.

Which meant keeping her away from him. Not hard; Robert didn't want her.

"I hope she doesn't get anywhere near you," said Elizabeth, "until she has a husband and three children, a house, four dogs, an established career and some sense."

"Well, tell her that," said Robert petulantly.

Robert could incite a saint to homicide, and Elizabeth was no saint. Somebody should have made him stand up to his responsibilities long ago—like his idiot mother, who fawned over him and believed everything he said. Elizabeth gritted her teeth. She wasn't going to do his dirty work.

"I will do no such thing, Robert," said Elizabeth. "I refuse. You call her back tomorrow and explain it to her yourself. It's your responsibility, and I'm not going to do it for you."

"I don't want to hurt her feelings," said Robert.

"You think I do?" Elizabeth asked. "Anyway, I am not going to tell her you don't want her. I think you've made it abundantly clear, but she's too trusting to see it. You call her. If you don't, I'll get you on the phone myself and see that you talk to her."

"You've gotten hard since you left me," Robert said nastily. "You don't seem to have any feeling anymore. No wonder you can't get a man to love you."

What a vicious, unprincipled pig.

"I mean it, Robert," she said. "Call her tomorrow at nine-fifteen. That's six-fifteen your time."

"Or what?" Robert sneered. "You can't tell me what to do."

"Or I'll call," said Elizabeth. Blood roared in her ears. "And since I know what a heavy sleeper you are, that misguided little cretin in your living room will answer, and I will talk to her."

There. Whoever said women couldn't bluff?

They both hung up at the same time.

Elizabeth sat straight up in bed, seething, until the phone rang again. No breathless anticipation this time. She snarled her hello.

"What'd I do?" asked Steve, who heard the anger pulsing in her voice.

"You called an hour too late," she said.

"Too late for what?"

"To forestall Robert, damn him!" she said. "He called."

"To ask for a reconciliation?"

"Don't be stupid," she told him, still full of adrenaline and ready to fight. "And don't try to joke. He's joke enough for one evening. Cara called him to say she wanted to go to California, and he called me to tell her she couldn't."

"Why didn't he tell her himself?"

"He doesn't want to hurt her feelings!" Elizabeth raged. "Well, he's not going to get away with it! He'll have to tell her himself he doesn't want her to come. I'll be damned if I'll be the heavy, even one more time!"

"Will he do that?" asked Steve. "Won't he waffle?"

Elizabeth sank into her pillows. Her ears were no longer roaring, but the receding adrenaline left her with an awful headache.

"He's not going to waffle on this one," she said grimly. "I refuse to talk about him anymore. It just raises my blood pressure."

"Want a minivacation?"

"Of course. Any vacation at all would be a relief."

"Why don't you and Cara ride the train into Manhattan early tomorrow? We'll go to a matinee and have dinner, and I'll bring you home."

"You are a fool for punishment," said Elizabeth.

"You don't want to?"

"Of course I want to, Steve," she said. "But spending the day with Cara dragging around refusing to enjoy herself doesn't sound like any fun at all. I wish," she continued plaintively, "I could do something about that."

He could be desperate, he thought, if he let himself. Elizabeth found Cara's opposition painful. How long would it be before she withdrew altogether, accepting a cold and present peace for the future happiness that he and Elizabeth could have together? It was too soon to say he loved Elizabeth, but it wasn't too soon for him to know that he was falling in love, and doing it slowly, easily and irreversibly. And he didn't want it to stop.

Something had to be done.

"I can understand that," said Steve. "As much as I dislike it. Look, honey, why don't you take her out to Lin's, then, and let her get to know all the little Vorklands? Lin thinks she can bridge the gap. I vote we let her try."

"It's a thought," said Elizabeth. "She loves babies and dogs."

"See there?" said Steve. "Once she sees Sammy and John the Toothed Avenger, even Melody won't be able to keep her away from them."

"All right. Any port in a storm." A new idea possessed her. If she couldn't have Steve all day, she'd have the next best companion. "You want me to get Sammy for you? You can pick him up when you get home."

Not only would she get Sammy for almost an entire day, she'd get to see Steve, if only for a minute. Maybe they could sneak a kiss behind the pantry door while Melody and Cara glared at each other in the den.

"Boy, you're fickle," Steve said, more than willing to employ Sammy as a binding tie.

"It was love at first sight," Elizabeth told him. "I couldn't help myself. It's okay then, if I bring him home with me?"

"Certainly. Next time I leave town you can keep him, if you want to."

"I'd adore it." She envisioned Sammy munching on bagels, all fuzzy and warm on the hearth rug. "Does he like lox? I'll lay in supplies. When will you be back?"

"As soon as I can," said Steve. "I miss you, Libby. If we can find some suitably hidden place when I get home, I want a nice warm kiss, with nice warm you all cuddled up in my arms."

"So do I," said Elizabeth, and meant it absolutely. "And I miss you, too." She wanted the man, she wanted the kiss. She wanted, she thought, much more than the kiss. But it was too soon for that. "The few kisses I've had have hardly been sufficient."

"I'll fix that problem," Steve promised. "In the meantime, will you do what I tell you to?"

"Absolutely anything." The truth.

"Are you all alone?"

All, all alone, and hating it.

"Yes. Cara's asleep by now."

"Where are you?"

"In bed, reading a good book."

"In bed," he said, and made it sound like a caress. "Put the book away."

She did.

"Turn the light off and snuggle into your pillows."

The pillow cupped around her head, holding it as firmly as a man's warm hand. The down quilt drifted lightly under her chin.

"I'm snuggled," she said.

"So am I," said Steve. "On a big wide bed meant for two people. Tell me what you're wearing."

"A flannel nightgown." A flannel nightgown which slid up past her thighs as she did as she was told.

"All ruffled and roomy?" Rough *R*s as deep as a leopard's growl.

"Plenty roomy."

"Is there room enough for two in it?"

"More than enough."

He was almost there beside her, gathering the yards of flannel in his clever fingers, pushing it above her hips, above her breasts, and tucking it there so he could free his hands to love her.

She heard him take a deep breath before he spoke. "Are you wearing anything else?"

"Panties," she said.

"What kind?"

"Bikini panties." Barely able to catch her breath. "Lace ones, black lace. But they're very small. Not room enough for two."

"Then they'll just have to come off," he said. Slow-burning words, wrapping her with heat. "Close your eyes and think about that."

In her mind, his hands slipped under the thin elastic, lifted the lace from her hot skin, cupped around her hips and stripped the panties away.

A long pause. "Ready?" he said.

She was ready. Her whole body screamed it.

"Raise your right hand." His voice was low and deep and pulsed through her like fire. "Now touch your fingers to your lips."

She laid the tips of her fingers against her mouth, remembering his kiss, the taste of him. And the desire she wasn't even trying to hold in check surged through her like a river.

"Now blow the kiss north toward Manhattan."

She blew.

Steve waited a few seconds before he spoke again.

"I got it," he said. Deep and audible physical passion passed wave by wave across the distance between them. "All hot and wet and just for me. Do you want one, too?"

"Yes," she sighed. "And hurry."

"Then here's yours." His voice sank to a whisper. "Reach for me, Elizabeth. I'm here, and you can touch me. Today and tomorrow and forever."

She could actually feel his mouth on hers.

"Sweet dreams," he said, and gently disconnected.

Dream? She couldn't even sleep, after that. She picked up *The Hail Mary Margin* and continued to read.

Did Steve look at her the way Jord Varic looked at Mira? Or had that chivalric love disappeared with his divorce?

At seven she got out of bed in the wonderful, room-enough-for-two, ruffled flannel gown and went downstairs to have a cup of coffee and read the paper. Whenever she looked up from the news of the day, she could see Steve, sitting across the table from her, sharing the quiet dawn.

Finally she ran out of time for the pleasant fantasy and went to wake Cara and dress for church. She didn't need to listen for the phone—she knew Robert would call. He didn't want the young girls he dated to know that he had a daughter nearly as old as they were. Sure enough, he rang up at nine.

Cara knew he was calling and waited eagerly by the phone.

"Hi, Daddy!" she said. "Are you going to send me money?" Pause. "Oh, wow. Great!" Pause. "But I want to come now. Okay. When?'' She sounded belligerent. "Well, where will you be?''

Robert must have done some fast talking, because Cara began to calm down. Damn it, thought Elizabeth. He tells her everything but the truth.

And so did she, she knew. Still—maybe she could keep juggling balls until Cara was old enough and distanced enough from Robert that the truth wouldn't be so devastating.

Cara got off the phone. "He said I could maybe come around Christmas.''

"You know he'll probably be too busy, honey," said Elizabeth, handing Cara her coat.

"He promised not this time," Cara said. "May we eat out after church?''

Elizabeth had already called Lin. "We've been invited to dinner," she said.

"It's not with stupid glophfy Melody Riker, is it?" said Cara suspiciously.

"She's in New York, remember?" Elizabeth said. "I guarantee you'll have a good time. And if you don't hurry, you're going to be late for Sunday School.''

On the way home from church, Elizabeth stopped at a bakery and bought two dozen bagels.

"We can't eat all those," said Cara.

"We're having company tonight, and he likes bagels.''

"Mr. Riker?" Cara narrowed her eyes.

"Not Mr. Riker.''

"Mr. Salvini?''

"I never saw such a pronounced case of hope springing eternal." Elizabeth grinned. "Not Mr. Salvini.''

"Who, then? Some man you have a date with?''

"You might say that," said Elizabeth, enjoying the game. "I just met him yesterday. It was love at first sight.''

"What's his name?''

"Samuel R. Canis." Elizabeth knew that Cara would adore Lin and Tom and the entire menagerie, but only if she met them before she found out who they were.

"Is he Italian?" asked Cara, who obviously hadn't been paying much attention in Latin class. "What does he look like?"

"Well, he has whiskers and a strawberry blond beard, and brown eyes and really bushy eyebrows and really curly hair. It's hard to tell much else. You'll see."

"When's he coming?"

"We've having lunch with his family. He's riding back home with us."

By the time they arrived at Lin's, Cara was avid with anticipation. And the greeting, as they got out of the car, was an exact repeat of yesterday's, plus Sammy. By the time Cara had sorted it out, she was captivated.

Her brow began to darken when she heard Lin's name and clouded to thunder when she met Sammy.

Then Johnny toddled onto the porch and wrapped both arms around Cara's legs.

"Me bite, me bite," he said, looking up at her with a winning grin.

Cara picked him up. "Are you going to bite me?" she asked, charmed.

"No," he said solemnly. He thought about it. "Bad Sandy," he said darkly.

"This is big bad John," Lin said. "We're trying to wean him from the taste of human flesh. Unfortunately he finds biting useful for defense."

"Maybe he likes it." Cara bounced him in her arms as Lin led them into the house. "Does it taste like chicken, Johnny?"

Elizabeth, Tom and Lin all laughed, and Cara blushed and glowed at their appreciation of her first real grown-up witticism.

"That's really funny," said Lin. "How clever of you."

"Maybe he'll be too full to gnaw on Sandy's arm after lunch," said Tom. "Since we're having chicken. Do you want coke or some hot chocolate?"

"Yes, please," said Cara, sitting at the table. Johnny squirmed off her lap. "Hot chocolate."

All four boys wanted hot chocolate, too.

"Git," said Tom. "It's too close to mealtime for you." He shooed them up the stairs.

Cara was immensely flattered. She'd suddenly been promoted to the adult table, and she was determined to live up to it.

"I told them you were coming, Cara," Lin said. "I'm afraid they'll pester you to death, because they adore Melody. She likes little kids, and they take advantage of it."

"I like them, too," Cara said, for once not minding the comparison.

"Well, then, you won't mind too much if they crawl all over you?"

Cara laughed. "Sammy and Miggy are crawling all over me, and I don't mind that."

Both dogs were trying to lick her face.

"They like you," said Lin.

"That's because I taste like chicken."

Everybody laughed again. There was scant resemblance between the smiling, charming, entertaining girl in the Vorklands' kitchen and the sullen little creature who slumped on the Harkness steps on Saturdays at noon. This was the Cara of the future, Elizabeth thought, and rejoiced.

"Miggy's beautiful," Cara told Lin. "How do you keep her so white?"

"She throws her in the wash when she bleaches the socks," said Tom, setting a huge steaming cup in front of Cara.

Cara giggled. "How does she really do it?"

"I put bluing in the rinse water," said Lin. She handed a stack of plates to Elizabeth, who spaced them around the long table.

Cara scratched under Miggy's chin. Sammy took exception to this diverting of attention. He put his huge front paws in Cara's lap and pushed his nose into her face.

"Aowrrr," he complained.

Cara hugged him. He tried to get the rest of the way into her lap. He managed most of his forequarters and snuggled his head into her shoulder.

"Mworp," he said, sounding satisfied.

"You've got that backward, Cara," Tom told her. "You should sit in his lap."

"He's a precious, sweet, baby dog," she announced, sounding exactly like her mother. "And he can sit on my lap if he wants to."

"He's big, all right," said Lin. "A big crybaby. Just step on his toe—he whimpers for a week."

"Here's dinner," said Tom, putting a bowl of chicken and dumplings on the table. "Let's feed the beasts and children."

Sammy sat in the back seat of the car and draped his head over Cara's shoulder. She kept one arm around his neck and chattered all the way home. Elizabeth hadn't seen her so buoyant in a long time—since the first of the school year, in fact. Lin's particular magic, Elizabeth thought gratefully.

She settled Cara and Sammy in front of the fire and cooked a frozen pizza. She and Sammy and Cara shared it. Then Sammy declared that the rug was too warm and the floor was too hard. He ambled to the couch and put one paw on the edge.

He glanced nervously at Elizabeth and slipped a second paw beside the first one. Then one back foot, seemingly of its own accord, joined the others. Sammy was astonished at its behavior; he looked at it with his mouth open.

Cara and Elizabeth held their sides, laughing.

Sammy collapsed on the couch.

"Murmph!" He sighed. He arranged himself comfortably and lowered his weary head to a throw pillow.

He didn't even move when Steve and Melody rang the bell. He waited until they were completely in the house, with the door shut, before he sat up on the couch.

"Rarff!" he said joyously. He bounded across the room to say hello. Cara looked desolate until he galloped back to her and buried his face in her shirt.

She grinned at Steve. "He had pizza and bagels for dinner."

Then she sat on the floor, as far from Melody as she could get without actually moving into the kitchen. Sammy shuttled anxiously between the two girls until he was tired of it, then he stopped equidistant between the separate poles and sank to the floor.

Cara and Melody inched imperceptibly toward him—his fuzzy teddy-bear looks were a magnet. Elizabeth surfed through the TV channels until she found a teen flick. The girls needed something to focus their attention off each other while she focused her attention on Steve.

He raised his eyebrows at her, and she beckoned with her head. He followed her into the kitchen.

Once they were behind the wall, he dipped his head and kissed her quickly.

"Did you find a suitably hidden place?" he asked. "Because if I don't get a real, honest-to-God kiss, I am going to go up in flames."

"We might go up in flames if we do," said Elizabeth, remembering the heat in her fantasies and the fire in her dreams. She took his hand and guided him down the back hall, opened the door and stepped into the garage. "Here we are."

"Perfect," said Steve.

"Anyplace would be perfect."

He took her into his arms. "Anyplace at all," he agreed. "Anyplace at all."

Their lips met. His mouth was hard and hungry, and his kiss was everything she had wanted it to be. But it was over too fast and left them both feeling incomplete.

For the next week Steve and Elizabeth established a clandestine routine: arrive ten minutes before detention ends, walk around to the back of the school bleachers, behind a concealing row of fir trees. One quick kiss quickly returned, rush back to one car or the other and hold hands and talk and yearn and desire and ache until the girls emerge, sour and unrepentant, to be driven home.

Steve still held out hope for the civilizing effects of a pizza parlor full of arcade games. Elizabeth held out absolutely no hope whatever. She expected the worst. It was what she'd become accustomed to.

On Saturday night, at six forty-five, Cara was still in her room, with the door locked.

Elizabeth sat on the top stair with her elbows on her knees and her chin in her hands, wondering just what to do next. The usual threats and bribes had failed. Finally she took the chignon pin out of her hair and unlocked Cara's door.

Cara was on her window seat, gazing out into the lowering night.

"You're invading my privacy," she said.

"Only adults are entitled to complete privacy. Children have to be monitored."

Cara's head snapped around. She sprang to her feet and slapped her developing bosom with the flat of one hand.

"I am not a child!" she announced, wild-eyed with insult. "I am a *woman!*"

She strode from the room.

Elizabeth managed to shut the door before she collapsed. She muffled her laughter by burying her face in a pillow and emerged some time later breathless and weak with hilarity.

"I will keep a straight face!" she told herself sternly, and left the room to deal with her obstinate daughter.

Cara sat hunched on the floor in the den, two feet from the television. The doorbell rang.

"Cara," said Elizabeth.

Cara got to her feet and headed for the stairs. Elizabeth blocked her path and took her by the shoulders.

"This will do you no good," she said evenly. "If you refuse to go with us, I am not going to make a scene by using physical force. We simply will all stay here, all four of us. In the same room. All night long."

Cara's eyes blazed. *If looks could kill*, thought Elizabeth, and continued. "If you go to your room, we will all come sit in your room. I personally will sit in front of the door so that you cannot leave. You and I together are going to spend the entire evening with the Rikers. If you find pizza and video games preferable to spending five hours trapped in your bedroom with Melody, then you'd better go and get your coat."

With that, she moved out of Cara's way and opened the door to Steve.

He scanned the room behind her as he stepped inside.

"Where's Cara?" he asked, tilting her face up to his for a quick kiss.

"Getting her coat, I hope," she said. "Your lips are cold."

"All of me is cold." He grinned. "If we weren't so rigidly chaperoned. I'd let you warm me up." He waggled his eyebrows at her and stage-whispered, "It wouldn't take much to do the job."

"Probably not," she acknowledged. "Where's Melody?"

"Sulking in the car." He didn't sound concerned.

"Cara's only coming because I told her we'd all sit in her room the entire night if she didn't."

Laughter rumbled briefly in his chest.

They heard Cara stomping down the stairs, and each thudding footfall resounded with rage.

"I can't imagine what you find to be amused about," said Elizabeth testily. "This is going to be like spending the evening with Truman and MacArthur."

"Freud and Jung."

"Tom and Jerry," said Elizabeth.

"Punch and Judy," said Steve. "Well, it's a first step, honey." He took her coat from her hands and held it while she put her arms in the sleeves. "We'll have a good time. Let 'em sulk."

Sounds like whistling in the dark to me, Elizabeth thought, as the three of them left the house.

Both girls were completely silent during the ride. At the arcade they leapt from their seats and slammed the car doors in unison. Melody hurried ahead of the group, and Cara dragged behind them, so no one would suspect that they were together.

"Table for four," said Steve to the hostess and had to repeat himself to be heard.

"This place is bedlam," said Elizabeth when they were seated.

And it was. There were forty video machines, all roaring and clanging and pinging in unison. Driving simulators were attached to car and airplane instrument panels and roared like high-tachometer engines. Pinball machines flashed with maniacal lights. Basketball games barked to the room, "Shoot ten baskets in fifteen seconds, win a free round." And they responded to a successful shot with the roar of a crowd and the excited voice of a sports announcer. A shooting gallery in the rear sounded like an invasion force. And in the center of it all, holding place of pride, was the virtual reality game. There was a small video monitor above the playing circle, which showed the computer action of the game.

An entire battalion, clutching their reservation numbers, waited in line for a chance to match wits with the computer. No one watched the monitor. Instead, they all stared fixedly at the Star Attack player, who stood in the center of a round plastic sensor mat several feet in diameter. He wore a helmet, which completely covered his eyes, and bulky astronaut-type gloves on his hands. All the Star Attack hopefuls watched him avidly.

As far as Elizabeth could tell, they were watching absolutely nothing. The player seemed deranged. He whirled and stabbed and fired an imaginary gun. A steady stream of exclamations, apparently unrelated to anything going on in the room, issued from beneath the opaque helmet.

Even Cara and Melody looked interested, when they thought they were unobserved.

"How does it work?" asked Elizabeth, fascinated by the spectacle.

"There's a virtual reality projector in the helmet. Sort of like the helmets jet pilots use that print all the plane's vitals on thin air in front of them. The player is actually inside a computer world, and he's responding to what he is seeing in his cyber-space universe." Steve pulled out a chair so that she could sit down. "It is so cool, you won't believe it."

"What kind of pizza you want?" asked the kid taking orders.

"I don't care," said Cara, tossing her head.

"I don't care," sniffed Melody.

"You choose, Elizabeth," Steve said. "I'll eat anything."

"Anchovies, artichoke hearts and hot Italian sausage," said Elizabeth, beaming at the boy.

"Anchovies!" chorused her three horrified companions.

"I hate anchovies," said Cara.

"I hate anchovies," said Melody.

"I'll eat almost anything," said Steve. "But not anchovies."

Elizabeth laughed. "Okay. Two large double pepperoni and mushroom pizzas and a pitcher of cola."

"You have a weird sense of humor," said Steve.

"How do you know I wasn't serious?" she asked, twinkling at him.

"Nobody could be serious about anchovies." He pushed his chair back. "Excuse me." In a few minutes he returned with two large drink cups filled with tokens and set one down in front of each girl. "Come find us when you've used these up," he said, then he held out his hand to Elizabeth. "Ready to play?"

"Do we have to stand in that line?"

"No, we have a number, which they will call when it's our turn. Those people are standing in line out of habit. Don't ask me why. There's certainly nothing to watch. Want to practice on the video games?"

"I've never really played many video games," she said. "I lose so fast that it seems like throwing quarters down a well."

"Nobody succeeds at first," he told her. "You have to practice."

"I've always wanted to. I just wouldn't spend enough money to get good at it. It costs a fortune."

"Well, here's a fortune," he said, handing her a cup of coins. He guided her to a formidable-looking console with supersonic planes darting across its screen. "This one's the best. You'll like it."

"Don't you want to play?"

"Let's get you started first." He placed her hands on the controls. "You ever fly an airplane?"

"Of course not. I've driven in New York City, though."

"Well, this is easier than New York. This is the yoke," he told her, patting her hands to indicate the wheel she held. "Use it to climb, dive and turn left and right."

"This thing like a steering wheel, only it's square?"

"Yeah. Now." He stood behind her and put his hands over hers. "This lever is the throttle." He pushed his left thumb down over hers, and the switch under her hand slid upward.

There were two buttons on the yoke under her right thumb. "What are these for?"

"Air-to-air missiles. Don't waste them. You only have six. For every enemy plane you shoot down, a friendly appears on the screen to help you. The deal is to get rid of six enemies, and then the friendlies do all the shooting so you can concentrate on your bomb runs. This is the bomb release. Target like this and then push the button."

"This is confusing," Elizabeth muttered.

Steve put two tokens in the slot. "I'll coach you. Okay. Here we go. Here comes the first plane. Bank left! Bank left!"

"Frog right," said Elizabeth. "Does that mean turn left?" ·

"Yeah, turn. Good, good! Now shoot. Shoot! It's the other button," he said kindly, as enemy missiles hit her plane and she blew up. "That one was for the bombs. You hit an orphanage and two hospitals. That cost you twenty-two thousand points. Ready to go again? Don't let 'em get behind you."

She began to get the hang of it about ten dollars later. The hospitals and orphanages were avenged. Elizabeth had destroyed two SAM sites, all six enemy planes and an ammunition dump before she lost her bearings and flew into the ground.

"I think you're ready for Star Attack," Steve said.

"I'm ready for a rest," she said. "That's really fun, Steve. No wonder you're hooked on it."

When they returned to their table, Cara sat unmoved, looking bored, with her cup still full of tokens.

"That rude brat," said Elizabeth, under her breath.

Melody was nowhere in sight, but they could hear her breathless voice. Over to their left she stood talking to a gaggle of adolescent boys, all of whom seemed enthralled with her presence. When the pizza appeared, Steve called her to the table. She came with her entourage in her wake. They saw her safely seated and then dissipated, chorusing "See ya."

"Those guys are from the Linwoody School," she announced. "They're coming to the Harkness Christmas dance." She helped herself to the pizza. "Me and Caroline Richards are practicing our dancing together."

"Caroline Richards and I," said Cara loftily. "Try to speak good grammar."

Melody gave Cara a poisonous look. "After *me* and Caroline practice tomorrow," she said to her father, "can I go horseback riding out at Aunt Lin's?"

"I hate horses," said Cara. "They make me itch."

"Good, because my Aunt Lin wouldn't let you near hers. They're blood stock."

"Is that the kind they use for dog food?" said Cara, with a curl of her lip.

"Yeah," said Melody. "I'll bring you some. What kind do you like to eat best?"

"Good grief," said Elizabeth to herself. "No wonder they drive Miss Westcott crazy."

"I think they're more Abbott and Costello than Punch and Judy," said Steve, who by then was laughing out loud.

Both girls viewed him suspiciously.

"Who are Abbott and Costello?" asked Melody, suspecting that she'd been insulted.

"Comedians," said Elizabeth.

"Well, I don't think she's funny," said Melody.

"So like I think you're funny," said Cara.

"Shut up and eat, Melody," said Steve. "Cara, you're young and fast, and I'm old and slow. Come see if you can beat me at the motocross game."

Cara, after one look at her mother's face, reluctantly pushed back her chair and arose.

Elizabeth smiled across the table at Melody. Melody gave a quick grin and ducked her head shyly.

"Have you played this Star Attack game your dad brought me here to see?" Elizabeth asked, cleverly avoiding all the obvious knock-'em-dead conversational stoppers like "How's school?", "How do you like living here?" and "Why can't you get along with Cara?"

Melody nodded.

"How do you do it?" Elizabeth wanted to know. "After I wait all this time, I don't want to waste my turn."

Melody munched thoughtfully on her pizza. "They have different levels," she said finally. "The first one, it has ships landing." She thought about it some more. "Like, it's a grid at first. Like a checkerboard. And you point your gun at the grid, but you have to wait till they land and the door opens. Then you shoot. Then the ship blows up."

"What if you miss one?"

"Then all the aliens get out and you're dead, because you can't shoot them all."

Melody leaned forward. "Then," she said, looking as enthusiastic about the game as Steve had, "when you get to the second level, there are still lots of ships, but the grid is three dimensional, so you only see certain angles. It's really neat. And also, I forgot to say, when you turn around, the pad senses where you are, and the screen changes. It is so cool."

"What pad? That plastic thing he's standing on?"

"Yeah. It has sensors under it, so it can tell when you move your feet. And also when you move your head, what you see changes, like it's a real world and you're really seeing it."

"No joke," said Elizabeth. Star Attack began to sound complicated. "Then what, after that?"

"I don't know. The second level's as far as I've gotten. Sometimes Dad plays it with me, because you can have two people compete. Dad's gone to level six."

"How many levels are there?"

"Ten. It is so totally awesome. I just love it." She grinned—Steve's wholehearted, appealing, completely entrancing grin. "Just as soon as I manage to make a zillion dollars, I'm going to buy myself one and play it all the time. I'm gonna buy Daddy one, too."

"How are you going to make a zillion dollars?" asked Elizabeth. Melody, separated from Cara, was charming. Well, she might have suspected that. Cara, separated from Melody, was charming, too. She wondered how Steve was faring and glanced across the room. He and Cara had their heads together, and Elizabeth could tell from the tension in competitive little Cara's stance that she was working as hard at the game as she worked at everything else.

"I think I'll design computer games," said Melody. "They're what I like best. I've already made up two games, and we play them at school."

"Are you good at math?"

She nodded, and there was no arrogance in her tone as she answered. "Yeah, really good. It's just like doing puzzles. My mom's good at math, too."

"How about your dad?"

"He's the best dad in the world, and I really love him, but he can just about add two and two, if he uses his fingers. He said he failed calculus in college, but the professor gave him a D so he'd graduate." She giggled.

Elizabeth privately wondered if the compassionate professor had been a woman.

"Cara says she wants to be a doctor," said Elizabeth, carefully introducing her main concern.

Melody was obviously torn between being truthful and being polite. She decided on truth. "I can't see that," she said.

"Why not?"

"I think doctors have to be nice to people." Suddenly her eyes had a shuttered look, and her mouth thinned into that obstinate, unforgiving line which Elizabeth knew so well.

"Melody," she said urgently. "I can't seem to get much about this out of Cara. Is there any reason why you two don't like each other? I have to know."

"She's not nice to me," said Melody.

"Are you nice to her?"

Melody was honest enough to say so. "It makes me mad every time I look at her. But I would be nice to her," she added, "if she'd be nice to me."

"That's what Cara says," sighed Elizabeth. "But you know, somebody has to start being nice first."

Melody didn't have to say, "Well, it's not going to be me," but Elizabeth could read it in her face.

"She chews with her mouth open," said Melody irritably. "Just to gross me out. It's so disgusting."

To Melody's astonishment, Elizabeth laughed. "And vice-versa, I understand."

Melody tilted her head and grinned. "Well, she started it."

"Oh, my," said Elizabeth, around her chuckles. "What in the world are we going to do with the two of you?" She wiped her eyes. "The only thing to do now is go play Space Invaders. I don't know any other games. Want to?"

"Sure," said Melody eagerly. "But I could teach you something else. There are lots of fun ones." She got out of her chair, then turned back to the table. "Here comes Daddy. I think it's our turn at Star Attack. We had number 164 and it's 162 on the board now."

Five minutes later, Elizabeth listened to the last of Steve's hurried instructions, fitted the virtual reality helmet over her head and allowed the attendant to adjust the bulky gloves to her grip.

Her world disappeared. All around her, now, blood red on black, like a nightmare scene at the back of her eyes, strange manlike creatures appeared out of nowhere and rushed toward her to attack. Their bodies grew huge as they ran, and they were nearly upon her, when the game began.

"All right now," said the voice of the attendant. "Here you go."

Alien ships dropped like cold blue rain from a thunderous sky. One by one, their black bays opened, and dimly lighted, inside them, Elizabeth saw things move.

She pointed her weapon at the nearest ship and fired. She caught a movement at the corner of her eye. She whirled and shot one alien which had escaped from an auxiliary module off a parent ship and turned to confront the main fleet again. Another module ejected and moved out of her view. A game, she told herself. This is a game.

"You're sweating," said Steve, when she removed the helmet.

"I got killed," she said. "Twice."

"You did good," said the attendant. "Better than most people the first time."

"Want to do it again?" asked Steve, grinning.

"I'd like to do it all night," she said. "Are you offering me your turn?"

"'Let not the marriage of true minds admit impediments,'" he said. "Of course."

She fitted the helmet to her head once more. And got killed twice, again, although it took the beastly little homunculi forty-five seconds longer this time.

While Melody played, Steve instructed Cara. She was bouncing with impatience when she got in the ring and could hardly stand still while Steve adjusted the helmet.

"Go get 'em, tiger," he said, and they could see her grin beneath the long black visor.

She spun and shot and crowed with victory when she hit a target, and made an inchoate noise of sheer frustration when she missed. Her eyes were glowing when she emerged.

"I got twenty of them the first round and twenty-three the second round," she said. "Next time, I'll do better." Steve held out his hands, and she slapped her palms against his.

"Pretty good, sis," he said. "Won't be long till you ace the whole game."

"Yeah," she said with satisfaction. "Maybe I won't be a doctor. Maybe I'll be a fighter pilot instead."

"Perfect job for you," Melody muttered.

"Melody," said Steve, in a warning tone.

The two girls locked eyes briefly, then spun apart and went to opposite sides of the room.

"Short truce," observed Elizabeth.

"They'll get longer," Steve told her. "Why don't you finish your pizza? I'll go pick up more game reservation numbers." He grinned. "You do want to play again?"

She nodded. "I'm hooked. I admit it."

Steve watched her walk across the room. Watched the glossy, black curls swinging across her shoulders; watched the narrow waist, the firm round adorable fanny cuddled in the tight jeans and the gentle, natural, primally female sway of her hips that always made his breath catch in his throat.

Watched as Joe Salvini appeared out of nowhere, with a wide, delighted smile, to intercept her. Watched as he put his hand on her arm and, as she tilted her head back to look at him, watched as her stance changed provocatively, unconsciously, as it always does when a woman is admired by an interesting man.

Watched with mounting ire as Salvini sat at his, Steve's, table. And began to eat his pizza.

And flirted with his woman.

To hell with Star Attacks. This was a real battle, with real stakes and real consequences. He lowered his head like a bull moose and charged.

Chapter Six

Steve, for the first time in his entire life, was jealous of another man. It rose unstoppably, bitter as gall, and burrowed steadily into his uneasy heart. He was unsure of Elizabeth, uncertain of her feelings, unable to know whether he could make her love him as he was beginning to love her.

"Is this part of the Westcott peace plan?" asked Joe, as Steve approached.

"Oh, absolutely," Steve said. "Elizabeth and I are trying to set a good example." He laid his fingertips lightly and possessively on her shoulder. "We're thinking of combining households so the girls can share everything."

Everybody laughed politely. Such a funny joke. Both men smiled; neither man's smile quite reached his eyes.

Steve patted Elizabeth's arm and dropped into a chair beside her.

"Here for the pizza?" he asked, knowing he was reacting like a bloody damn Neanderthal. He couldn't help it. He felt like laying about him with a club and throwing Elizabeth over his shoulder to cart her off to his cave.

She must surely be slack-jawed with amazement beside him. He couldn't make himself look.

"I'm here for Star Attack." Joe gave Steve a shrewd assessing look from his sharp black eyes. "Have you played it?"

"Once or twice," said Steve modestly, recognizing a challenge. "Very difficult."

"How're you doing?" Joe asked.

"I've crept my way to level four," said Steve. "Hanging on there by my toenails."

Cards dealt; bets placed.

"We ought to be pretty evenly matched," said Joe. "I've clawed up to level four myself. Want to try a round or two?" There was satisfaction in the eyes of both men. The first bluff had been called, and each of them thought he'd carried it off perfectly. They sauntered toward the sensor circle on the floor.

Elizabeth, wide-eyed, watched them walk away. Neither man had so much as looked at her, but she knew without question that the entire subtly hostile interchange between Joe and Steve had been about her. She knew now how Helen of Troy had felt.

And she knew, with a little surge of smug exhilaration, that Helen had liked it.

"Is that Mr. Salvini?" asked Cara, who had come up behind her. "Cool. Is he going to play Star Attack with Mr. Riker?"

"Yes," said Elizabeth. "Want some cola?"

Melody and her cadre of admirers appeared. "Hey, was that Mr. Salvini?" she wanted to know.

"Yeah," said Cara. "He's gonna ace your dad at Star Attack."

"He will not," said Melody. "My dad is really good."

"Yeah, but he's really old. He's got wrinkles."

"He is not really old," said Melody hotly. "He's just sort of old."

"Older than Mr. Salvini," Cara said. "That means he has slower reflexes. He won't win."

Elizabeth got to her feet. "I'm going after more cola," she said to the little group around the table. She got a firm grip on Cara's upper arm. "Cara, come help me."

"Do you know how rude you're being?" Elizabeth whispered furiously, once they were out of earshot.

"I'm not, either," said Cara. "I'm just being truthful. You told me always to tell the truth. He is old. Really old. He's old enough to be your father, almost."

"Do not say one single word more about Mr. Riker, do you hear me?" Elizabeth ordered. She gave Cara's arm a little shake for emphasis. "I am sick to death of this idiocy, and I don't want to hear another word about him. Now take this tray of glasses back to the table." She thrust the tray into Cara's hands, then picked up two pitchers of cola and followed.

She glanced at the sensor circle as she passed. Steve and Joe were still battling. The game operator said, "You guys started out too low. I'm bumping you up to level seven." The small crowd around them cheered.

And cheered at what? Elizabeth wondered sourly. There wasn't a thing to see, except two presumably sane men whirling and stomping and shooting at nothing with a pair of toy guns. She herself was engaged in a real battle, with real combatants and real fighting. Felt like Helen of Troy, did she? Well, the present war was likely to turn out just as badly.

Cara set the glasses on the table. Before she could separate them to hand them around, Melody plucked them from under her nose and distributed them to the boys with a sunny smile. The boys were transfixed. Cara scowled. As Elizabeth filled each glass with soda, Melody said, "I told you my dad was good. Mr. Salvini just got penalized for stepping out of the circle."

"Don't talk about your dad," Cara sniffed. "My mom says she's tired of the idiot and doesn't want to hear another word about him."

Elizabeth gasped. "I said idiocy, not idiot, and I also said I didn't want to listen to you two fight anymore."

"No, you didn't," Cara insisted. "You said, 'I don't want to hear another word about him.' I remember exactly."

Melody's eyes were narrow with concentration. She was committing every syllable to memory. It didn't take much imagination to predict the conversation Steve and Melody would have, when Melody got him alone.

Elizabeth sat, stunned, for about thirty seconds, looking at the two perfectly horrible, thoroughly exasperating little girls. She loved one of them dearly; she knew she would have no trouble learning to love the other. And they were both just absolutely dreadful. Better dreadful than boring, she supposed. Who wants boring kids?

Then to her surprise, she giggled. The giggle sprouted a chuckle, gained energy, budded, bloomed and blossomed wide. She abandoned herself to it. She leaned back into her chair, threw her head back and laughed. And the more she laughed, the funnier she thought it was: the dagger stares, the suspicious adolescent vigilance, the secret, stolen kisses. Her sides ached; her jaws hurt. The laughter filled her to bursting, supplanted the tension, banished the irritation and left muscles weak with hilarity behind.

When she was able to raise her head and look around her, the boys had fled. Only Cara and Melody remained, and they were shocked and embarrassed. Elizabeth found that comical, too.

"What's so funny?" asked Steve from behind her. He handed her a napkin.

She wiped her eyes and giggled again. "Location joke. You had to be there. How was the game?"

"He beat me," said Steve evenly, sitting down beside her. He knew he was the perfect picture of urbane congeniality; black rage burned in his heart.

"Well, it wasn't easy," said Joe. "Level four? Right. You cheated."

"So did you."

Joe grinned. "Yeah. I did. I flew fighters for the Navy for ten years. Still do it on weekends. Gave me an edge I didn't tell you about."

Cara, Melody and Elizabeth all swiveled their heads in unison.

Steve smoldered under the facade of good-humored content. Joe Salvini, damn him, was interesting, intelligent and competent. Under any other circumstances, Steve would have enjoyed his company.

But it was Elizabeth who enjoyed Joe's company, and she enjoyed it entirely too much.

And Melody and Cara listened with open mouths, hanging on to Salvini's every word.

Damn that irresistible Italian charm, thought Steve. The man's a Pied Piper.

"You did, really, fly fighters?" asked Cara. Her big green eyes got bigger and greener, and her black brows winged upwards. "That's what I want to do."

"Go ahead," Joe said. "Be a fighter pilot or an astronaut or anything. Tell you a secret." He leaned forward. "Did you know that when the space program started, NASA did a lot of tests to see whether men or women made better astronauts?"

"They did?"

"Yep. And the women won," said Joe. "They were just as good at science, flying and math. They were smaller, so it didn't cost as much to send them into space, they had better coordination and hand dexterity, and they worked together as a team better than the men did."

"So how come all the astronauts weren't women?" Cara was captivated.

"Well, being an astronaut was a big he-man-type job, and the men who ran the program weren't about to admit that women could be better at it, so they hid the report and hired men. That, my dear, is called prejudice."

"It's better now," said Cara.

"It's better. But don't give up," Joe told her. "You have to keep reminding a lot of people that you can do anything. And you remind them by being good at what you do."

"At everything?" she asked.

Joe grinned. "Even history."

Cara blushed. "I'm not very good at history."

"You could be."

Elizabeth frowned. "Exactly how bad is she?"

Joe turned his attention from Cara.

Steve, watching them from carefully impassive eyes, had to admit he couldn't disagree with a word the man had said. He wished he'd said them himself. Maybe, he thought, with the sudden detachment that seized him when an idea for a novel struck, he'd make his next book about a woman. The kind of woman Joe talked about. The kind of woman he hoped Melody would become—and Cara, for that matter—honest, skillful, clearheaded, competent. Like Elizabeth.

The melancholy ebbed, the jealousy abated; the idea capered enticingly through his consciousness, driving everything else before it. He leaned forward himself and eyed Joe with professional interest.

"Tell me about learning to fly," he said.

Cara stood in line for Star Attack two more times and replayed all three games, shot by shot, on the way home. In the front seat, surreptitiously, Steve and Elizabeth held hands.

"Bor-ing," said Melody, yawning.

"Just because you're not as good at it as I am," Cara said.

"You're just jealous," said Melody, "because all those guys don't talk to you. That's why you played so much."

"That's enough, Melody," said Steve, in an I'll-brook-no-more-nonsense kind of voice.

Both girls subsided. They folded their arms and scowled silently at each other from their corners of the back seat. When Steve stopped the car in front of chez Fairchild, Cara was up the front steps with her keys in the door before the engine quit humming.

Elizabeth and Steve followed slowly up the sidewalk.

"Well," said Steve, as they approached the porch. "Want to make a statement?"

Elizabeth looked at Cara, waiting impatiently by the open door. Looked at Melody, who glowered from the car window.

"I'll pay for it later," she said, with resignation.

"Try to remember that you're the mommy here," said Steve. "Want the kiss, or not?"

"Oh, yes," she sighed, turning toward him. "I definitely do."

He took her face between his hands and kissed her gently on the lips. It was a tender kiss, undemanding, understanding and nurturing.

I'm falling in love, she thought. *Oh, God, what shall I do?*

"Good night, sweetheart," he said quietly. "Call me if you need me."

She watched him walk back to the car and drive away, then closed her eyes for a second before she turned to see Cara's outraged face.

Cara slammed the door after Elizabeth was inside.

"You let him kiss you!" said Cara furiously.

"Yes, I did," said Elizabeth.

"That's disgusting!" said Cara. She radiated anger like a blast furnace radiates heat. "He's disgusting!"

"Now, look here, Cara," Elizabeth began.

Cara threw up both hands. "You don't need to tell me anything!" she shouted, wild-eyed and raving. "I already know what you're going to say—wouldn't I like to have a father? Well, I've already got a father, and I don't need another one!"

And with that she ran up the stairs. The bang of her bedroom door rattled the house.

Elizabeth wandered disconsolately down the hall to the den and collapsed into her favorite chair. The television remote control had slipped between the cushions, and when she sat down, her weight pressed all the buttons at once. The TV surfed maniacally through all sixty-four channels at full volume.

A metaphor, she thought, digging in the chair. For my entire existence. Loud and confusing.

The bowels of the upholstery were full of pencils, coins and old squashed popcorn. As her fist closed around the remote control, an upholstery staple sliced under the quick of her ring finger. She jerked the remote control to the surface and examined the finger; it was bleeding. It hurt. She stuck it in her mouth. Then she squirmed into the chair, pointed the control like a magic wand and zapped the television into silence.

She wished handling Cara were as easy. Steve had said they were in for big trouble if they didn't take control. Well, he was wrong. They were already in big trouble. She could control what Cara did, but not what Cara thought or felt. Precious, volatile, quicksilver Cara, who seemed unalterably opposed to the man Elizabeth was beginning to love. If she could possibly quit falling in love, go away from him and forget all about him, she would. But going away wouldn't help. He was in her mind and in her heart, and no separation would erase that. When she closed her eyes, all she could see ahead of her was the misery of loving a man she couldn't have. And a love which should have been delight promised agony instead.

For a minute she leaned her head against the back of the chair and let misery wash over her. Then she pulled herself together and went to the kitchen and brewed a restorative cup of tea. With the tea and the third book in the *Fireman* series, *The Lion's Whelp*, she could escape from her troubles long enough to regroup and mount a new assault.

Steve's face smiled out from the back cover. Interesting how he changed from book to book. When he wrote *The Lion's Whelp*, he was a young father, full of great hope for Melody. And in *The Lion's Whelp*, Jord had to protect the most precious treasure in all the Allied Universes—the One Child who would grow up to defeat Kalik the Destroyer. Elizabeth could read between the lines: Steve's great love for Melody, his fear that he would somehow fail her and that through some mistake of his, she would never realize her promise.

She sighed. It was every parent's fear; had been through all of human history, she supposed. Jord's struggle touched her heart and increased her anxiety.

Would loving Steve be that fatal error that somehow devastated Cara?

Music pulsed from upstairs, loud and angry. Elizabeth pushed herself out of her chair and went to the kitchen, where she pounded on the ceiling underneath Cara's room with the handle of a broom. The noise abated marginally. Elizabeth rapped on the ceiling again, and this fitful com-

munication eventually yielded a compromise: music that
was too loud for Elizabeth and not loud enough for Cara.

After a few minutes of listening to it, enough to allow
Cara to save face, Elizabeth poured two cups of chocolate
milk and heated them in the microwave. Then she took one
to Cara, told her to turn the music off and drank her own
hot chocolate while she soaked in a bathtub full of water hot
enough, she hoped, to soothe her into sleep.

The tub was a huge old claw-footed dinosaur, long and
deep and comfortable.

Big enough for two, she thought, and immediately pushed
the idea out of her head by submerging herself up to her
neck. She leaned her head on the curved enamel edge and
closed her eyes. Steam filled the bathroom and clouded the
mirror. Heat clouded her mind, and she felt almost weight-
less in the calming water.

"I've gotta get out of here and go to bed," she said aloud.
The water knew she didn't mean it and folded her warmly
and seductively, and she sank deeper into it and drowsed.

The phone rang.

Maybe I won't answer it, she thought.

It rang again.

The water gave her up reluctantly, clung to her, ran sullenly onto the floor. She wrapped herself in a bathtowel and
ran for the phone on the nightstand by her bed.

Steve.

"Hi," he said, in a voice full of high good humor. "This
is the extremely wrinkled old idiot with slow reflexes. I'd
mention my name but I understand you're tired of it and
don't want to hear it."

"Damn!" said Elizabeth, with fervor. She dried herself
with one hand, half-freezing in the cold room. The water got
its revenge: her damp body erupted into goosebumps.

"Was that the location joke?"

She began to laugh again. "Yeah. Apparently you've
heard a somewhat edited version of the conversation. I'm
sure you can imagine the rest. I was stricken speechless."

She snuggled naked between the white sheets and pulled
the heavy comforter under her chin. "So while I was sitting
there, unable to think of a thing to say, I had this sudden

image of us sneaking around all over town, hiding from those two terrifying brats, looking over our shoulders like a couple of fugitives, snatching kisses in out-of-the-way places and pretending we don't know each other in public. Exactly like a bad spy movie. Struck me as funny. Still strikes me as funny."

Another peal of laughter roiled up from her midsection and exploded into the room. After a minute she said, "Do I sound hysterical?"

Steve's deep chuckle rolled across the line. "Yep."

"Not surprising," said Elizabeth, trying to catch her breath. "They're driving me crazy."

"You're not going crazy. That's battle fatigue."

"Why don't they like each other, do you suppose?" asked Elizabeth.

"Because they're both so obnoxious," said Steve. "They're exactly alike. How could they like each other?"

"Think they'll outgrow it?"

"God, I hope so," he said. "I'm graying fast."

"I haven't noticed any gray," said Elizabeth, wishing she could tangle her hands in every hair he had.

"You're not looking in the right place."

"What place is the right place? Gray hairs grow everywhere, once they start."

"Yep." A chuckle.

The right place? The right place? There was a sudden silence as Elizabeth realized what he meant.

"You're blushing," he said.

"Not I," she said. She wasn't blushing. She was salivating. Her imagination ran amok, and she galloped right along with it. It wasn't only his hair she wanted to get her hands on. She wanted to get her hands on all of him. All. Her mind's eye saw him clearly and liked the view.

"What's the name of that church you and Cara go to?" asked Steve. The laugh was still in his voice. "What time does it start? Melody and I will come tomorrow."

"Saint Cyril's. Ten o'clock." She ventured to stretch her legs. The sheets were like ice. She curled up again in the warm hollow she'd made for herself.

"What'd he die of, old Cyril?"

"Froze to death, I expect," said Elizabeth, observing the rime on the outside of her windowpane.

"Is that an oblique reference to the weather, or do you want me to get off the phone?"

"Weather, of course. There's ice on the outside of my window."

"How about you?" Steve asked. "Are you nice and warm? Wearing your long flannel nightie and your bed socks and your mobcap?"

"Actually, no. I was bathing when you called, and I dried off in this refrigerator and now I'm in bed, and I'm going to be a pretzel tomorrow because the sheets are so cold I can't move. What's a mobcap?"

"One of those Martha Washington hats, ruffled around the edges. Looks like a shower cap. Keeps your head warm.

"It's not my head that's cold. It's my feet."

"Where's the flannel nightie to warm up the rest of you?"

The rest of her was beginning to be a little chilled. "I'd have to get out of bed to get it, and I don't want to. I'd freeze for sure."

"Does this antique house of yours have a furnace?"

"Don't you know sleeping in a hot room is bad for you?"

"Are you sure your distant ancestors didn't come out of the Massachusetts Bay Colony?"

"As a matter of fact, they did. Why?"

"Only a Puritan could equate comfort and affliction."

"Bah, humbug."

"You don't have an electric blanket, either, I'll bet."

"Electromagnetic waves after your molecular chemistry," she said. "I read that in one of your books."

"Bah, humbug. That's bad science, but useful fiction," said Steve. "Since I'm not there to warm your feet for you, I'll tell you what to do."

"What?"

"Climb into the tub long enough to warm up, put the roomy flannel nightie on and get back into bed. Then drowse and think of me, sharing the nightie, all night long."

"I might consider it, if I didn't know it would keep me awake all night," she said, admitting deprivation. "Old Cyril, as you so disrespectfully term him, is the first church on the right past Ardmore Square. On Montgomery. Meet you there?"

"Yeah," he said. "Good night, darling."

She did exactly what he told her to. Then, comfortable and warm, she switched off her reading lamp and blew a kiss off her palm into the dark, trusting that it would find its way to Steve's lips. And when she slept, his endearment echoed like a benediction through her dreams.

Steve, lying in his own cold bed, had an irresistible vision of Elizabeth rising from her bath, rosy and warm and dripping wet, for him to dry. He had a vivid visual imagination: he could see every sweet curve, her round, full breasts, her tumbled hair; could see her lifting her arms and stepping forward, smiling, to meet him.

He groaned and turned over in bed. Heat flooded through him, lacing his belly and clotting his loins with an intensity that was more pain than desire.

Was she thinking of him now, fantasizing as he was, dreaming of touching him, holding him, making love? Or did she still dream of Robert, of his body and his kiss? She sounded indifferent when she spoke of Robert, but the mind and the heart often have opposite goals. Elizabeth was a passionate woman; Steve had seen that passion and tasted it. If the memory of Robert subconsciously evoked that passion, then perhaps Joe Salvini did, too.

Cara had a crush on Salvini, because he looked so much like her father. Why wouldn't Elizabeth react to that subliminal stimulus, too? Elizabeth, Steve knew, would never let Robert into her life again, despite his charm. But Joe was everything Robert wasn't. How could Elizabeth help but respond to him?

Damn Salvini. And damn Robert. And damn, too, this primal adrenaline-charged competitive urge to fight for a woman, which God had built into even the most reasonable of men.

At least, he thought, with what scant humor he could muster, I used to be reasonable. Now I'm just another victim of testosterone poisoning.

He groaned again and closed his eyes, and couldn't sleep. And tossed. And turned. And dozed uneasily. He dreamed of being tied up and attacked by angry wasps, and woke to find the alarm buzzing and himself tangled in the sheets.

An eight o'clock wake-up? Mild irritation. On Sunday morning? Extreme irritation. He scowled at the ceiling until he remembered. Oh, yeah, church. He swung his feet to the floor and felt his way to the shower. When he had on his suit and tie, he went to waken Melody.

"What?" she said, when he tapped on her door. Her voice croaked.

Steve entered and sat on the edge of her bed. Only the top of her head showed. The rest of her was snuggled under a patchwork quilt that his sister had made and the thirty or so stuffed animals she wouldn't sleep without. He pulled the quilt down to her chin, and she squinted at him like a sleepy little owl.

She had squinted like that as a baby, as he'd rocked her and fed her her 6:00 a.m. bottle. The little round baby face, topped with soft blond fuzz, had turned miraculously into a pretty girl, inevitably growing up and away from him. He wasn't sure how it had happened so fast. He'd just become accustomed to the baby, and suddenly she was a pigtailed child, with Barbie dolls and roller skates and jump ropes and shrieking friends. The Barbie dolls and roller skates gave way to lipstick and boys long before he was ready for it. He smiled. She still had the shrieking friends.

Daddy's girl, he thought, with that melancholy pride all men feel as they watch their children grow into competent adults.

He rubbed his knuckles gently on her scalp.

"Time to wake up, honey," he said.

"It's Sunday," she said, closing her eyes.

"Yeah. We're going to church."

"Church?" she repeated. "What church?"

"St. Cyril's Episcopal."

She rose from the bed like a cannon shot. All traces of the cuddly baby were gone. Her hair stood out and her eyes were wide open and her teeth were bared. Her braces glittered in the lamplight.

"Cara's church!" she said. "I won't go!"

"You most certainly will," said Steve, in what his ex-wife once had called his ex cathedra voice.

"Why do we have to start going to church now?" roared Melody. "We never did before!"

"Church is a place where you learn the virtues of unselfishness and self-control," said Steve, standing up. "Those are two concepts to which it is time you were introduced."

"Cara's been going since before she was born, and she hasn't learned anything yet," said Melody, gesturing wildly. "What's the point?"

"Sometimes it takes a while to get the message across," Steve told her. "I want you out of that bed, showered, dressed and downstairs in an hour. Understand?"

He stayed long enough to get a sullen affirmation, then went down to his coffee and newspaper, shaking his head all the way.

Dealing with Cara and Melody was like trying to tunnel out of a cave-in: slow, hard and dangerous. There were hazards at every turn. It didn't matter. He'd keep digging. He intended to have Elizabeth and a couple of bullheaded little girls weren't going to stop him.

At nine o'clock, as ordered, Melody appeared. Steve rose to fix her breakfast and got his first good look at her.

She had on a gray wool skirt that was rolled up until it was five inches above her knees. The legs underneath were bare of stockings. The roll of wool around her waist was badly concealed by a black patent belt, and the combined fabric and leather bulged out around Melody's middle like a bicycle inner tube. Her hair looked nice—curled and brushed. But her face was adorned with all the drugstore makeup her allowance would buy. Thick eyeliner ringed her eyes, zigging and zagging where her unskilled fingers had faltered. Mascara glopped in blobs on her long brown lashes. Blue eyeshadow winged out nearly to her ears and met a russet blush which reddened her cheeks like an unhealthy fever. The toilette was completed with a violent pink lipstick which made his eyes hurt.

Her appearance was not exactly a surprise. She had been born wanting four-inch heels and rhinestone earrings.

"Oh, geez," Steve said. "There is no balm in Gilead. You've used it all."

Melody began to look contentious.

"Your hair looks nice," he said. "But the rest of you needs considerable repair."

"Oh, really, Daddy," said Melody, flouncing toward the table.

"Oh, really, yourself," said Steve. "Go upstairs and wash that goop off your face, put on stockings, roll that skirt down and get a blazer. Right now. I want you back down here in ten minutes, looking like an ad for a temperance union. Go."

"Everybody wears makeup," Melody countered. "Besides, I look like a ghost without it."

"You look like a Ringling Brothers clown act with it," said Steve, mining the archetype for the same image Neolithic fathers had used when their daughters first stained their lips with berry juice.

Melody's lips trembled and her eyes filled with tears.

"You just don't understand!" she wailed, and fled upstairs, weeping.

"Oh, damn," Steve said. He remembered his father and his sister Lin having exactly the same argument, with exactly the same results. History repeating itself. No wonder philosophers feared for the future of humankind. He sank his teeth violently into a tough piece of toast.

She reappeared with a clean face, a wounded pout and her skirt rolled down, but not all the way. Steve looked at it and decided to let it pass.

"Let's go," he said.

The church was Christmas-card perfect, a white-steepled Colonial vintage building which had been carefully preserved. Surrounding it was a low stone wall, which also encompassed a graveyard with apple, oak and walnut trees grown tall among the ancient headstones. If Steve had been in a better mood, he'd have been charmed. Instead, he wondered sourly if Episcopalians had a patron saint of lost causes. Unpleasant pictures of Elizabeth smiling at Joe had populated his unwelcome dreams, and dreams like that were hard to forget.

He looked around for Elizabeth. She stood at the door, looking like a fantasy in a soft pink wool dress. Its flared skirt swirled enticingly around her beautiful legs as she came to meet them. Her hair wound around its curly self into a prim chignon, secured by a silver and amethyst comb. But the toothed discipline of the silver was insufficient, for a few wispy tendrils had escaped and asserted their independence, and they curled and frothed and beckoned in the breeze.

Steve sighed. She looked good enough to eat. The tough piece of toast and a pitched battle with Melody were hardly any more nourishing to the spirit than the nightmare memory of Joe Salvini holding Elizabeth spellbound with his charm. His vexation condensed and knotted itself securely just behind his consciousness.

Beside Elizabeth stood a tall redheaded girl about Melody's age. Elizabeth pointed, and the child bounced down the steps, all smiles.

"I'm Gigi McClellan," she said. "Are you Melody?"

Melody nodded, too shy to speak.

"Well, actually, my name's Ginger, but I changed it. That's a horse's name, even if my mom doesn't think so."

Melody giggled. "My Aunt Lin has a bay horse named Ginger."

"See? I told you," said Gigi. "Sunday School's upstairs. They have doughnuts. And after, the whole class is going for pizza and a movie. It costs five dollars. You want to come with me?''

With her face shining, Melody turned towards Steve. He had the money out of his pocket before she asked. Then, without a backward glance she ambled off, with Gigi chattering like a castanet.

''Do you know how to ride horses?'' asked Gigi. ''I've always wanted a horse, but I have four brothers, and we don't have enough money to feed five animals that eat like horses, my mom says.''

Steve watched as the two girls climbed the stairs.

''Good morning, Madam Magician,'' he said, smiling for the first time that day.

''Gigi could talk to a rock,'' said Elizabeth, looking satisfied.

''How about the four brothers?''

''They're too busy eating to talk at all. She wasn't kidding. Our rector calls them, collectively, the genial young giants. And he isn't kidding, either.'' She pointed toward the parking lot. Across the churchyard toward them came two of the said young giants, who had driven themselves to church. They were laughing at something and poking at each other and looked as wholesome as Tom Sawyer and Huckleberry Finn.

''Easy to recognize,'' said Steve. ''They're as carrot topped as Gigi. Are they going to be at this Thanksgiving dance Melody keeps talking about?''

''Geordie is, I expect.'' Elizabeth led Steve into the church common room for coffee and pastries. ''He goes to Linwoody Boys' Prep, and he's a second-former, like Cara and Melody. Or so Cara tells me.''

She looked suddenly troubled, as she said that.

''What's the matter?'' Steve asked. The moody knot swelled with the addition of more trouble and nudged at his forebrain. He picked up two foam cups and filled them with coffee.

"I have this uncomfortable feeling that Cara mentioned Geordie once, with high praise for his general romantic appeal."

Steve raised his eyebrows. "And Gigi will introduce Geordie to Melody."

"And Melody, having a general romantic appeal of her own," Elizabeth said, "will probably appeal to Geordie, who has shown no general interest in Cara's appeal, and while I'm on the subject of appeal, I think I'll appeal to God for help."

"Yeah?" said Steve. "And what are you going to pray for?" His stomach knotted up again.

She thought of Melody and Cara, of loneliness, of wanting Steve. Of sex and desire and sleepless nights and love.

"Deliverance," she sighed, stirring milk and lots of soothing sugar into her coffee.

Chapter Seven

The rector, an exhausted father of newborn twin daughters, had spoken of fortitude as the most important of the cardinal virtues.

"A lot he knows about fortitude," declared Steve, as he and Elizabeth watched the busload of eighth-graders pull away from the church. "Wait till those infants are thirteen. Then we'll see what he has to say."

"Grumpy," said Elizabeth, amused.

"Dealing with Melody," Steve pronounced, "is exactly like riding a half-trained horse. People think you're doing all right, but you know you're not in control, and so does the horse."

"Having a little trouble today, are we?" asked Elizabeth sympathetically.

He treated her to a recital of the morning's conversation.

"She'll outgrow it," Elizabeth said, although she had no proof of that. Her own experience led her to believe it would last forever.

"Before she drives me crazy?" asked Steve. It wasn't only Melody driving him crazy. There were Cara and Joe Salvini and Robert Fairchild and loneliness and longing and jealousy all waiting their turn to discomfit him. The restive knot which had nudged at him all morning swelled blackly over his future.

"She's not going to drive you crazy," said Elizabeth, slipping her hand into his.

No, but wanting you and not having you will, he thought to himself. Aloud he said, "I have to go home and let Sammy out. If you want to come with me, I'll buy you a sandwich." He knew he snarled when he said it. He was in a terrible mood—nothing in his life was going right, and he didn't seem to be able to do anything about it.

"Why are you so irritable?" asked Elizabeth, suddenly cross herself. Very surprising she wasn't terribly cross all the time, she thought. Irritability was the inevitable result of worrying about Cara during her waking hours and dreaming about Steve during her sleeping hours and trying to sandwich productive labor into the tiny spaces that were left.

"The pot calling the kettle black," returned Steve. "Are you coming?"

She tugged at her hand; he elected to keep it.

"Let go," she said, with emphasis.

"I refuse." He opened the passenger door of his car and tucked her into the seat.

"Now I'll let go," he told her. "But I want it back as soon as I start the engine." He fastened her seat belt for her, then he got Sammy's blanket out of the back seat and tucked it around her legs and feet. "There," he said. "You can relax and enjoy the ride."

"You act like you're trying to get me back to the asylum without upsetting me," she said, after he'd started the engine.

He reached across the seat to take her hand. "You know how sensitive animals are to emotion."

She scowled. "You ought to be worried about me, not Sammy."

"I was talking about me," he said. "There was an earthquake once, when we lived in California, and Sammy didn't even wake up. If he had a clowder of cats doing a cancan in front of him, he'd pant and try to learn the steps. He's a doof. I've had a bad morning. You ought to be nice to me."

Her scowl lessened, and she produced a throaty humph that was almost a chuckle.

"What I like about Sammy," she said, "is that he's never out of sorts, he's always glad to see me, and he doesn't want anything but a little petting now and then."

"That's all I want," said Steve, wondering if he were ever likely to get it. "Just a little petting. And I am always glad to see you, despite the increasingly unlikely circumstances."

"Sammy has other charms," she said. "He has a vocabulary bigger than mine. *Armph* and *oomphf* and *rauff* and *mrowrrmp*. He's a scholar and a gentleman."

"Try to remember that no matter how many times you kiss him," said Steve, "he will never turn into a prince."

"He doesn't need to turn into a prince," said Elizabeth. "He already is one. Have you noticed how attached he and Cara have become?"

"Yes. I wish I could say that it's progress." He sighed. "She shows no sign of becoming attached to me." He pulled to a stop in his driveway. "Or Melody."

That was true enough. Cara remained obdurate, despite the wiles of Sammy and Johnny and the considerable Vorkland charm. She regarded Steve and Melody as an affliction on the unfortunate Vorklands and pitied their circumstances.

"I don't want to hold out any hope," Elizabeth said soberly, as she got out of the car. "When I talk to her about us, I still get that shuttered look, and she turns around and goes into another room."

Sammy heard them coming and barked madly. Steve opened the door and pushed past him. Sammy capered, leapt and whirled, rearing like a colt. He dashed around the room, looking for something to play with, and snatched one of Melody's socks off the coffee table.

"Gimme that," said Steve, grabbing at him.

Sammy feinted and ran. Steve hooked the end of the sock and tugged. Sammy gave the sock a shake to show that he still claimed possession and dropped it on the floor.

"Mwrorp," he said, nosing at Steve's ankles.

"That means out," translated Steve.

"What happens if you ignore him?" Elizabeth wanted to know.

"I'm afraid to find out," said Steve, opening the door. "He always sniffs my ankles first."

Sammy trotted disdainfully into the small yard, lifted his leg, and galloped back to the comfort of the house.

He presented himself to Elizabeth with an elephantine wriggle.

"Him's a big precious boofums baby dog," she crooned, rubbing her knuckles on the top of his big nose.

"Him's a shameless, opportunistic, conniving hound," said Steve, amused by this sudden rupture of Elizabeth's syntax. "Don't let Cara hear you talk like that."

"I'm in love," said Elizabeth. She dropped to her knees and ignored any possible damage to her stockings and her pink dress.

"Good," said Steve. "Marry me."

"And spend my declining years as a referee?" she said, refusing to look at him. "No, thanks. I think I'll just take up with Sammy, instead, and go live on the *Busted Flush*. You think he'd like a boat better than he likes your backyard?"

Every muscle tightened, from his ankle to his ear. A warning cramp nibbled at his neck. "I somehow think Travis McGee would object to the five of us."

"Yeah?" she said. "Maybe we should move in with Meyer."

"Maybe we should move in together." His tone was hard and flat.

She canted her eyes upward. He was smiling, but there was a certain ominous rigidity about his mouth. She quit petting Sammy and stood, to find herself literally and figuratively backed against a wall.

"How about the sandwich?" she said, trying to defuse a dangerous situation.

His eyes glittered. "How about answering me?"

"That can't have been a serious suggestion." She tried to move away. He put one large hand flat against the wall and kept her where she was.

"Why the hell not?" he snapped. "It's time for you to start thinking about loving me, Elizabeth. Past time for you to think about getting married again. And far past time for you to resolve the conflict that keeps you single and celibate in that ancient sexless brick house of yours."

"I don't want to talk about it," she told him, battered by her emotions. "What if we're never able to bring the girls to reason? It's a real possibility—I don't know why you won't face it. It's not fair of you to demand that I love you."

"Not fair? What's not fair about it?" The cramp bit at his neck again.

"I have too many other problems. I can't think about either romance or marriage now." She would look at the ceiling, she thought, the floor, anything but Steve's face. "I don't seem to be able to think coherently about anything. It's stress."

He stepped across the dog and took her by the shoulders. "You have to think about romance and marriage." He pulled her, almost roughly, into his arms.

He made her look at him, look into gray eyes as hard and cold as flint. Overlying the passion and desire was anger and purpose and uncompromising resolution.

"We are falling in love," he said. "Surely you've noticed. We've been dancing politely around it, trying to ignore it, for months, and we have to do something about it. Either give it up or continue with it. It's time for you to decide what you want to do."

"Why just my decision?" she said. "What about you?"

"I made my decision the first time I kissed you. I want you, now and forever. In my heart, in my life. In my bed."

She turned her head. "I have to think about Cara."

"I'm tired of thinking about Cara and Melody," he said. "I want to think about you and me. It's time we gave ourselves a break."

Elizabeth rolled her eyes. "Oh, do try to be sensible," she said.

"You think I'm not sensible?" he said. The words rumbled menacingly in his chest and emerged as a subsonic roar. "Would you like to try to explain to me why it's sensible of you to let Cara control what you'll do and whom you'll love?"

"I don't recall asking you for any advice," said Elizabeth icily. "I'll let you know when I want anything from you."

"You don't know what you want," he said disdainfully. "You're too busy trying to figure out what Cara wants."

She stared at him for a minute, then her green eyes flashed.

"Yes, I know what I want. I have a child to raise. I want to do it right. And if that means doing without you, then that's the way it will have to be."

The pressure in Steve's chest spread to his head and his hands. He fought himself to keep from holding her too tightly.

"That's not all you want," he said, through a pounding anger.

He wrapped his big hand around her jaw and forced her mouth to his. At first she was paralyzed by the sudden aggressiveness of the kiss, then she opened her mouth fully to his demanding invasion. His tongue plunged phallically, deeply and strongly, until she was violent with wanting him. She clung to him, seeking and wild, he slid his hands over the soft pink dress, cupped her warm, rounded buttocks, and pulled her solidly against him. He hungered, he burned, he desired. He wanted her to feel that desire hard against her, and he wanted her to hunger for it, too.

He wanted her to remember it at night, in the desert wasteland of her bed. He wanted her to covet him, dream of him, lust for him until she was savage with need and aching for him to come to her.

"If you think you're going to let Cara decide for you, Elizabeth," he said, between his teeth, "and sleep in that big, cold bed all by yourself for the rest of your life, you're wrong. I'm going to have you, and nothing Cara or Melody can ever do will keep you from me."

She pulled away from him with her heart pounding. When she looked at him, he was breathing hard, and his mouth was tight and bloodless at the corners.

He walked away from her and jerked open the door. "Stay, Sammy," he said.

Sammy slunk to his chair, looking sideways at Steve from eyes wide with alarm.

"He thinks you're mad at him," said Elizabeth, full of reproof and glad of diversion. "Poor baby."

"He was born with a guilty conscience," Steve told her.

Her heart still thudded dangerously in her breast . . . and intensified when she let her body remember the hot touch of his hands.

"He should split it with you," she said. "You need a conscience worse than he does."

He snorted at that. "I'm ridden with conscience, God help me," he said. "Are you coming? I want to eat."

She gave Sammy a last comforting pat before she put on her coat. "Where are we going?"

"To a steak house. For good, red meat, so rare it's barely warm to the touch." He got behind the wheel. "A virile, hearty, manly meal, to sustain me through weeks of trial by combat." Irony surfaced, gained strength and treaded water. But his sense of humor, he thought, was permanently gone.

"Appeals to the caveman in you, does it?" she asked acidly.

He considered Robert and Joe Salvini.

I'll take them to the zoo, he thought. *And feed them to the tigers.*

"Yes," he said, with satisfaction. "It does. How long are those two brats going to be at the movies?"

"We're supposed to retrieve them at three." She looked out the window at the elegant facade of the restaurant Steve had chosen. "We can't eat here. This place is terribly expensive. Besides, for food like this, I should be in a better mood."

"You don't have to be in a good mood to eat," said Steve.

"I do if I want to enjoy it."

"Bah," said Steve, whose appetite had never been affected by his emotions.

PLAY

$ BIG BUCKS $

AND YOU COULD WIN THE

$1,000,000.00

PLUS JACKPOT!

ONE MILLION

ONE MILLION

YOUR PERSONAL
GAME CARD
INSIDE....

SILHOUETTE

HOW TO PLAY

IT'S FUN! BIG BUCK$ IT'S FREE!

It's so easy...grab a lucky coin, and go right to your BIG BUCKS game card. Scratch off silver squares in a STRAIGHT LINE (across, down, or diagonal) until 5 dollar signs are revealed. BINGO!...Doing this makes-you-eligible for a-chance to win $1,000,000.00 in lifetime income ($33,333.33 each year for 30 years!) Also scratch all 4 corners to reveal the dollar signs. This entitles you to a chance to win the $50,000.00 Extra Bonus Prize! Void if more than 9 squares scratched off.

Your EXCLUSIVE PRIZE NUMBER is in the upper right corner of your game card. Return your game card and we'll activate your unique Sweepstakes Number; so it's important that your name and address section is completed correctly. This will permit us to identify you and match you with any cash prize rightfully yours! (SEE BACK OF BOOK FOR DETAILS.)

FREE BOOKS PLUS FREE GIFTS!

At the same time you play your BIG BUCKS game card for BIG CASH PRIZES...scratch the Lucky Charm to receive FOUR FREE

Silhouette Special Edition® novels, and a FREE GIFT, TOO! They're totally free, absolutely free with no obligation to buy anything!

These books have a cover price of $3.75 each. But THEY ARE TOTALLY FREE; even the shipping will be at our expense! The Silhouette Reader Service™ is not like some book clubs. You don't have to make any minimum number of purchases–not even one!

The fact is, thousands of readers look forward to receiving six of the best new romance novels each month and they love our discount prices!

Of course you may play BIG BUCKS for cash prizes alone by not scratching off your Lucky Charm, but why not get everything that we are offering and that you are entitled to! You'll be glad you did.

Offer limited to one per household and not valid to current Silhouette Special Edition® subscribers. All orders subject to approval.

▶ DETACH AND MAIL CARD TODAY!

EXCLUSIVE PRIZE # 31 859936

BIG BUCKS

$

TWO WAYS TO WIN BIG BUCKS!

1. Uncover 5 $ signs in a row...BINGO! You're eligible for a chance to win the $1,000,000.00 SWEEPSTAKES!

2. Uncover 5 $ signs in a row AND uncover $ signs in all 4 corners...BINGO! You're also eligible for a chance to win the $50,000.00 EXTRA BONUS PRIZE!

HURRY!
This jackpot must be claimed!

Scratch here

LUCKY CHARM GAME!

Claim 4 FREE books AND a FREE Mystery Gift!

YES! I have played my BIG BUCKS game card as instructed. Enter my Big Bucks Prize number in the MILLION DOLLAR Sweepstakes III and also enter me for the Extra Bonus Prize. When winners are selected, tell me if I've won. If the Lucky Charm is scratched off, I will also receive everything revealed, as explained on the back of this page.

235 CIS AS3N
(U-SIL-SE-07/95)

NAME _____

ADDRESS _____ APT. _____

CITY _____ STATE _____ ZIP _____

NO PURCHASE OR OBLIGATION NECESSARY TO ENTER SWEEPSTAKES.

© 1993 HARLEQUIN ENTERPRISES LTD.

PRINTED IN U.S.A.

"We need reservations." She put one foot on the ground, but didn't get out of the car. Steve extended a hand to pull her up.

He shrugged. "So I'll bribe the headwaiter for a table."

"Bribe him?" said Elizabeth, in a voice which shuttled between amazement and rebuke. "Do you do that sort of thing?"

"Bah!" Steve repeated irritably, and Elizabeth watched as money did, indeed, change hands.

Outside the window by their table, a vigorous little stream rushed past a willow copse. Glaze ice tipped the branches. They moved and glittered, the water leapt and glittered, as Steve watched. The muscles around his mouth began to relax. A skein of geese beat into the wind, headed southeast, and their wild cries echoed like a homing call in the cold November air.

Steve followed them until they were out of sight, then he sighed and leaned back in his chair.

Elizabeth sighed, too, and beckoned for the waiter.

Cara returned from the movies tight-lipped. Elizabeth didn't have to wonder why: Geordie bounced off the church bus behind Melody and melted under the warming power of her thousand-watt smile.

They watched the disaster from the front seat of Steve's car. It unfolded in front of them like a grade-B movie melodrama.

"God help me," said Steve, shaking his head. "Melody's too young for this and I'm too old for it."

"For what?"

"Geordie. Puppy love. I can't even handle my own romance, let alone hers," he growled. "Why does she have to bother me with this now? I've got enough on my mind. Why can't she just wait until she's older?"

"How old?" asked Elizabeth.

Across the parking lot, Melody and Geordie, charmed with each other, postured and flirted.

"Till she's twenty-five," said Steve. "That's a good, safe age. Mature. Sensible."

"Are you sure that's sufficiently distant?"

"It isn't kind of you to laugh at me."

"I'm not laughing at you," she said.

"I know. You're laughing near me. You know what Lin says?"

"What?"

"She says, 'This, too, will pass, and something worse will come to take its place.' "

Elizabeth shuddered. "Thanks for sharing," she told him. "I'll dream about that at night."

"It's not situation specific," said Steve. "She uses it about any trouble with her kids."

"Wonderful. Is she justified by subsequent events?"

"Sorry to tell you. Yes."

"Terrific," said Elizabeth, who was certain Lin was right.

Cara marched towards Elizabeth's car. Her back was ramrod straight, her head was high, her jaw was firm and her eyes were miserable.

"There's the 'something worse,' " said Steve. "Bless her heart."

"Bless all our hearts," said Elizabeth, opening her door. "I'd better go."

Steve bent and kissed her quickly.

"I love you," he said. "Think about that, every time you get a chance."

She turned away from him and left; her back was straight, and her head was high. He couldn't see her eyes.

"I hate Melody," said Cara the following Wednesday, as she got in the car. She had stood outside in the rain, waiting for Elizabeth. Her hair was wet, and water puddled on the floor under her shoes.

No big surprise there, thought Elizabeth. The wipers beat frantically at the windshield; water sluiced away and the rain fell even harder.

"You know what she said?" Cara asked, wrathful both in tone and form.

More adolescent outrage. Elizabeth couldn't stand it.

"She said her dad said I was a slow learner," Cara told her mother. "He said that was the reason I've gone to church all my life and never learned anything, because I'm stupid.''

Gray shadows glanced off the rain slick streets. Cara's wool coat, which had been crumpled in the bottom of her locker for nine hours, stank like a wet dog.

Cara and Melody and their endless sniping were very tiresome. Elizabeth looked at Cara, irritated.

"Don't pay any attention to what Melody says her father says. If you want to know what he really said, go ask him yourself."

"Because she's such a liar all the time, right?" said Cara hopefully.

"No, Cara," Elizabeth said with impatience. "Because messages get garbled in translation. Get your word from the horse's mouth. Mr. Riker wouldn't say such a thing. He likes you very much. If you want to know the truth of something, go to the source instead of depending on hearsay."

"And you know what else?" Cara said. "She knows I like Geordie, because she saw me talking to him on the train."

Now, there was an idea common in every preschool: if you want something, it belongs to you. A dynamic idea, which had caused endless wars and hatreds. A seductive and ruinous idea—ask anybody in any one of a thousand contested world trouble spots just how destructive it could be.

Not, of course, that Cara could understand that now. Early adolescence, with its raging irrationality, wasn't exactly the best time to try to teach anyone to view personal disaster with philosophical detachment. Elizabeth certainly wasn't about to try.

She couldn't dredge up much interest in philosophic detachment herself, she thought gloomily. Steve was right about one thing she wanted: it hadn't taken any soul-searing kiss for her to acknowledge the liquid desire that melted her whenever she even thought about him. She knew all about desire, much more, really, than she'd ever wanted to find out. And if she was kept from realizing the desire?

She wished the possibility were unthinkable. Unfortunately, she could clearly see herself riding off into the sunset—alone.

The car hit the curb and lurched as she turned into her driveway. "Bah," she said, much as Steve had earlier.

"There's a big box on the porch," said Cara, suddenly elated. "I bet it's my birthday present from Daddy."

Over a month late, as usual. Too much stuff, as usual. Chosen by the current girlfriend, as usual. Elizabeth could tell a lot about the women Robert dated by what was in the Christmas and birthday boxes.

Cara was out of the car almost before it stopped moving. "It is from Daddy! Look how big it is!" she squealed.

She was ripping at the strapping tape before Elizabeth could unlock the door. When the house was finally open, Cara tugged the box into the foyer and tore into it.

"Oh, cool!" Cara grabbed the item on top and held it up. "Clothes."

Oh, God, Elizabeth thought. The Tin Ear must have picked out that horror. It was a matched set, a thin knit T-shirt and leggings, like cheap long underwear (probably exactly its function in a previous incarnation), splattered with purple and pink dye and ripped artistically in strategic places. The second garment to emerge was a hot pink body suit to wear with the—thing—and meant to show through.

Manchester Park, read the label. Rodeo Drive. It must have cost a bloody fortune, and it wasn't fit for a charity donation.

That was just the beginning. The box was full of the sort of clothes for the sort of woman Elizabeth had always thought you'd find on the street corners in bad districts of large cities.

And Cara would fight to wear them.

Robert had sent clothes before, and they were always awful. But these—these were definitely the worst yet. Stupid damn Robert—didn't he ever look at what his money bought? Even he couldn't have been idiot enough to sanction this shipment. She would like to take every piece back to California, thought Elizabeth, and poke each despicable thread down his throat until he was so permanently plugged up that he'd be constipated forever.

"I wish I didn't have to wear a skirt and blazer every day," Cara lamented. "Can't I please go to a public school next year?"

"Don't be silly," Elizabeth snapped.

"I don't see why not," said Cara, in the mood for a fight.

"I ... will ... not ... argue ... with ... you ... about ... this. Take those clothes upstairs," said Elizabeth, and silently added, *then throw them out the attic window.*

"Look at the card Daddy sent," said Cara, for once deciding to retreat. She dumped the clothes into the box and hauled it upstairs.

Elizabeth read the card and with difficulty resisted the urge to claw it into confetti.

"Give all my bestest love to Mom," it begged. In italic type. Even the signature was typed: "Dad." Elizabeth said aloud for the first time the sort of word she had always thought would be said only by the sort of woman you'd find on the street corners. And found it very appropriate to the situation.

Robert had never said *bestest* in his life.

She went to the phone to call Steve, an innocent civilian who needed to be informed that the battle was rejoined. It rang before she could get it off the hook.

Joe Salvini. Cara picked up her bedroom extension and quickly replaced it.

"Are you calling to tell me her grades are awful?" asked Elizabeth, after Cara was safely off the line.

"No. Actually, her grades are much better," said Joe. "She seems to be interested in what we're doing. I'm preparing next semester's lesson plans. You said you had some Civil War artifacts. Still want to share them?"

"Sure," she said. "I have quite a few things, but the letters are the most interesting, I think. They really show what was going on, both at home and in the army. Lots of details of family life. When do you want it?"

"I'll come look at it on Monday evening, if that's okay."

"I could bring it to school for you."

"I have to be in Philadelphia all day. I'll come by on my way home," he said. "I want Cara to present this to the class herself. Will you have time to help her with it?"

"Absolutely," said Elizabeth. She'd look forward to it.

"Good," said Joe. "It'll be good for her to learn to speak to a group. See you Monday night, then."

As soon as they disconnected, Cara exploded down the stairs.

"What did he want?" Dancing about, unable to stand still.

"The Civil War stuff," said Elizabeth.

"Oh." Deflation. "Do you want me to take it to school?"

"No. Mr. Salvini's coming by to look at it."

"Oh. He is?" Renewed hope. "Did you like talking to him?"

"Of course. He's very nice."

"He's really good-looking, too, don't you think?" asked Cara. "I mean, really."

"Very nice, yes," said Elizabeth, trying to turn Cara away from the subject of Mr. Salvini. "Have you started your homework?"

"I did it in detention today," she said. "I want to show you something. Dad sent a dress." She shot upstairs.

Detention. No wonder Cara's grades were better, thought Elizabeth. That's the one benefit to the feud that she hadn't considered.

Cara clattered down the stairs again, clad in an outrageous blood red organdy and satin dress. It made Elizabeth's head hurt to look at it.

"I'm going to wear this to the Thanksgiving Dance," said Cara, spinning around.

"Darling, that's really precious," said her crafty mother. "It looks just like the kind of dress a little girl ought to wear."

Cara looked thoughtful. Elizabeth pressed the assault.

"I think your father would love to have a picture of you in this. It's adorable. You had a Sunday School dress very much like it when you were in first or second grade. Imagine his remembering that." She walked around Cara, smiling. "You look very sweet and nice in it."

Sweet and nice were two things Cara seldom wanted to be.

"Can I go shopping Saturday?" asked Cara. "Just in case I decide I don't want to wear this?"

Elizabeth grabbed her daughter and hugged her fiercely. "I adore you," she said. "Despite linguistic trials. Did you know that?"

Cara put her arms around her mother and snuggled into her shoulder. Elizabeth dropped a kiss on the curly soft hair.

"Yes," said Cara. "Can I go by myself with just Gretchen and Megan and Sara Fane? I'm old enough to pick out what I want."

"What about detentions?"

"I'm not gonna get one," said Cara confidently. "I'm being really, really careful."

Elizabeth laughed and gave Cara another squeeze before she let her go.

"Homework time," she said.

"I know, Mom," said Cara. "You don't have to tell me." She went into the kitchen. "I don't have very much, anyway."

Since Elizabeth had used that strategic ploy herself with her own mother, she knew it was not to be believed.

"Your book bag," she said to Cara, with more than a touch of suspicion, "is bulging."

"Library books," said Cara. "Honest, Mom." She went upstairs loaded with enough food to sustain her through a two-year famine.

Elizabeth settled herself in a chair by the fire and opened *Kalik the Destroyer*. Lot of nerve she had, telling Cara to do her homework, when waiting upstairs in her office was the accounting system of the McNulty Paper Box Company, waiting to be dragged into the twentieth century. She felt guilty for a nanosecond, then opened the book.

Steve's picture on the inside cover told a story, all by itself. The jaunty boy shown on *Fire in the Hole* was gone; the young confident man pictured in *The Hail Mary Margin* and *The Lion's Whelp* had vanished. This Steve was grim-faced and sad and weary. His lips were painfully compressed, his eyes were hooded; she could tell where the lines on his face would be when he was old.

Elizabeth knew from reading Steve's other work just how emotionally autobiographical the books were, and the first few pages of *Kalik the Destroyer* were painful. Jord had

failed, for the first time. He was fighting on in a disinte
grating world to save its children, of whom there were only
seven left. One of the seven was the link to the One Child's
future, but Jord didn't know which one. And he was des
perate to save them all. All the early optimism was gone
Jord was fighting just to stay alive.

Elizabeth put the book down. She couldn't stand any
more. It was obvious to her that Steve had written *Kalik* a
his marriage was breaking up. All his pain and fury and
helplessness was condensed and magnified through Jord
Varic, and Elizabeth could feel his despair as intensely as i
it had been distilled and fed into her veins.

It was a terrifying book.

She was too emotionally uncomfortable to keep reading
McNulty and his boxes would be a distraction from Kalik
and his hatefulness.

Besides. The One Child was in grave danger. Elizabeth
knew it was stupid, but the book had really shaken her. She
wanted to see if Cara was all right.

She stopped at Cara's door and tapped lightly.

No answer.

"Cara—get started on your homework."

No answer.

Elizabeth tapped again. No answer. She pushed the door
open and peeked in.

Cara was sitting cross-legged on her bed, with her nose in
a book. It didn't look like a textbook.

"What are you reading?"

Cara looked up, startled. "*Dragonflight*. It's really good
I'm going to read all the books she wrote."

"Who?"

"Anne McCaffrey." She dipped her head again and said
absently, "You ought to read this, Mom."

"Well, I might. I find that I'm becoming a science fic
tion fan myself." Elizabeth withdrew quietly and went to her
office to turn on her computer.

Cara read until it was time for bed, came home with a new
set of books on Friday, read until Elizabeth made her quit
and got up early on Saturday so she could finish her book
before she had to go shopping.

Her book bag had been crammed every night, all week. Elizabeth investigated: most of it was science fiction. If she hadn't known how competitive Cara was, Elizabeth would have worried about her grades. But the grades stayed up. Cara worked more efficiently—her words—so she'd have more time to read.

Saturday morning she saw Cara out the door with a credit card and a headful of admonitions: don't buy anything tight, don't buy anything black, don't buy elbow-length gloves; don't buy lipsticks, you have them; don't leave the mall; stay in a group; meet Dr. Fane exactly at three in the Food Court and don't keep her waiting.

"You forgot to tell me not to talk to strangers," said Cara, grinning.

"I forgot to tell you to have fun," said Elizabeth, kissing her. Cara sprinted to the Fanes' car, all elbows and angles. She looked two inches taller than she had a month ago and leggy as a young colt.

Almost all grown up. It was such a short time from diapers to dances, from dances to graduation. Be lonely here, Elizabeth thought, with Cara gone and away from home for good.

Be nice to be able to share the big house with Steve, to have Cara and Melody whirling in and out as they went through college, to sit around the table with them and listen to them talk about their careers and their husbands and their babies.

They'd be more likely to catapult peas at each other with soup spoons. Elizabeth went to her computer with a heavy heart. She couldn't see that the girls were any less hostile than they'd ever been.

She clicked the mouse to bring up a spreadsheet and concentrated on its symmetric form. Steve and Sammy were coming for lunch, after Steve dropped Melody and her friends off at the mall. If she could forget about everything except Wilson-Markam Industrial Consulting for two and a half hours, she'd have a good start on next week's work.

She was through Wilson-Markam and well into Reddy, Mann and Steegle, Attys. at Law, when she heard Sammy barking outside. She closed the file with satisfaction and bounded down the stairs with Cara's energy.

"Hi," she said, beaming at Steve, but reaching for Sammy, as she opened the door. She put her arms around his fuzzy neck, and he nuzzled at her happily.

"I wish you'd pet me like that," said Steve.

He unleashed Sammy, then opened his arms to Elizabeth.

"I've missed you for the past few days," he said, kissing her.

She circled his waist with her arms. "A telephone conversation simply can't compete with a good, long, wet kiss."

"Certainly can't," he agreed. "Let's do it again."

A second later she said, "What in the world is banging against my shoulder blades?"

Steve withdrew an arm. "This," he said, holding up a bottle of wine.

"Why in the world did you bring that here?" she asked.

"If I'm going to drink that nectar of yours," he said, taking off his coat, "I want to be able to pay proper attention to it. This is commiserating wine."

"What are we commiserating about?"

"Did you know that you said Melody is an awful liar and nobody can trust anything she says?"

"I think," said Elizabeth, considering, "that I may kill Cara."

"There are laws against infanticide."

"I know why they come as babies. Because if you couldn't remember how sweet they were when they were little, you couldn't survive their adolescence."

"The English have the right idea. They ship 'em off to boarding school as soon as they get obnoxious."

"I couldn't send her to boarding school. She'd think I had abandoned her. Besides—" there was the vision of the empty house, with Cara grown and gone "—I'd be lonesome."

That was Steve's greatest fear. He knew she was lonely. And if Cara and Melody didn't somehow make peace, that loneliness would sooner or later drive her right into the arms of another man. Of Joe Salvini, perhaps. Melody, with self-important virtue, had repeated a "conversation" with Cara over lunch: Salvini, said Cara, had been calling Elizabeth, and Elizabeth was really glad to hear from him, and they talked on the phone a long time.

Steve could practically hear Cara's voice ringing in his ears. And while he knew intellectually that there was more—or less—to the phone calls than he understood, emotionally, he wanted to build a moat around Elizabeth's house and fill it with sharks.

He wished he could chalk it up to paranoia.

Unfortunately what he feared was possible. More than possible.

He watched while Elizabeth expertly uncorked the wine. As she stretched for the glasses, her shirt separated from her jeans, and he was filled with a physical passion so great that it made him dizzy.

All he had to bind her with was to create in her a real, sustained and irresistible physical desire so great that she wouldn't want any other man, ever. Beginning now.

Quietly and deliberately, he took her glass from her hand and set it beside his. Then, with her luminous eyes looking deeply into his, he put his hands at her slender waist and pulled her into his arms.

She could feel every inch of his long, hard body, feel her effect on him, feel his quickened heartbeat and uneven breathing as he put his lips to the soft crescent of her ear. The pressure of his palms flirted with her breasts as his hands wandered from her hips to her shoulders, to lift her arms and loop them around his neck.

She clung to him, fighting the urge to arch her burning body into his, and yielded to his searching touch. His lean fingers continued their long, slow progress, trailing up her arms, grazing the sides of her full breasts, dipping into the hollow of her tender throat, brushing the high cheekbones, heating the throbbing pulse at her temples and threading into her hair. His hands tangled roughly in the slick, black silk of it, and he pulled her head back to look into her face.

Her lips, red and wet with wine, parted to meet his. For a short second she gazed into his heavy-lidded eyes, then her thick, black lashes fluttered and dipped in surrender as he covered her mouth with his.

His hungry demanding mouth moved slowly across hers, pulling the sweetness from her, tasting her, knowing her. Ravenous herself, she pressed against him. His hands moved from her hair to her hips, pulling her into his loins, and the adamant, vital, essential maleness of him, uncompromised against her belly, flooded her with passion.

He slipped his hands underneath her flannel shirt, dipped into the waistband of her jeans and rubbed at the dimples on her bottom.

Her thoughts frothed like a storm-whipped sea. Oh, he was splendidly hard against her, and his heart pounded and his hot breath rasped against her ear. And oh, she was covetously, selfishly, voraciously desiring. Her own pounding heart and hungry mouth and clinging form had made that very clear.

She had forgotten. She had forgotten what it was like, the delight of physical passion, the complete immersion of intellect in emotion, the perfect and wonderful triumph of her heart.

Breathless, she pulled her lips from his and buried her face in his shoulder. He relaxed against the door and held her to him gently. She put her arms around his waist and squeezed.

"Meltdown," he said, with a low breathy chuckle.

"Dangerous radiation," said Elizabeth, her voice muffled by his shirt.

What now? asked her intrusive reason. What...now that she admitted her heart's desire. The decision she made would affect the rest of her life and Cara's, too. Would give her either happiness or misery, and God help her, she couldn't possibly say which side happiness lay on. She had always been able to call home for help—but she couldn't ask her mother about this one.

Her mouth was dry, suddenly.

Steve hugged her again, hard, and handed her a glass of wine and held her while she sipped it.

"Aormm," Sammy complained, squirming between them. "Murmphf."

"It upsets him when he's ignored," said Elizabeth, detaching herself from Steve. She badly needed some relief from the intense physical and emotional pressure. "Poor baby."

"I wish you had half as much sympathy for me as you do for him," said Steve. "I'm upset when I'm ignored, but do you drop everything and pet me? No."

"He's a great deal cuter than you are," said Elizabeth heartlessly.

Sammy lifted his nose and followed it unerringly to the kitchen. Steve and Elizabeth followed to find him barking at a pot on the stove.

"Kielbasa and chili," said Elizabeth. "May Sammy have some?"

"He's not supposed to beg," said Steve.

Sammy sat by the stove, grinning and ingratiating.

"I don't think he knows that," Elizabeth said. After she filled her plate and Steve's, she chopped the rest of the hot dog buns with a little chili and some bites of kielbasa.

"We don't want to make him sick," she explained to Steve. To Sammy she said, "There, darling. Eat the good yums-yums all gone."

Which he did, in forty seconds flat. He belched, licked his vast chops and collapsed on the floor under the table.

"Unbelievable," said Steve. He fetched the filled plates off the stove, where they had languished while Elizabeth fed Sammy. "Would you like to come to the table and eat your good yum-yums, too, or do you plan to spend the afternoon fawning over that furry Casanova?"

"Jealous, are we?" asked Elizabeth, her eyes twinkling.

"You're very fickle," said Steve, settling in a chair. Under the table, Sammy snored. Steve nudged at him to make him roll over.

"He's better looking than you are," said Elizabeth. "And easier to get along with and bigger. Why shouldn't I throw you over?"

"You forgot *smarter* and *has bigger teeth*," said Steve, picking up his hot dog. "However, as you have just witnessed, he snores. I don't."

"How do you know you don't?" asked Elizabeth reasonably. "You're always asleep when you do it."

"There's one way we could find out," said Steve. "Want to take a nap?"

Yes, she did. Very much. And there wouldn't be any time to snore, either. But she said, "Sorry. As appealing as you are, no."

"Why not, Elizabeth?"

She gazed across the table at him: handsome, sexy, desirable, almost irresistible Steve. Damn it. She wanted to go to bed with him. And didn't see how she possibly could. At least he deserved to know why.

"Because of the girls. Because if we can't bring them around, then we have no future together. And if we have no future—I can't bear..."

She didn't finish, but Steve could fill in the blanks. And he knew exactly what she meant. It was hard for him at night, to think of her, to open his mouth to phantom kisses, to reach for her with his caressing hand and find only an illusion created by his inflamed desire.

But if he were to take her to his bed, to cover her body with his, to kiss her naked breasts and have her rise to his touch. To feel himself enclosed by her and rock her fiercely under him, to possess his love and complete his heart.

How could he bear to have her taken from him then?

That, surely, would be deepest hell.

Chapter Eight

Giggles foamed like bubbles from Cara's room. Elizabeth could hear the rustle of their petticoats and the soft tap of their slippers as Cara and Sara Fane dressed for the dance.

Cara had bought a silky, deep teal brocade with a full skirt and off-the-shoulder puffed sleeves, which made her look like an eighteenth-century belle.

At last she floated down the wide stairs. She had a thin gold bracelet around each wrist and her great-grandmother's little cameo hanging from a gold chain around her neck. Her black curls cascaded down her back, almost to the wide lace sash around her waist, and satin slippers glimmered on her small feet. Her green eyes glowed, and her eager little face was pink with excitement. Small and graceful, the edges smoothed, the angles softened, she was in every way a herald of the woman she would become.

She was so lovely that Elizabeth, watching her, had to blink to stay the tears.

"It's tea length," said Cara shyly, twirling to show her mother. "Does it look all right?"

Elizabeth surreptitiously wiped her eyes, and she had to clear her throat before she spoke. "You look absolutely beautiful," she said.

"Yeah," said Cara, with a child's ecstatic bounce. "I do, don't I?"

"Wait right there," said Elizabeth, leaving the room. "I want to take your picture." She had wept twice before, looking at her daughter: once with joy and astonished love, the first time she cuddled newborn Cara in her arms, and once with pride and a helpless sense of time passing, the morning Cara started kindergarten. And she felt it all now: the joy, the love, the pride—and the relentless time that was sweeping Cara so inexorably away from her. She wiped her eyes again and fetched the camera.

Three frames later, Sara appeared, in a pink dress the color of peonies. The two girls fluttered together, each with an arm about the other's waist, and quivered like butterflies poised for flight. They belonged in an old-fashioned summer garden, among the roses and the larkspur and the bluebells and the buttercups, and they cast the light of growth and life into the cold November night.

No one would ever believe, looking at them, that there was ever a damp, drizzly November in any soul, thought Elizabeth, as she bundled the girls into their coats and led them to the car. The trouble might reappear tomorrow, but for tonight—even in November—they could have moonlight and roses. Cara would spend a delightful evening with cake and punch and awkward, eager boys, and Elizabeth would spend an even more delightful evening in front of the fire with Steve and a good meal and a good wine and a number of excellent kisses. She didn't even have to go out to retrieve Cara from the Harkness gym: Sara's parents were on pick-up duty. So she dropped Cara and Sara at the gym door with a light heart and the prospect of an entire evening spent in comfort and pleasure.

She had just laid the fire and poked it into life when Steve rang the bell.

His hands were full of bags laden with Chinese food.

"This stuff is leaking on my coat," he said, bending his head to kiss her.

"It's leaking on everything," she told him. She led him into the kitchen and let the bags drip into the sink while she sponged at the front of his trench coat.

"That's not doing much good, Libby," he said.

"Nonsense," she said, scrubbing at the dark stain. "This coat's designed to be impenetrable."

"I can tell you from experience that it's not." He took the coat off and threw it across a chair. "See? My shirt's wet from the rain."

"Oh, look at you," she said. "You're dripping." She threw the sponge into the sink and picked up a cup towel. "Here."

"I don't need that," he said.

"You certainly do," she said.

"Come here," he said. "You must need a closer look." He gathered her to his wet shirt, cup towel and all.

"I can't see it all from here." She put her arms around his waist and smiled up at him.

"You can share the rainwater with me then." He looked into the clear green eyes and saw all his hope and desire there. His hands dipped below her waist and massaged her round bottom through her jeans. "Am I getting your sweater wet?"

"It's untreated wool," she said, seeing the desire in his eyes and feeling the evidence of it against her. "Slaver just rolls right off it." Only she was the one drooling, she thought. She wanted him. Wanted, wanted, wanted him.

"Well, aren't you lucky it's waterproof?" he asked, gliding the tip of his tongue across the separation of her lips.

She took a long, deep breath and opened her mouth to him. Still he wouldn't kiss her, but teased her with his tongue, dipping it just slightly into her mouth, withdrawing when she leaned closer, fanning it gently against the corner of her smile and moving slowly across her bottom lip again. It made her crazy.

She wanted to run her hands down his hard bottom, to press him closer to her, to unfasten his jeans and hers and lie with him, there on the soft new rug.

Why couldn't she have what she wanted? For a short second she was enormously angry at Cara and Melody, then the anger passed. No sighs, no regrets, no recriminations; she needed just the will to keep fighting.

"I need another kiss," he said, nuzzling at her neck. "A real one, this time. Not like the short ration I got at the door."

"Oh, and whose fault is that?" she asked. "It isn't as if I haven't offered." *It isn't,* she said to herself, *as if I haven't begged for that kiss, with my heart and with my body.*

She put her hands behind his neck and pulled his head to hers. And the kiss that followed made them both dizzy.

"The food's getting cold," she murmured after a while. "We ought to eat."

"I'd rather do this." He sat in a kitchen chair and straddled her across his lap. The weight and warmth of her against him made him gasp.

"We can always do it later," she said, but she leaned into his arms and kissed him again before she got up.

She moved across him, of necessity grinding against his belly and down his thighs as she parted the distance between them, and the pressure was nearly more than he could bear.

"Oh, can we?" he said, groaning. *Enough, already.* Reluctantly he took his hands off her and let her go.

"Well, I don't see why not." She was well aware of the effect of her squirming, and delighted by it. "We have hours and hours. We have time for any number of things. Shrimp chow mein and Szechuan chicken and fortune cookies and a bottle of wine and a little discreet hanky-panky in the parlor. I'm sure we can think of a way to amuse ourselves through a long winter evening."

"I hate discreet hanky-panky," he said, moving painfully out of his chair. He got bowls from the cabinet and emptied the cartons.

"Discreet hanky-panky is better than no hanky-panky at all." She rummaged in a drawer for chopsticks and placed them in soldierly rows beside the bowls.

Steve, still in some discomfort, wasn't sure about that. *Discreet hanky-panky,* he thought, *was like having half as much food as you needed to keep from starving, or half as* much air as you needed to breathe. Instead of relief, it just sharpened your torment.

Elizabeth leaned against the cabinet and sniffed at the chow mein. "That smells wonderful."

He picked a shrimp out of the bowl with the chopsticks and carefully conveyed it to her mouth.

"I love shrimp," she said.

"Do you?" He fed her another.

"Yeah. And scallops and oysters."

"I thought it best to stay away from oysters," he said, starting for the table with two plates. "In view of your theoretical aversion to physical involvement."

Her lips tightened slightly. "All I do all day is fight," she said. "I can't stand any more of it." She loaded all the food onto a big tray. "Let's go into the den. The wine's on the coffee table."

The firelight bathed the room in gold. The smug old leather chairs squatted on either side of the hearth like a couple of old men, snoozing in a napping place they'd occupied for nearly eighty years. The couch stretched out comfortably between them, its down cushions plump and inviting. Elizabeth put the tray on the two ancient steamer trunks, which, covered with glass, served as a coffee table, then sat cross-legged in front of the feast and reached for a plate.

Steve read the label on the wine and shook his head. A wonderful Chablis. With Chinese food, out of boxes, drunk by people in jeans instead of tuxedos. He filled his glass and closed his eyes and breathed deeply of summer pastures and sunlit fields and wind and rain and curling vines. He came to himself again when Elizabeth chuckled.

"Are you hypnotized?" she asked.

"Damn near it." He took a sip of the wine: pure Olympian nectar. He closed his eyes and let the bouquet of the wine close around him again.

Elizabeth raked Szechuan chicken and chow mein onto the plates and handed one across the table to Steve.

"You only love me for my wine," she said.

"It's a great attraction, I'll admit," said Steve. "But not the only one."

"I wish I could hypnotize Melody and Cara," said Elizabeth. "You're much easier to please than they are."

"God is easier to please than they are," Steve said. "You know we shouldn't go on hiding from the girls, Libby. They have to get used to us as a couple."

"What makes you think they aren't?" Elizabeth asked. "We're together all the time."

"Cara, for one thing," he said. "She nearly exploded from rage when she saw me kiss you." He fed her another shrimp. "We should be holding hands in public, honey. Kissing each other hello and goodbye in front of them. It won't hurt them to see a little affection between us. Might even help reconcile them to the inevitable."

"Which inevitable?"

"The inevitable in which we get married and produce a bunch of little Johnnys and Sandys and build a loving, happy home."

She thought of the Vorklands and longed for that future Steve envisioned.

"Do you think the girls would get used to it?" she asked wistfully. "The holding hands, I mean. They're so terribly opposed. I can't get through to Cara at all."

"Well, I've made a little progress in understanding," said Steve, between bites of chicken. "I've been talking to Melody. She doesn't mind sharing me with you, but she refuses to share me with Cara."

"That makes sense," said Elizabeth.

"It does not," said Steve irritably. "Why would she think I can't love the two of them at one time?"

"Why did Cain and Abel think it?" said Elizabeth. "Or Jacob and Esau?"

Steve considered that. "I guess it has been around a long time, rivalry like that. The question is, what will we do about it?"

"The world is full of people who have less to wrangle over than Melody and Cara, and still they fight," said Elizabeth gloomily. "It's not you Cara doesn't like. It's Melody."

"Can't say that I blame her."

"How can you say that about your own daughter?" asked Elizabeth.

"How can you say it about yours?" Steve countered.

"Well, in her case, it's true. She's been an absolute beast about this."

"She's nice to me," said Steve. "It's Melody who's awful."

"Melody," said Elizabeth truthfully, "has always been perfectly lovely to me."

Steve tweezed the last shrimp on his plate and put it into Elizabeth's mouth.

"Maybe we could work a trade," he suggested.

For a second Elizabeth the Beleaguered almost considered it.

"No," she said. "Nobody could love Cara in her present state except a mother."

"Or a father," said Steve. "Marry me."

"And live in a war zone?" she asked. "As appealing as you are, I don't think I could handle it." She sipped at her wine. "I believe I'll lock myself in the cellar with a bottle opener and a thousand pounds of Stilton and stay there until that '79 Chambertin matures. Cara ought to have grandchildren by then, assuming she can induce anyone to marry her."

He looked at her troubled face. It was no wonder that she wanted to escape the stress caused by their two obstreperous daughters. It was a natural reaction. He didn't mind if she ran for shelter, as long as he was the shelter she took.

"And apples," said Elizabeth suddenly. "I'll have them roll several bushels of Granny Smith's down the air lock twice a year."

"No crackers for the cheese?" Steve asked.

"Maybe crackers," she said. "And a cat for company."

Steve reached across the coffee table and handed her a fortune cookie. "Maybe this will give you some ideas," he said.

She broke it in half and silently read her fortune. *Confucius say, if a man takes no thought about what is afar, he will find sorrow close at hand.*

"What's it say?"

She handed it over to Steve. "Think ahead, it says. Good advice, I say. Confirms my plans. I'll take two corkscrews in case one of them breaks."

Steve arose to put another log on the fire. "Speaking of thinking ahead, Melody's spending the night with Caroline," he said. "I suppose it's too much to hope that Cara will go home with Sara."

"Entirely too much. They're coming here."

"What bad planning." He poked the fire into life and came to sit down beside her.

Elizabeth grinned. "We have enough time to accomplish quite a bit between now and then. What do you want to do? Reform the Congress? Reduce the deficit? Downsize the military? There are all kinds of problems we could solve."

"Why?" he asked, leaning her across his lap, so that he could look into her eyes. "Who wants to talk?"

He teased at her lips again and she grabbed his sandy hair with both hands and pulled it firmly.

"Did you ever take tennis lessons?" she asked.

"What in the world has that got to do with this?"

She tugged at his hair, and he moved his head until the tip of her nose was firmly against the tip of his.

"Did you?" she growled.

"Yes. You look cross-eyed." He laid his hand flat on her stomach and rubbed gently.

"Don't try to distract me," she said. "Didn't your coach ever tell you about the importance of follow-through?"

She moved her head just slightly; their lips met. And the follow-through, she acknowledged, was spectacular. He kissed her deeply, his tongue probing, exciting, taking her breath. She raised herself to circle his neck with her arms and pulled herself completely to him. He lifted the thick sweater to ease her shirttail out of her jeans, and his long, clever fingers tickled gently at her ribs and back before he unfastened her bra.

"My God, it's hot in here," she gasped.

"That's because you're wearing full-plate armor." He sat her up and put his hands to the hem of the heavy sweater. "Raise your arms."

"I'm not sure this is a good idea," she said. "I don't want
to start something we can't finish."

"We'll finish it," he said. His touch and voice were
tender, but under the tenderness was energy held rigidly in
control. "Hold your arms up, Elizabeth."

She held up her arms.

Steve threw the sweater aside and leaned his back against
one of the sturdy old chairs.

"Come here, baby," he said, shifting her to face him.
"Want to ride astride again? I liked the results the last time
we tried it."

"I rather liked them, myself," she said.

She slung a long leg across him and slid into position. Her
jeans were too tight; she felt tender and swollen. Her breasts
seemed to grow and throb, needing the touch of his hand
and tongue to ease them. The pressure of his body against
hers made her want to grind herself into him to give her release. Every nerve in her body shouted hurry! hurry! and
she fumbled with the buttons on her shirt, trying to unfasten them.

He curved her hands in his and kissed each fist as he
leaned forward so that she could wrap her legs around him.
Then he pressed her palms low on his belly and attended to
her buttons himself. He worked quickly, but each small
button seemed to Elizabeth to take an eternity to escape its
slitter, and she occupied herself while she was waiting by
working at the buckle of his belt.

At last the shirt fell open, and she shrugged it away. Her
bra was a mere wisp of satin and lace, soon discarded. He
reached for her eagerly, but before he could put his hand to
her soft curves, she smiled impishly and said, "Hold up
your arms."

Goodbye to his rugby shirt; goodbye to the T-shirt underneath. She ran the flat of her palms slowly over his chest
and polished gently at his nipples. They sprang immediately erect; he could feel the tight pull of them in his groin.

The fire inside him burned fast and hot; her teasing hands
made it leap completely through him, in his chest, his
throat, his mouth. He massaged her breasts, cupped them

tightly together, kissed them slowly, covering them tho
oughly with his open mouth, teasing at each pink areola.

"Steve!" she said urgently, wanting more.

He ran his tongue down the cleft he had created an
sucked lightly at each nipple.

I'm crazed, Elizabeth thought. She wanted him to touc
every inch of her, wanted to touch him, all over, every
where, wanted his kisses, wanted to be loved by his bod·
and she wanted it all, immediately, impossibly, at one tim·

"Lie down," she said.

"That's supposed to be my line," he said, but he turne
away from the chair and lay back on the floor.

She slid down until she was lying on top of him, and l·
her mouth search his chest. His nipples were as erect as her·
and as she teased them between her lips, she could feel h·
heart thundering under the thick muscle of his chest. H·
rose inside his jeans, splendidly hard and strong, and he p·
his arms around her and rolled her onto her side.

With one hand he held her head, and he kissed her deep·
as his other hand slipped open the buttons on her jeans. H·
teasing fingers smoothed across the lace of her pantie·
traced the pattern of the woven flowers, followed the curv·
of the seams, slipped under the elastic—

And let it pop against her leg and grinned.

She opened her eyes and scowled at him, then grabbed·
fistful of the hair on his chest and pulled sharply.

"Ow!" he said, prying her fingers loose.

"Try that again," she told him, "and you'll be bald as·
baby from the neck down."

"I'll try something else instead," he said. He stood an·
brought her with him. "It's been a long time since I did thi·
but I just remembered we have to take our pants off."

"Oh, yeah," said Elizabeth. "I knew there was som·
thing else." She unfastened his jeans and the snap on h·
shorts and pushed them down.

Then she rubbed her hands around his hard, flat bo·
tom, loving the feel of it, before she moved her touch an·
her attention to the more entertaining anatomy of his front·

Steve kicked his clothes away and knelt in front of her. H·
removed her jeans efficiently. Too efficiently, she though·

disappointed: she liked to be undressed slowly, wanted his hands moving across her so thoroughly that he missed nothing in his exploration of her body.

Then inch by inch, he satisfied that desire. He rubbed his hands over every square millimeter of her silk panties, dipping his fingers under the waistband, under the elastic at her thighs, slowly, slowly drawing a line between her legs. And slowly, slowly, he pulled the whispering silk across her heated skin. His hot mouth followed the unhurried descent of his hands. At last, at long, long last, he pulled her down beside him on the thick carpet in front of the fire.

And turned away from her.

She gasped when his hands left her body. He turned back to her in less than two seconds. He kissed her tenderly, then showed her a condom, which he held lightly between the forefinger and middle finger of his right hand.

"Ah," she said, understanding. "Do you always carry those?"

"Only since the day I met you," said Steve. "I found a good discount, and I've bought a lifetime supply."

He flicked the foil packet lightly across one distended nipple and she shuddered from the lightning flash that went through her.

"A lifetime supply?"

"Yeah. Enough for thirty years, with nine months subtractions here and there for additions to the family." He grinned. "I figure after thirty years, we can resume skin to skin contact for the thirty years after that."

"Sixty years?" Picturing them at ninety, doddering joyfully to bed, hoary-haired and wrinkled.

"Assuming I can bring you to your senses and convince you that marrying me won't cause irreparable emotional damage to those two brats we've spawned."

"Don't you think sixty years is a bit optimistic?" she said. "Not that I'd mind, you understand, but what makes you think you can hold up that long?"

He bent to kiss the breast he'd been teasing.

"My great-grandfather, God bless his soul, fathered a set of twins at the age of ninety-two." He kissed her belly and toyed at her with his tongue.

"Gimme a break." She was so liquid, she thought she'd melt there on the floor and miss the delight that was to come. Hurry, hurry, hurry! she urged him silently.

She tugged at him, and he resisted. Didn't he want to make love? Why didn't he hurry?

He circled her breasts with one lazy finger, spiraling a figure eight around them. "No lie. Both those babies looked just like him."

"Bald?" she said, grabbing at his hand to force him into action. "And no teeth?"

"Right," he said, smiling, and kissing as he smiled. "He had to marry the lady in question and support her for the rest of his life."

"And how long was that?" she asked. "Did it take as long as you're taking?"

The indolent spiral continued, farther and farther up the mound of her breasts, climbing inexorably but too slowly toward her tender nipples. She knew the electric pull that would occur when he touched their pink tips, the intensified desire which would lace through her. Why didn't he hurry?

"My, you're impatient," he said. "Two years. I won't be that long."

"You're sure about that?" she asked. Her heart was in her throat. She couldn't breathe without panting. "Doesn't seem like you're moving very fast to me."

"Not long. I promise." He handed her the packet.

"I take it you want assistance." She felt fumbling and uncoordinated; she didn't see how she could manage it.

"No, I want you to do the whole thing." He stretched out full-length on the carpet, all rampant male, before her. "I find it incredibly sexy."

She knelt beside him. Her hands trembled from the tension of her need, but there was nothing uncertain about her touch. When she was through, he beckoned.

"Come here to me," he said, and opened his arms. His lazy hands covered her again, sweeping, caressing, probing, teasing, before he slipped his fingers between her willing thighs and rubbed gently at the little hooded peak he found so surely. It grew and throbbed and she pushed against his gentle hand, wanting, needing, craving the release which only he could give her.

He gathered her under him. His every move was exquisite. He filled her, swelled inside her, excited every nerve, inside her and out, until the very air around her body crackled like a wildfire.

The phone rang, rang and rang. Elizabeth moved restlessly, disturbed but not distracted. The ringing stopped for a few seconds and then began again.

"Forget that," said Steve, into her ear. "Concentrate on me."

She clung to him beyond speech, except for a gasping "Oh! Oh! Oh! Steve!" She held him fiercely to her, arching to meet him, the miracle inside her rising, rising, rising until it peaked and exploded and rushed beautifully through her belly and buttocks and thighs.

For a few seconds she lay spent and tingling, and then Steve kissed her deeply and moved inside her again.

"My turn now," he said, his voice low and harsh.

He thrust hard and fast, his breath ragged, his heart pounding, until his unabated vigor exploded, and since she was still tender, still sensitive, the fine rushing came over her again.

They lay still for a minute, smiling at each other, their satisfaction complete.

"I don't care what happens," said Elizabeth. "I'm glad we did it."

"I love you, did you know that?"

She linked her hands behind his neck. She was never, she decided, going to let him go.

"Yes," she said. "I love you, too." Her voice faltered. That was indeed a tentative, uncertain declaration. But she was worried about Cara and worried about the future. She cleared her throat and said it again. "I love you, too."

He appeared not to notice how her voice had hesitated.

She reached across him and pulled an afghan off the chair to cover them. "It's cold in here. Snuggle me up."

"How could you be cold, my heart?" he asked. He was still burning up. But he spread the afghan across them and tucked it firmly behind her. "How about a postcoital kiss or two?"

"Or three or four or fifty?" She would never get enough of his fabulous, tantalizing, absolutely stupendous kisses, but she could try. She could try every single day for years and years.

He looked at her lips, warm and red and luscious.

"One," he said, kissing her. "Two. Three. Four."

"Are you going to count them all?"

"Five," he said.

"These," she told him, "are not adequate kisses. Quit counting. I think it distracts you."

"Six," he said. A slow, thorough kiss, sensual and delicious. "Was that adequate?"

"Yes," she said, suddenly hungry again. "I want another one just like it."

She got what she wanted, and then some.

"I hate to sound depraved," she said, gasping a little. "But what's your refraction time?"

"Fifty kisses," he told her, running a hard hand from her hip to her breast. "We'd better keep working on it."

He took her soft breast in his hand and began to massage it. He'd be ready for her, long before fifty kisses had passed. And he'd be sure that she was ready, too. Years of this, he thought, and a surge of joy made his heart dance.

"So far," Elizabeth murmured, "you're only up to twelve. I want another kiss." Her hands behind his neck pulled his head to hers again. The kisses, she decided, got better as they went.

"Only one?"

"More than one."

"How many more?"

"Fifty."

He was well into the next one when his cellular phone blatted.

He raised his head and looked annoyed.

"Melody's the only one who knows that number," he said. "I can't imagine why she's using it. I told her I was going to be here, and she knows your telephone number."

"Maybe she was on the other end of the ringing phone," said Elizabeth. "Something must be really wrong. You'd better check."

"I guess so—she ought to be in seventh heaven. Geordie met her at the door." He got to his feet and grappled for the small phone in his jeans pocket. He frowned at the number displayed on its pager function; it wasn't one he recognized.

Elizabeth's phone rang again before he could dial, and he answered. "It's Cara," he said. "She's upset."

Elizabeth rose and wrapped the afghan around her.

"Cara?" she said, into the receiver.

Sobbing and incoherent, hysterical babbling coursed into her ear.

"Cara!" she said again, alarmed. "What's wrong?"

More sobbing. After a minute's coaxing, Cara produced a few words of somewhat lucid speech.

"Come get me," Cara gulped. "Right now!"

"But, darling, why?" Elizabeth asked. "What's wrong?"

"I can't tell you over the phone!" Cara wailed. "Just come get me right now!" And she hung up.

"What's going on?" asked Steve.

"I don't have any idea," said Elizabeth, rushing to dress. "But I have to go after Cara this minute."

The phone rang again. Elizabeth was certain it was Cara with some kind of explanation, but before she could get to the phone, Steve said, "Melody, does this have anything to do with Cara?" A pause. "All right, honey, all right. Calm down. I'll be right there." He turned and Elizabeth tossed his clothes to him.

"Shall we go in one car?" he asked, jamming one leg after the other into his jeans.

Elizabeth stopped buttoning her shirt long enough to gape at him. "You must be crazy. Of course not."

"Just a thought," he said.

"Oh, do try to be sensible!" she said as a parting shot. She grabbed her keys and purse and bolted out of the house.

Steve locked the door after her.

"Tempest in a teapot," he thought irritably.

* * *

Elizabeth drove too fast, ran yellow lights and slid around stop signs without coming to a halt. She couldn't imagine what Cara and Melody had done. Terrible scenarios coursed through her mind; mutual verbal assault? Slapping? Down and dirty wrestling? A melee involving all the company of the dance? Nothing she could imagine was believable, but Cara and Melody had produced the unbelievable for several months now. She should be prepared for the worst.

She pulled up to the Harkness gym in record time. Outside the door were two knots of students, each harboring, presumably, either Cara or Melody. Elizabeth couldn't see either girl, but Miss Westcott was in plain view, looking nettled.

Steve drove up behind her and parked. Miss Westcott pulled a whistle out of her dress pocket and blew into it with all the vigor of a semester's frustration behind her breath. It was deafening. The children whirled, alarmed.

"Your parents are here," she said.

The crowds parted. Melody and Cara appeared simultaneously, shot a hostile look at each other and burst into tears.

They were dressed exactly the same.

Their identical dresses shimmered as they rushed from the porch. Their identical slippers flashed as they ran, and the identical bows in their hair and the identical tears on their faces reflected the school security lights as they fled.

They both were wild with rage and humiliation.

"This is the wrong time to laugh," said Elizabeth, chuckling in spite of herself. She could see Steve in the side mirror, trying to keep a sober face, as she leaned across the seat and opened the door. Cara spilled inside and tried to conceal herself from the gathered crowd.

"I hate Melody Riker!" she sobbed, as they drove away. "I really, really hate her."

Definitely the wrong time to laugh.

Cara shed the dress before she was out of the foyer, cast it to the floor and flew up the stairs in her underwear, weeping. Elizabeth hung the dress from the knob atop the newel post and followed.

Cara lay across the bed, crying into her pillow. Elizabeth was quite at a loss for words. She couldn't think of one thing to say that wouldn't increase the flow of gallons per minute all the way to the U.S.-Hydrologic-Survey-estimated flood level. So she sat on the bed and rubbed Cara's back.

Finally Cara said, in a voice full of fury, "Melody did this on purpose to make me look stupid."

"Come now, Cara," said Elizabeth. "She is just as upset as you are. It's just bad luck that you both bought the same dress."

"It was not," said Cara.

"Of course it was," soothed Elizabeth. "It's a very pretty dress, darling. Anybody who saw it would want to wear it."

"I never want to see that dress again!" stormed Cara. "I want you to cut it up into bits and throw it in the garbage before I come downstairs."

"Now, really, Cara."

"I do!" she shrilled. "And I don't ever want to see Melody again, either. I won't see Melody again! You can drag me with you everywhere you go, and I'll just squeeze my eyes shut and I won't open them and you can't make me!"

Great God in heaven, thought Elizabeth. They are surely going to drive me mad. She gave Cara a last pat on the bottom. "Come downstairs, darling. I'll make us some popcorn."

"I'm never coming downstairs," said Cara. The hysteria was fading; she sounded sulky. "I'm never going to school again. I'll just have to change schools."

"You'll feel differently about it once you sleep on it."

Hysteria again. "I will not! And I'll just go live with Daddy, if you won't let me change schools, because I never want to see anybody from Harkness again as long as I live!"

Oh, God. Things just seemed to get worse and worse. To have this disaster after the idyllic evening she had spent with Steve was overwhelming. Now she knew she loved him, deeply and dearly, and perhaps for the rest of a lonely, heartbreaking life. Cara and Melody grew more hostile toward each other with every day which passed.

Kalik. Kalik the Destroyer was at work in their lives; every breath they took was a fight against him. How much longer could they last? Before, when she and Steve had talked about it, showing the girls their affection and love for each other seemed sensible and appealing. Now?

She was frightened, she knew, that Cara and Melody would guarantee her a bleak future bereft of the man she loved.

"We'll talk about it later," said Elizabeth. The bed squeaked as she rose; the door creaked as she pulled it closed behind her. Have to oil this, she thought, seized by mind-saving irrelevance. Oil all the doors in the house.

Her head ached. Every squeak stabbed at her temples.

She got the afghan off the floor and collapsed on the couch. The room smelled of woodsmoke and the very slight but lingering perfume of sex. She rolled to her side and cuddled one of the couch pillows to her stomach. She did love Steve. She knew it, had known it for some time. She'd been afraid to admit that love, afraid of the malevolent spirits whose joy it is to confound human happiness. Afraid Cara and Melody would drive them irrevocably apart, and she'd spend the rest of her life in helpless longing.

But now she knew that even if the worst came to pass, if for some reason she couldn't have him, even if they never made love again—she knew that this short, wonderful time spent in his arms had been worth all the pain it was likely to cause.

Chapter Nine

Elizabeth was depressed, and the depression was exhausting. It was just eight-thirty, and she was ready to go to bed. Only the knowledge that she'd have to trudge up the stairs kept her on the couch.

The phone rang six or seven times, quit for a few seconds and started again. She lay on her back with her eyes closed, considering whether she wanted to go to the trouble to answer it. She didn't want to talk to anyone. Especially not to Steve.

She wanted him to come over, to take her in his arms and comfort her. And he couldn't. He had huge responsibilities of his own, responsibilities just like hers. Responsibilities that—if either of them had any sense—would keep her out of his arms forever.

She was afraid if she heard his voice she'd cry.

She glared at the phone on the small table at the end of the couch.

"Shut up, damn you," she said, nudging it with a toe.

It wouldn't.

Finally she sat up and grabbed the thing. She lay down again with it on her stomach and listened to it ring twice more before she answered.

"Elizabeth?" said Joe, from the other end of the line. "Is Cara all right?"

Damn it. She didn't want to hear from Joe.

"Of course," she said, and she barely kept from snapping. "Two girls wearing the same dress is hardly a disaster."

"It is, if you're thirteen," Joe reminded her.

"I am tired of thirteen," said Elizabeth.

"You'll survive it," he told her. "It's just a phase."

Elizabeth thought of Cara at the age of one, flushing a tennis ball down the upstairs toilet. At two, bringing a hose inside to water the houseplants. At three, painting the cut crystal bathroom faucets with red fingernail polish. At six, when she stored eggs, milk and bologna in her toy refrigerator until the smell of them became so horrible that Elizabeth thought a sewer line was broken and called a plumber.

"I'm an expert survivor," said Elizabeth. "However, what Steve's sister says about phases is that this, too, will pass, and something worse will come to take its place. So far, all my experience makes me think she's right."

"This, too, will pass, and something *better* will come to take its place," said Joe kindly. Cara and Mel can't keep this up forever.

He sounded so—untroubled, Elizabeth thought. So confident. Like a man with no wildlife experience, who thought tigers were cute and would be fun to have as pets. "Don't underestimate them," she said grimly. "They'll eat you alive."

"Goodnight, Elizabeth," he said, with gentle sympathy. "Things will look better in the morning."

Everybody always said that, thought Elizabeth irritably. As if they were offering some sort of guarantee.

She stared at the ceiling. Falling in love was such a simple process. It happened without effort and with no warning. And forever after, you couldn't just consider yourself and your love. Other people important to you bombarded you with their own needs and expectations. They had to be handled skillfully, so they wouldn't be hurt. You spent a lifetime picking your way through an emotional mine field, never knowing what was going to cause an explosion.

A gloomy picture. Ishmael's November was skulking in her soul. She needed Christmas, with carols and bells and excitement and joy and hope, and it wasn't even Thanksgiving yet.

The phone still squatted on her stomach, and its bell vibrated through her ribs as it rang again. This time it was Robert, who wanted to know if Cara had gotten her birthday package. Elizabeth definitely didn't want to talk to Robert, that frequent and careless layer of mines.

After she called Cara to the phone, she ran a tub of hot water and immersed herself to her chin.

Kalik the Destroyer was impossibly paralleling her life, and it was horrible. Jord Varic felt exactly as she felt: hopeless, helpless and filled with the fear that she had little chance of success.

She rubbed at her shoulders and told herself the heat would soothe her tight muscles.

Instead, the tension maliciously compressed itself and moved to a particularly vulnerable spot just behind her ears. The heat went wherever heat goes and took its small comfort with it. When the water became uncomfortably tepid, Elizabeth put on her footie jammies, swallowed three aspirin and climbed into bed.

Into the big, cold bed. She could hear Steve saying it, his voice as cold as the icy, white virginal sheets. Sleeping all by herself in the big, cold bed.

She hated it.

Steve looked in on Melody twice. She had the quilt pulled over her head.

Both times she heard him open the door, and both times she said, "Go away! I want to be alone!" It was an order no less forceful for being muffled by her bedclothes.

He looked at her dress, which was in a heap in the corner, and went downstairs to call Elizabeth, shaking his head all the way.

If two boys, he grumbled to himself, happened to wear the same suit to a dance, they wouldn't start World War III over it. They probably wouldn't even notice. When boys showed up identically dressed, they were pleased; it meant they could know they were dressed properly, and it made them feel secure. Girls really were inexplicable. Why would they care who wore what, anyway, as long as both of them looked nice in the damn dress?

The Fairchild phone was busy. He snarled at it impatiently. It had been busy for an hour and a half. Whom would Elizabeth be talking to at this hour? She wouldn't have called her mother; it was four in the morning in Paris.

She didn't necessarily have to be talking to Salvini, he told himself—though he knew if he'd been Joe Salvini, he'd have called her. Elizabeth had lived in Philadelphia all her life. She knew dozens of people.

Some of those dozens, including Salvini, were men. And not one of those dozens, including Salvini, was in a war zone. Steve had brooded on the phrase since he'd heard it pass Elizabeth's lips.

But he and Elizabeth were living in a war zone, and no mistake—unwilling noncombatants enduring life under two generals who never called a cease-fire. He would never give up the hope that Melody and Cara would come to terms. But how long would Elizabeth tolerate battle conditions, when she could end the war by surrendering to Cara's demands?

Elizabeth was distressed now beyond all measure. He wanted badly to go to her and comfort her. To take her in his arms and kiss her and brush the hair away from her face and hold her quietly while she relaxed into slumber. To cuddle her close and provide her with serene, restful, untroubled sleep.

But she was out of reach.

Her phone line was still busy at eleven, at midnight, at one o'clock. Steve had an enraging vision of Salvini, giving Elizabeth the comfort he wanted to give her himself.

At last he went to bed. There was no serene, restful, untroubled sleep for him. He tossed under the covers and listened to a heavy rain rattle against the roof of the house.

Unpleasant images chased through his half-sleep and transformed into nightmares whenever he dozed.

The next morning he forced Melody into dress clothes and drove them both to church. She didn't want to go.

"Everybody will laugh at me," she sobbed, before she would get out of the car.

"I keep telling you that nobody would have noticed, if you and Cara hadn't made such a scene," he said calmly, when what he wanted to do was shout at her. "And nobody cares now. It's a new day. They have other things to think about."

"No, they don't have other things!" she said. "Everybody noticed. And they'll all laugh at me! I'm not going!"

"Damn it," Steve muttered. Then, holding out what he thought was bait, he said to Melody, "Here comes Geordie."

"Oh, no!" she shrieked, and ducked under the dash. "Don't let him see me!"

Steve felt like gibbering. In the past few months, Melody had become a wild-eyed cross between Greta Garbo and the Red Queen. How long would it go on? He dreadfully missed the nice, funny little girl she'd always been, with her cheerful face and her sunny sense of humor. What if little Miss Hyde had moved in to stay?

So he wanted to marry Elizabeth and have two Hydes in the same house? What a horrible prospect. He could picture them, snarling around corners, stamping up the staircase, slamming doors and hurling insults, which were, as Miss Westcott had said, too various to relate. With that incentive before him, he could stop writing science fiction and start turning out horror stories. There would certainly be plenty of ideas to draw from.

He supposed the years from twelve to eighteen were nature's way of making sure everybody was glad when the kids left home for college. But was every child consumed by adolescence to such a degree that it depressed paternal immune systems and made their fathers' hair thin on top? Or was it just Melody? What an awful hypocrite he was, telling Elizabeth how to handle Cara, when he couldn't do a thing with Melody. He wasn't ever going to offer any more advice. He wasn't qualified.

Elizabeth passed in front of his car, huddled with Cara under a huge black umbrella. He tapped on the horn, and she turned and stopped and waited for him. Cara and Melody shot apart like negative particles, unable to bear such close vicinity. Steve and Elizabeth watched them run in different directions through the driving rain to separate church doors.

He turned the umbrella slightly sideways, to shield them from onlookers and kissed her good morning. She held her face up willingly, not disturbed in the slightest by their public environment.

"I'm practicing what you preach," she said, smiling, when he raised his eyebrows at her. "Public affection."

"And I was just beginning to despair," he said, his tension dissolving under her touch. "I didn't get a lot of sleep last night."

She smoothed her gloved hand across his cheek and left it there while he kissed her again. Then, arm in arm, they went inside to listen to the priest, a learned historian, lecture on the roots of enmity between Araby and Israel.

"Sort of speaks to our situation," said Steve, over the post-service coffee. "Not quite as bad, though."

"What happened to they'll-come-around-I'll-see-to-it?" asked Elizabeth, who hadn't had much sleep herself. "I may not be actively despairing right now, but I sure considered it all of last night."

"That's not despair," said Steve. He looked for Cara and Melody, who sulked in separate corners of the room. Geordie, obviously acting on a man's instinct for danger, was nowhere in sight. "It's battle fatigue. You need some R and R."

"Had some yesterday, thanks," she said. "Can't see that it dissolved the tribal friction. But—" with a thoroughly delighted grin "—it certainly dissolved a different problem."

"Friction does have its uses," he said solemnly. "We'll have to try it again."

He ached for her, all the time, in every way—with his body, with his mind, with his heart. He caught a glimpse of Cara passing in front of Melody, her head down, her shoulders stiff, and of Melody, her lips tight and thin and white.

He had learned to love Elizabeth, and it had been an easy lesson. All his happiness was bound up into the future together—and now Kalik the Destroyer had appeared in his life again, with its gnashing teeth and devouring jaws, to tear and swallow the hope of his soul.

Anger and fear pulsed through him. He sublimated them into strengthened resolve. He would wrestle and kill Kalik, kill that monster which hated love and destroyed it; he would vanquish Kalik with perseverance and strategic planning. He could do it. He would do it. The Kalik of his past had been beyond his control—Melody and Cara weren't.

"It's not just the sex," she said. "It's the love."

"You need more of both," he said gently.

"No doubt about that." Her hand trembled. Coffee dripped onto her beige kid gloves.

"I'd have discussed it with you last night," said Steve, unable to stop the words from coming from his mouth. "But your phone was busy."

So he had tried to call. She immediately felt better.

"Joe called, to see if the girls were all right."

"He didn't call me," growled Steve. He took the coffee from her hand and blotted at her glove with a napkin.

"And Robert called, to see if Cara got the package," she continued. "I could almost see his tan from here."

He wanted to ask, which one did you talk to for three hours? But he wasn't quite that crazed by jealousy yet. He looked at Elizabeth, slender and beautiful in an English tweed suit, and wondered how long it would take him to get to that humiliating point.

He was a patient man. He knew that. Patience was made up of self-control and steely determination. Controlled anger. Controlled fear. Controlled movement, thought and action. He'd learned that as a schoolboy playing football and refined it in the Navy, as a Seabee, doing things so dangerous that impatience could send you to an early grave.

He could be patient with Melody's hysteria, with Cara's hostility and with Elizabeth's anxiety.

He could be patient. And, he thought, glancing at the old cherrywood altar framed by the open sanctuary doors, he could ask for help.

"Want to spend Thanksgiving with Melody and me?" he asked, considering how to calm the hurricane by Thursday.

Elizabeth looked at him with longing in her eyes. "I'd adore to. And Lin has already asked."

"I thought just the four of us."

Elizabeth actually laughed out loud. "You, me, Melody, Cara, Kalik and poor Sammy cowering in his chair with his paws over his eyes."

So she'd been thinking along the same lines.

"Kalik," he said, with a good deal more certainty than he felt, "can be vanquished."

"Maybe," she said doubtfully. "I hope so. I told Lin not to buy a big turkey, though. The girls will spoil my appetite."

"That's good. The girls will be too busy glaring at each other to eat at all," he said. "And I'm really not that crazy about turkey."

They laughed, but it wasn't really funny.

Elizabeth said, "As much as I hate to leave, I have to go home. I'm helping a client set up a new accounting system tomorrow, and I'm going to have to work for the rest of the day and most of the night to customize the software."

"Sounds imposing," said Steve, who customized his own software by calling a technician.

"Is imposing," she said. "Also fun."

"Better you than me," said Steve, smiling at her.

"Well, I'd hate to have to write a book," she said. "Even an ABC book. I don't see how you do it."

"You know, you're the first person who's ever said that to me," he told her. "Usually they inform me that they could write something much more profound than mere science fiction, if they just had the time."

She tilted her head bewitchingly. "Oh, come on. Is that really true?"

"Yeah, and then they tell me that since they don't have time, they'll just give me their idea and I can write it and they'll let me have half the profit."

"What do you say?" asked Elizabeth, much amused.

"I tell 'em my mind's not sufficiently developed to be able to handle such complicated material," he said. "Then I trot right off to the nearest bar, buy a stiff drink and admire their guts."

"I've read through *The Lion's Whelp*," she told him. "It's very thought provoking."

"I was so unsure of myself as a parent when I wrote that," Steve said. "Used to be, I thought I knew everything, and now I find that I don't know anything at all."

"I'd laugh at that, if it weren't so true." She glanced around her. All quiet. "I read *Kalik the Destroyer* a few days ago. It was hard to finish. It's frightening."

"I wrote that as my marriage was breaking up. My entire world was breaking up with it. Sure a change from jaunty Jord in the first book. He knew everything. I've often envied him."

"Are all your books autobiographical?"

"Well," said Steve, shaking his head doubtfully. "I don't intend for them to be, but a lot of the time, it works out that way. Jord seems to be, more than most."

From across the room, where the kids were congregated, came a burst of laughter. Cara, who was standing to the side, fled through the vestry and into the churchyard. Melody came to her father with her face flaming.

"I want to go," she said. "Right now."

Steve handed her the car keys. She left without another word.

"I guess that means we're going home," he said regretfully. "I guess it also means old Dad tossed a ball that missed the basket."

"What basket?" said Elizabeth, putting on her trench coat.

"I told her today was a new day, and nobody cared what she wore last night, they all had better things to worry about."

"Why in the world would you tell her that?" demanded Elizabeth. "Surely you knew better."

"It sounded good at the time," he said.

"You need a keeper." *Men,* she thought, and not for the first time, *have no sense.*

"Want to volunteer for the job?"

"Then I'd need a keeper."

"I'll volunteer for that job."

"I know you would. We'll think about it." She retrieved her umbrella from its repose in the foyer. "You want me to walk you to your car?"

"Supposed to be the other way around, isn't it?"

"You can only be the walker if you have a bumbershoot," she said. She stepped outside with the umbrella and pushed the magic open-it-up Mary Poppins button. "Otherwise you have to be the walkee."

"Oh," he said. He took the umbrella from her hand and put his free arm around her waist. "I didn't understand the protocol.

Through the foggy drizzle that remained of the storm, they could see their cars. Neither girl was visible.

"Where could they be?" Elizabeth asked, worried, as they walked toward Steve's car.

"If the theory of precedence has any value," said Steve, "Melody is under the dashboard."

"Of course. Stupid question," said Elizabeth. "Cara never wants to see anybody from Harkness again as long as she lives. She wants to change schools and says if I won't let her, she'll go live with Robert."

"She knows how much you love her," he said. "You going to let her blackmail you like that?"

"That's not blackmail, it's an attempt to escape her embarrassment," said Elizabeth, dismissing the thought. "She couldn't go, anyway. Robert doesn't want her. Responsibility makes him break out in hives."

Now that they were next to his car, Steve could see Melody hunkered down in the back seat. Lucky Mel. Both her parents loved her, wanted her and needed her. He had custody only because he worked at home and was more accessible to his daughter. Marian had always tried hard to act in

Melody's best interest, even when Marian herself was hurt by it.

Feisty, rebellious, hot-headed Cara needed a father as well as a mother, Steve knew, to guard her and guide her and help her grow up. Steve wanted to take Cara into his own heart and let her dig a little safe place there and know without question that she had a father who would love her and help her until he died.

Robert was going to break Cara's heart, and Steve didn't see how to prevent it. It enraged him.

He handed Elizabeth the umbrella, and breaking his vow not to give her advice, asked, "Have you told her that?"

"Of course not, Steve," Elizabeth said. "Why hurt her feelings for no reason? I just tell her I won't allow her to go, and that's that."

"She's sure to find out what he's like sometime," said Steve.

"Not from me, she won't," Elizabeth said decisively. "Besides, he does love her, in his fashion."

"Listen to me, Libby. If you don't tell her about Robert, it's going to cause a significant disaster some day," Steve said. "Please think about it." He curved his hand around her soft cheek and found it chilled. "Kiss me quick, darling, and get in your car. You're cold, and you're getting soaked."

"I hate quick kisses," Elizabeth complained, turning her face up to his.

"Better than no kisses at all," he said.

"I hate a Pollyanna," she said, half meaning it.

"Shut up," he murmured against her lips. "You're wasting time."

She certainly didn't want to waste time. Who knew how much time she'd have with him? As soon as he'd kissed her, he left, and with a sigh as mournful as the November wind, she watched him drive away.

When she reached her car, Cara was lying on her back on the front seat, with her coat wrapped around her head and her feet pressed against the cold window of Elizabeth's door. She swiveled to a sitting position as her mother opened the door, but the coat remained in place.

"You're going to smother," said Elizabeth.

"Good!" said Cara, folding her arms across her chest.

"Fasten your seat belt," Elizabeth said, starting the car. "Cara, what happened to make you leave?"

Cara ripped the coat off her head. Her hair frizzed electrically around her face and her green eyes glittered. With rage, Elizabeth was happy to see, and not with tears.

"They called Melody and I the Bobbsey Twins!"

For once, Elizabeth was too dispirited to correct her grammar.

"That wasn't very nice," she said.

"They said she was Flossie and I was Freddie, and they're going to call us that all the time." She slid as far down in the seat as her seat belt would let her. "I hate Melody. This is all her fault."

Elizabeth declined to say that it would all blow over. She wasn't sure she believed it herself. Children were quite capable of fastening on such an incident and carrying its effects well into adulthood. She could imagine Cara and Melody, attending the fiftieth reunion of their Harkness class and being greeted by old friends. "Hey, look, girls! It's Flossie and Freddie!"

God preserve us all from that, she thought. Being a teenager was hard enough without being deliberately humiliated on a daily basis.

"If anybody calls you Freddie," she said. "Just refuse to answer. They'll quit."

"No, they won't," said Cara. "I want to change schools." She scowled. "It fits Melody, though. Flossie the Cow."

Elizabeth wanted to slap her.

"If I ever hear those words out of your mouth, or hear that you have said them to anyone," she told Cara angrily. "I will personally remove from your life the telephone and the television for the next entire year."

Cara looked at her, her eyes as shuttered as a steel safe door.

"I mean it," said Elizabeth, more calmly. "It would be wrong and malicious. I don't care how much you dislike Melody, I will not have you being deliberately slanderous. Do you understand me?"

Cara nodded sullenly.

Elizabeth hoped that guaranteed compliance.

Cara locked herself in her room as soon as they got home. Elizabeth, on her way to her office, tapped on the door. Cara needed something to do besides ponder her trouble.

No answer, but she hadn't expected any.

"Would you go downstairs and put a frozen pizza in the oven, please?" she asked. "I don't have time to fix lunch. And would you bring me a cup of tea and some pizza when it's ready?"

Cara would, she knew, delay until just before Elizabeth became annoyed enough to take action. How the child could gauge her mother's state of mind so exactly was a mystery, but she had a genius for it.

Elizabeth went into her office and switched on her computer. The McNulty Paper Box Company, had moved up in the world and, in keeping with its new dignity and increased importance, had become McNulty Paper Container Manufacturing Corporation. They still made boxes, but now they made more sizes, and they had new customers, and they had for the first time issued stock. Elizabeth stuck a disk in her floppy drive, opened their books and began to work.

At a quarter till three, her stomach began to complain of neglect.

Fifteen seconds, she said to herself, and I am going to be really cross with that girl.

And as if by magic, Cara's door opened and Elizabeth could hear her thumping down the stairs to the kitchen. After considerable noisy activity, she appeared with the pizza and an entire pot of tea, two cups and two plates, and set them carefully on Elizabeth's desk. She had folded the napkins in the shape of campaign hats, put pizza on the good china and arranged the entire assembly atop a lace doily on a black lacquered tray.

Elizabeth thought the gesture was a tacit apology.

"Thank you, darling," she said. "That looks wonderful."

Cara munched on the pizza and considered her mother speculatively.

Uh-oh, Elizabeth thought, and her suspicion was soon confirmed.

"That was Sara Fane on the phone," said Cara.

"Yeah?" said Elizabeth warily.

"Yeah," Cara told her. "She said Dr. Fane said I ought to go to a public school next year. Because of Melody. She knows. She's a doctor."

"Oh, is that right?" asked Elizabeth. "Well, she's a very good orthopedic surgeon. I'd trust what she told me. Did she say if you stayed at Harkness that it might cause hip dysplasia, scoliosis or rotator cuff injury?"

"Probably something like that," said Cara, encouraged.

The elegant tray was no apology. It was a bribe, softening her up for the touch.

"I guess we'll have to take the chance," said Elizabeth. "It would be awful if any of those things happened, but one must sacrifice for a good education."

She grinned as Cara stomped out of the room.

At seven o'clock, she instructed Cara in the womanly art of tuna-noodle casserole, asked for a small glass of wine and considered calling Steve.

Later, she thought, her head still filled with McNulty and his boxes. *Soon as I finish this.* If she once heard his voice, she'd stay on the phone for an hour, and she didn't have an hour to spare. Besides, a good talk with him would be her reward for finishing up with McNulty.

Cara brought the casserole and the wine. Elizabeth ate with one hand and entered data with the other. After a while, her back started to hurt. Got to get one of those ergonomic chairs, she told herself, and glanced at her watch: eleven forty-three.

"Good grief," she said. It was much too late to call Steve. Considerate of him, she thought, to leave her alone so she could work. But still, she wouldn't have minded a call just to let her know he was thinking about her.

The television nattered downstairs. Cara was still awake. And tomorrow was a school day. She made Cara go to bed, then worked for two more hours before she finished and could get some sleep herself.

She arose stiffly the next morning at six, dropped Cara at school and carried to Mr. McNulty and his boxes their new accounting software. That evening she staggered home exhausted, laden with carryout tacos from Pancho's Mexican Villa.

"I'm going to take a short nap," she said to Cara. "Save me a taco and wake me up if Mr. Riker calls." She lay on the couch where she'd be sure to hear the phone and woke up, cold, at half past three. Cara had long since gone to bed.

She hadn't heard from Steve in two days. There was a limit to consideration. At six, when she got Cara up, she intended to call him and demand an explanation.

But Cara came into Elizabeth's bedroom just before the alarm went off.

Elizabeth sat up in bed. She was so groggy that she couldn't focus her eyes. "What do you want for breakfast?" she asked, squinting at Cara.

"I can cook my own oatmeal," said Cara. "So you don't have to get up. I want to do everything for myself this morning."

"I'm certainly happy to comply with that," said Elizabeth. So I'll just call Steve, right now, she thought. Then her heavy eyes slammed shut and she fell unconscious onto her pillows until after ten o'clock.

"Oh, God. McNulty!" she said, as she leapt out of bed.

The floor was icy. The furnace was off. She leapt into bed again.

Steve.

To hell with McNulty. If he had a problem, he'd call. She'd never had a shy client yet. She'd call Steve this minute. She didn't care if he was in the middle of saving an alternate universe. She didn't even care if he were in the middle of saving *this* universe. She didn't give a damn if her untimely interruption delayed the publication of his new book by three years. If he was in some arcane writer's trance, and she was the hateful Person from Porlock who made him mess up the best work he'd ever done, then too damn bad. She was going to force him to surface and demand some attention.

She had to go downstairs to turn on the furnace, but that could wait. Who needed it? She put wool socks on over her pajamas, stuck her feet into her snow boots and bypassed her bathrobe in favor of a full-length down coat with a drawstring hood. It was as ugly as a city dump and so poofy that it would have made Olive Oyl look fat, but it was really, really warm.

Then she sat cross-legged on the bed, picked up the receiver and discovered that the line was dead.

"Rats," she said to the universe she presumed Steve was now saving and went to search out the cause. The last place she looked was Cara's room. The bed was neatly made and the phone lay on the coverlet, disconnected.

There was the problem. She set the phone on Cara's bedside table, stretched out on the bed and called Steve.

"This is the Person from Porlock," she said.

"I was about to resort to carrier pigeon," he told her. "Your phone's been busy since Sunday."

"Since Sunday?" Elizabeth said, puzzled. "I don't know why you couldn't get through on Sunday, but Cara was on it half of Monday night. And I was certainly here last night, all night long. Maybe there's something wrong with the line."

"Maybe," said Steve. "You ought to get it checked."

"I will, if it happens again. I wondered why you hadn't called. I was beginning to get my feelings hurt."

"And vice-versa," said Steve. "I've missed you."

"I've missed you, too," she said. "When I wasn't too tired to feel anything at all."

"Get the program finished?"

"Yep. It's up and running. It only needs watching for glitches for a couple of days. McNulty, *et al*, are very pleased." She yawned hugely. "Actually, all the work has been therapeutic. It's kept me out of touch with developments."

"Such as?"

"Well, I understand from Cara that Sara Fane's mother says Cara will have orthopedic problems ranging from tennis elbow to housemaid's knee if she doesn't go to a public school next year."

Steve chuckled.

"All right for you to laugh," said Elizabeth. "Melody isn't bugging you for a transfer."

"No," said Steve. "She wants to skip a grade. She's smarter than Cara, you understand, and much more suited to the rigors of advanced scholastic work and the more sophisticated social milieu of the Third Form."

"I see," said Elizabeth, perversely happy to realize that he had kindred problems.

"She did mention that Geordie ought to skip a grade, too," said Steve. "I believe she plans to talk to him about it."

"God help us," she said.

"He will," said Steve confidently. "Want to have breakfast with me?"

"Can't," she said. "I'm trouble shooting at Mr. McNulty's fancy new container corporation, and I am at this moment one and a half hours late. Soon to be two."

"Thought the program was up and running," said Steve, very disappointed. "I also thought we'd have breakfast at home. Do you realize I haven't had a kiss in almost forty-eight hours?"

"Better than you do, I expect," Elizabeth told him. "Why don't you and Melody come have supper tonight? I'll fix some spaghetti or something."

"No opportunity for kisses there," said Steve.

"We can play footsie under the table," she promised. "Best I can do, I swear. I'm going to be at McNulty's until at least five."

"I think my hero is going to be in a violent battle today," said Steve. "He's going to let an entire universe be wantonly destroyed because he hates all the life forms in it."

"Sublimating a bit, are we?"

"Don't you read Freud? War is a substitute for sex."

"We have to talk about that," said Elizabeth.

"Freud and his theories?" asked Steve. "Or sex?"

"Sex."

"Sex is not a conversation topic. It's an action sport. I'll show you next time I have a chance."

"Yeah, well, the next time we have a chance is what I want to talk about."

"What's the matter? Postcoital remorse?"

"Don't be stupid. I never felt less remorseful about anything. I just know where it's leading, that's all."

"God, I hope so. You're incredibly dense if you don't."

"I'm concerned about setting a good example for the girls. I've been telling Cara since she was ten that premarital sex is not a good idea."

"Marry me now, then," said Steve. "Solves the problem neatly."

"Do not bug me about this. I have enough trouble."

"Look, Libby," said Steve reasonably. "You and I both know that what's appropriate for children and what's appropriate for adults is different. I agree that we shouldn't carry on a physical affair in front of them, even after we're married. But with sufficient discretion, we can have what we want and need. All parents, married and unmarried, walk that line. We can do it, too."

"I agree with that," said Elizabeth. "But I think I ought to practice what I preach, and so I feel a little hypocritical. I've always been honest with Cara."

Steve was silent for a long minute. Finally he said, "Have you, now? What about the way you've deliberately misrepresented Robert?"

There was an immediate explosion, born of guilt and uncertainty.

"How dare you?" Elizabeth asked. Her rage made her voice shake. "I've done what's best for her. I've protected her all her life. And I'm going to keep doing it, despite your misguided advice to the opposite."

"You think that's good for her?"

"Of course it's good for her!" Elizabeth said furiously. "Do you think a child ought to know its father is a congenital liar and incapable of fidelity? Let her love him as long as she can. She'll find out soon enough. And I hope she'll be forgiving enough to love him regardless of his faults, when she does."

"What about you, Elizabeth?" said Steve, asking outright about his greatest fear. She had said she loved him—

and he had noticed the uncertainty in her voice when she spoke. "Do you love him, regardless of his faults?"

"I despise him, as you well know," she said. "I'm not going to fight with you over the phone."

"Fine," said Steve.

The soft click of a disconnect sounded in her ear.

She looked at the phone incredulously and shook the receiver.

"Damn it to hell!" she said, aware that she shouted, and slammed the receiver onto its hook.

Chapter Ten

Five minutes later Steve was at the door. His eyes glittered like hoarfrost.

"Damned if I'll spend the day stewing about Robert," he said.

"I refuse to argue about it here in front of all the neighbors."

"Scared?" he challenged.

"Of you?" she said, sneering.

"That they might report to Cara," he said. "I know you're not scared of me."

"Go home."

"I won't," he said. He pushed inside the door and nudged it closed. "What are you got up as?" he asked, looking her over.

The fat, down coat flapped open to show her thick pajamas.

"My furnace is off. Where's your coat?" demanded Elizabeth, speaking much as she would have to Cara.

"I was in a hurry." He kicked out of his shoes. They were wet, and his socks were wet.

"You'll freeze, you idiot," said Elizabeth crossly, seeing the socks. "Give me those." She pointed.

He handed her the socks and expected her to hang them on the fireplace screen, behind which last night's coals still drowsed. But she took the socks and his shoes and put them in the microwave oven.

"You'll melt them," he said, alarmed. They were his boat shoes, old and comfortable and treasured.

"I will not," she countered. "I've done this a thousand times. How'd you get this wet? It isn't even raining. Don't you have any sense at all?"

"Not where you're concerned," he said. He still looked annoyed, but as he opened his arms to her, his eyes softened. "Kiss me. I'm cold."

She went willingly into his embrace. "Only if you promise to stay off the subject of Robert. It maked me mad to hink about him."

Steve's face and hands and lips were cold, his hair was cold under her hands. He wrapped himself around her and hugged her hard.

"Two or three more kisses ought to take care of the chill," said Steve, helping himself to another one.

"It's certainly taken care of my chill," said Elizabeth. How good it felt to be in his arms, to have her cheek against his chest, to hear the slow strong beat of his heart in her ear as he kissed her hair. "Are you going to stay long? Because if you are, I want to get the fighting over with all at once."

"I don't want to fight, Libby," he said. He linked his hands loosely around her back and let her lean against them. "I'm over here because I can't work if I'm mad." He kissed her again. "Can you?"

"I'm not mad," she said. "At least, not now." She snuggled up a little closer.

"Also," he began, and she drew away warily.

"Also, what?" she asked. "Caveats on the kisses? Another we-have-to-take-control lecture?"

"Well, we do."

"I knew it," she said. She broke away from him and leaned against the cabinet. "All I get is trouble. The fur-

nace. Robert. Cara. Miss Westcott." And most heartrend-
ingly, she accused, "You."

He held up his hands, placating. "I just want you to do
one thing."

"Like what?" she said.

He'd heard that tone in Melody's voice lately. He was
smart enough not to let it make him smile.

"I want you to promise me that you'll let Cara find out
what Robert is really like."

"Give me a break, Steve. What am I supposed to do?
Catalog his faults? She can't even understand half of them,"
Elizabeth said belligerently. "You want me to get her out of
bed tomorrow and while she's brushing her teeth, tell her
that Robert's an uncaring, unfeeling jerk?"

"You won't have to tell her anything, sweetheart," he
said. "Just quit making excuses for him. Let her draw her
own conclusions—I guarantee they'll be the right ones.
Cara's a very bright kid. All those late birthday and Christmas presents and all the payoff money because he doesn't
want her around—she'll get the idea."

"I don't know why you think she needs to find out now,"
said Elizabeth, still fighting to protect Cara's innocence. "It
can't hurt for her to wait until she's older."

"It does hurt her. It hurts her, because she's believing in
a fantasy. It hurts all of us."

"Oh, Steve, really," she said. "She never sees him. You're
overstating the problem."

"Am I?" he asked. "I don't think so. Tell me this, Elizabeth, how is Cara going to learn to love and trust me if she
has this fantasy father in her head? And he is a fantasy. You
invented him for her."

There was a new, uncomfortable thought, and it made
sense. Of course Cara would never let herself love Steve, as
long as she believed that Robert wanted to be completely
involved in her life. He was definitely a fantasy father, and
he was no substitute for the real thing.

Steve was the real thing.

"Spaghetti tomorrow," she said. She moved back into the
circle of his embrace. "Don't forget."

He kissed her again, gently. "I hope this means you agree with me."

"I'm not sure I agree completely, but I will quit making excuses for Robert. I suppose that's sensible."

"All right," he said, satisfied with this small advance. "Kiss me again, and I'll fix your furnace."

"I can fix it," she said, turning her face up to his.

"In that half-acre coat? You'd set your sleeve on fire." He brushed her lips with his.

"That wasn't a kiss," she complained. "You couldn't even light an idea with that, let alone a furnace."

"It lit an idea for me," he said. "First, I'll start a fire and get the furnace going. Then after a while, we'll have coffee in front of the fire and enjoy the comforting sound of a furnace that's doing its job."

"Then what?" she asked, clumping after him in her snow boots. She caught a glimpse of herself in the mirror over the piano. Quite a sight, she thought, grinning at her reflection: her face barely showed above the upturned collar of her coat, and her hair frizzled wildly around her head.

"Then I'll fix the kiss." He stacked logs on the grate and applied a match to the kindling.

She started toward the stairs to her room, and Steve reached out a hand to stop her.

"Where're you going?"

"To dress. I have to go to work."

She said this regretfully. The fire had blazed and caught and spread its lovely warmth into the room.

"Wait" he insisted. "I might need some help downstairs."

Thus enjoined, she followed him into the basement and watched as he dealt efficiently with the furnace.

"You don't need me," she said, turning to go.

He grabbed the hem of her coat. "Yes, I do. And you need me."

"I do? What for?"

A glimmer of a smile from Steve.

"To help you take your boots off," he said.

She pretended to ponder. "I suppose that could be a help."

"Also to help you unbutton that coat." He tugged at it, and like Gibraltar, it proved immovable.

She nodded solemnly. "That might be a help."

"And the pajamas." He reached under the coat and fingered the fabric covering the inside of her thigh. He tugged at that, too, and it didn't go anywhere, either. A great challenge.

"Mighty thick and heavy, those pajamas." He wrapped his big warm hand high around her thigh and rubbed gently between her legs. "Wouldn't want to exhaust yourself struggling to get out of those pajamas."

The furnace roared to life, and Steve peered at its innards for a minute to make sure it wasn't faking. When he was satisfied, he patted the ridiculous coat somewhere in the region of Elizabeth's fanny and urged her up the stairs to the kitchen.

"What now?" she asked, though she had a pretty good idea.

"That depends entirely on how good your furnace is, how warm your bed is and how hot the water in the bathtub is," he said. "I might need a little help, myself."

"You think so?"

"I'm almost sure of it," he said. "You'd better give old McNulty a call and tell him the handyman won't be through fixing things at your house until noon."

He handed her the phone and listened as she talked. There were definitely rewards for being self-employed that more than compensated for the security of a salaried position.

Beneath them, the furnace hissed. The fire crackled in the warm living room. Steve tangled his hands in her luxuriant hair and pulled her head back.

"That's a dangerous smile," she said.

"I'm in a dangerous mood," he told her. "It needs taking care of." He swept his hands down the length of the coat to her hips, which he could barely identify through the layers of feathers. "This is an atrocious garment. What possessed you to buy it?"

"Protection from the cold. It was useful in its day."

"Its day is past." He picked her up, like a bride about to be carried across a threshold, and started up the stairs.

"You're the one who's going to wear yourself out," she warned. "And you don't even have pajamas."

"Honey," he said, with absolute conviction. "I don't think I have to worry about either pajamas or energy."

And indeed, when they reached the high, old bed, only Elizabeth was out of breath.

He helped her out of her boots, laughed at the socks and pulled them off her feet. Her blue-footed pajamas made him laugh again.

"What, another layer?" he said. "What's under this?"

"Another layer," she said. "Like an onion."

"Okay. So I'll peel you." He busied himself with the coat. "Should I peel you?"

"Why not?"

"Well, for one thing, it's freezing in here."

"Believe me, my pet. I am in no condition to notice." He cast aside the coat. The pajamas were like a baby's sleeper: a long zipper started at the neck. He shook his head, chuckling. "I can't believe you wear this."

"Just wait," she said, unbuttoning his shirt and unfastening his jeans. "You will soon not just understand but crave these pajamas."

"I crave what's in the pajamas." He tossed his shirt away and stepped out of his pants.

Elizabeth touched him covetously. "Sex two times in one week. I can't believe it," she said.

He pulled the zipper all the way down and let the blue pajamas fall to the floor. She shivered.

"Get in bed, quick," he told her. "I'm freezing. And *I* can't believe it, either. It's almost too good to be true."

He pulled the down comforter up to their chins and snuggled her into his arms.

"No Kalik here," she murmured, kissing him.

"He hates love," said Steve. "He won't come around."

"Your feet are solid blocks of ice," she said.

"The rest of me isn't."

"I can tell." She put her hand behind his hip and put a little forward pressure on it. "Come here," she said. "Right now."

He did. Their combined heat was more than adequate, the reward left them awash in delight, and afterward, neither of them gave a thought to McNulty or Jord Varic or Cara or Melody or anything but each other. They slept.

Steve woke, drowsily content. Elizabeth stirred beside him and realized that the fifty kisses, while desirable, weren't really necessary.

"What time is it?" she asked.

He looked across her at the clock. "Eleven-thirty. Want fifty kisses?"

She trailed a teasing finger across the joining of his thighs. "I doubt seriously that I'll ever get fifty kisses all at one time," she told him.

"You could, if I do it really fast. Like this." He ducked his head under the covers and demonstrated on her ribs.

She squealed and giggled and grabbed his hair. "Stop that!" She tried to turn over, to get away from him, but he wouldn't allow it.

"Want me to find something else to do?" His voice was muffled, but she could tell he was laughing.

"Anything else."

He did.

After a minute, she said, "Don't stop that."

He didn't.

Steve lay back, breathing hard. "Want to try another fifty kisses?" His eyes wouldn't open; none of his muscles wanted to work.

"I'm too tired." Elizabeth draped herself across him and rested her head on his chest. "Besides, I'm beginning to feel depraved."

"As long as you're not feeling deprived." He felt bone heavy, and for once, completely sated.

The bed moved as she sat up. It was actually warm in the room. He wasn't sure how much of it was due to the furnace and how much due to the considerable heat he and Elizabeth had generated. Which explained his lassitude. All that tempestuous energy had been transformed into heat, and everybody knew that heat was exhausting. He needed time to recover. Fifty kisses? He didn't know if he could even deliver one of good quality.

He didn't even open his eyes when she got up, but he did hear water running into the bathtub. It splashed as she stepped into it. He willed himself out of bed. There were some opportunities, he knew, that a man should never pass up.

The old-fashioned bathroom was as cloudy as a castle in the air, and mist wreathed and curled around him as he came through the door. Pink light from the two small lamps on her dressing table danced from the moving water and twinkled from the mirror and the gilded claws of the old, footed tub. The rising air was lilac scented from her soap— pure essence of Elizabeth, and he shut the door behind him with magic in his heart.

Elizabeth looked up, smiling, and moved forward in the tub. He slid in behind her, around her, and pulled her back against his chest.

A fountain of curls tumbled out of the wide pink ribbon which bound her hair on top of her head, and the ribbon was tied with a big, untidy bow that trailed its ends above her right ear.

She relaxed against him. Her curly hair was irresistible. He hid his face in it for a minute and wrapped his arms around her, under her breasts.

He held her firmly. She needed to exert no energy to keep from slipping deeper into the soothing water. She put her arms over his and closed her eyes and let her languid body float. She felt without weight, without care, with no past to lament, no future to fear, enchanted in a glorious here and now of savor and delight. His mouth grazed across her neck and ear, tugging at the ribbon, teasing at her skin, murmuring love words and sprinkling kisses. She turned her head, seeking for him, and his hands covered her breasts as his mouth found her lips. She half turned toward him and he cradled her with one arm as with the other he dipped a soft cloth into the water and wiped it gently across her face.

"Funny way for an idyll to start," she said dreamily. "With a fight about Robert."

"You can summon an idyll from the most unlikely inspiration," said Steve, patting at her cheeks with the warm cloth. He turned her to faee him and picked up the soap. The water lapped at the dark tips of her breasts. He dipped his head and tasted the sprinkled drops which frosted them.

Then he lathered the soap in his wet hands and smoothed its creamy sweet-smelling froth across her breasts and shoulders. She let her head fall back, arching her throat. He kneaded gently at her neck with his fingers and rubbed under her chin with his thumbs.

"You look like a cat," he told her. "The very expensive kind, with the huge eyes and long thin necks."

She slanted a green glance at him and picked up the soap herself.

"You look like a bulldog, the kind with a thick neck and bristly jowls." She didn't lather her hands; she scrubbed at his chest with the soap, using it like sandpaper. He snatched at it. A slippery tug-of-war ensued. When it was over, they were both covered with soap and breathless with laughter.

"Well, I'm clean," said Elizabeth, rinsing herself vigorously. "And that ringing in my ears is sure to be McNulty and his boxes. I really have to get out of this water."

Steve lounged at the end of the tub, still covered with bubbles. She splashed water at him.

"Don't you have a book to write, you lazy thing?"

"I'm working on ideas right now," he said.

"The last idea you came up with had nothing to do with a book."

"A man can have more than one idea," said Steve, thinking of his vision and greatly desiring to have it fulfilled. He remembered with exquisite clarity how in his mind she had risen, an enticing Venus ascending from her magic bath. The water streamed from her like liquid silver, and her skin glowed pink, and her languid emerald eyes drowsed between lush black lashes, which the mist had tipped with dew.

The water did indeed stream from her like liquid silver, now, as she stood. But the emerald eyes were laughing, not drowsing, and she stepped out of the tub before he could move.

"Come on out of there!" she commanded, shaking a towel at him.

He lay back, smiling. She looked more like a vigorous young Amazon than a pliant, malleable Venus. The Venus certainly was a sweet vision, but all things considered, the Amazon was a great deal more fun.

She swung the towel around her head like a lasso, pretended to rope him, and tugged. "Don't make me come in after you," she growled.

"Don't shoot," he said. "I'll come quietly." He heaved his bulk from the water and a cascade fell onto the floor. He looked at his feet. "We've made an awful mess in here."

"Yes, but wasn't it fun?" She threw the towel over his head and yanked. "Come here."

He came. "Just what I wanted," he said.

"No ideas," she warned, fending him off with a quick hand. "One fast kiss, a loaf of bread and McNulty." She leaned forward from her waist and let him peck her on the lips.

"Hardly worth the effort," he said.

"Don't complain." She flicked him with the towel.

"You know," he said, drying himself. "I have a lot of money. Maybe I'll buy McNulty and his damn boxes. We can have all our conferences in that bed."

She considered. "Good idea. I'll ask him if he'll sell. What shall I say if he wants a partner?"

"Don't be lewd, madam," he said. He held up a pair of red bikini panties he'd spotted on the dressing table. "Yours, perhaps?"

She grabbed for them and he held them out of her reach.

"Awful small," he observed, holding the scanty silk aloft between his thumb and finger. "Is this it? Where's the rest of them?"

"Gimme," she said. "You bully."

"Scandalous," he told her. "Might as well not wear anything, as these."

"You wish," said Elizabeth.

He grinned. "I do, indeed." He spread the panties in two hands and squatted, holding them for her. "Here. Step in."

She put one hand on his shoulder and balanced first on one foot, then the other. He pulled the red gossamer into place and kissed her, just below her navel.

"There," he said. "All fixed, to my intense regret. What next?"

She reached in a drawer behind her and fished up a bra. He put out his hand and she gave it to him.

He looked at it with pure masculine satisfaction. It was red, and it matched the panties. He held it by the straps, so she could put it on.

"You do know, of course, that I'd rather be taking this off you?" he said from behind her as he fastened the catch.

She spun away from him, into the bedroom. He followed and put on his clothes as he watched her dress.

"How would you like to live in Hawaii?" he asked. Elizabeth clad only in a small red bikini every single day was an enchanting idea.

She grinned over her shoulder, having divined his meaning. "Don't be lewd," she said.

It was full dark by five o'clock. Elizabeth built a fire against the chill and started the spaghetti sauce. Cara came downstairs, and Elizabeth pressed her into service as a salad maker. The doorbell chimed just as Cara had finished, and she ran to answer it.

Elizabeth could hear her delighted welcome.

Joe Salvini. Damn. He had come to examine her Civil War memorabilia, of course. She had forgotten all about him.

Cara led him into the kitchen, chattering. "You're why Mom made me make so much salad," she said.

"Am I invited to dinner?" he asked, when he saw Elizabeth.

She welcomed him cordially. Maybe this was just the break she needed—Cara and Melody, with Joe to think about, would be too busy to fight with each other.

"I hope you like spaghetti," she said.

"You ask an Italian that?" he said, grinning. He was dressed in a really wonderful suit. His shirt was starched, still fresh and gleaming white, and his cuff links were small, discreet and obviously real gold.

Come to think of it, he'd been dressed just as expensively on Parents' Night. Elizabeth had just been too agitated to notice. Must be some restaurant his parents own, she thought.

Curiously she asked, "What's the name of your restaurant?"

"Con Amore," he said.

Con Amore. Of course. It wasn't just a restaurant. It was *the* restaurant, and as she recalled, his family owned at least five different places that were famous. World famous, actually. She had read about them in Fortune Magazine, once, in her dentist's office.

"We're taking a class of kids to cook in *Con Amore?*" she asked.

"Why not?" asked Joe. "I learned to cook there." He took off his coat and rolled up his sleeves. "May I help with dinner?"

"Help?" said Elizabeth. She handed him a spoon. "I'm not about to give you bottled spaghetti sauce. You'll have to cook it yourself."

"Now, now," he said. "Don't be a food snob. We can do very well with this and a few extra ingredients."

"I'll bet your mother never used a bottled spaghetti sauce," said Elizabeth, watching as he opened the cans.

"If she did, she never let me know about it," he admitted. "But I'm not the purist she is."

He poured the sauce into a saucepan and asked for a big skillet, which Elizabeth produced.

"Now what?" she asked.

He dripped a little of the sauce on his finger and tasted it. "Not too bad," he announced. "You and Cara can dice onions and garlic."

Before Elizabeth could move, Cara got a knife and chopping block and put them down on the cabinet beside the stove.

"Here, Mom," she said. "I'll get the onions." She raced for the onions like a manic squirrel, deposited them and when the doorbell rang, ran to answer it with the hasty admonition "You stay there and chop, Mom. I can do everything else."

Elizabeth, considerably aggravated, watched her go.

"Determined little thing," said Joe, amused but sympathetic.

"Disastrously," muttered Elizabeth.

"In a few years she'll have her own life to worry about," said Joe. "Then she'll ignore yours."

She could hear Lin saying, "This too, will pass, and something worse will come to take its place."

"I don't know whether that's comfort," Elizabeth said. She lifted her head and listened. "That ought to be Steve and Melody at the door." She handed the chopping knife to Joe. "I'll go see what's holding them up. It's too cold to stand outside."

As she passed through the corridor into the den, she heard Cara's clear, cold, arrogant dismissal.

"You'll have to come back some other time," she said. "My mother has company, and she doesn't want to be disturbed."

"Cara!" Elizabeth said. Even for Cara, that was tremendously rude. She looked at Cara's hostile face and told Steve and Melody to go into the kitchen and help Joe chop vegetables. Then, furious and embarrassed and feeling helpless, she grabbed Cara by the upper arm and dragged the dreadful child to her room.

She removed the telephone and said, as calmly as she could manage, "I will give you ten minutes to pull yourself together, then I will expect you downstairs with two apologies, one for Mr. Riker and one for Melody. You are confined to the house for two weeks, no telephone and no television. For every extra minute you delay, I will add an extra week. I will not tolerate these bad manners, and you'd better make up your mind to change your behavior, right now."

Cara had that hard, shuttered, wooden look. For a second Elizabeth was almost frightened, both of her own rage and of Cara's relentless intransigence. The rage would pass without incident. Elizabeth was a grown woman. She had long ago learned to control herself.

But Cara—that was another matter. She had always been willful and stubborn, but she was mathematically analytical. She could generally be reasoned with. But if she believed herself to be in the right, she fought without quarter, and didn't know when to quit. Elizabeth harbored the hope that as Cara matured, reason would conquer. She wondered, as she shut Cara's door and went downstairs, if she'd been too optimistic.

Steve had set the table. If anything could have amused Elizabeth at that moment, it would have been the sight of the two big men on domestic KP with kitchen towels around their waists, stirring sauce and making salad and laying out utensils while the lone female in the area sulked at the table, as sullen as a storm cloud.

"Ready to resume chopping?" asked Joe, holding up the knife.

"Naw, I'll chop," said Steve, taking over her station beside Joe. "You go pour us all a big glass of wine, Libby. Some of that '66 claret from the basement." He patted her on the fanny of her tight jeans and directed her toward the basement door.

Elizabeth looked over her shoulder, to see Joe and Steve grin at each other.

"Making a statement?" asked Joe.

"Yep." Satisfaction.

"Well, you don't need to," said Joe equably. "I've figured it out already."

"Good," Steve said. He juggled three of the onions briefly. "Tell me how you want these chopped."

"Chunks the size of your thumb." He looked across the room at Melody. "You've certainly set yourself a problem, haven't you?"

Elizabeth didn't want to hear any more about problems. She shut her ears against their speech and went after the wine. Once she was in the basement, she didn't want to come up again. She considered using the phone to send out for apples and cheese and hibernating there, in the eerie half-light, until reason prevailed in the upper world.

It would be a long, long stay. With a knot in her stomach, she climbed to the surface to find Cara lurking outside the basement door, at the bottom of the back stairs.

Elizabeth, looking at her big forlorn eyes and hunted face, almost felt sorry for her. She had been crying. Elizabeth hoped that indicated repentance rather than defeat.

"You want to walk in with me?" she asked.

Cara nodded.

"You understand you're to stay?" said Elizabeth. "After all, we do have guests."

Cara nodded again. She wiped her sleeve across her nose and stood.

Her back was straight and her head was high. No penitent, she. She was one hundred percent righteous dissenter, made to do a repugnant deed by forces beyond her control.

"May I presume you've made up your mind to be polite?" Elizabeth persisted, seeing danger in Cara's stance. The potential for subversive action was still alive and well, even if the requisite apology was imminent.

Cara stared at her, balefully. Then she swiveled her head forward and marched into the kitchen.

Oh, well . . . half a loaf. Elizabeth followed her daughter through the door.

Cara stood like Nathan Hale before the British hangman, with her feet apart and her hands behind her back and her chin elevated and made her declaration in a voice that was strong, if expressionless.

"Thank you, Cara," said Steve gravely.

He turned his gaze on Melody and waited.

Melody looked at the table and mumbled. "Thank you, Cara," she said.

Cara sat as far away as she could get from the Rikers, folded her arms and stared at the wall. Over by the stove, Joe shook his head.

"I think the thing to do," he said to Steve and Elizabeth, "is to pretend they're not here. They'll either loosen up and join the conversation or sit here and stew all night. It's up to them." And suiting action to words, he handed Steve a bowl of garlic cloves. "You want to mince these for me?"

"All of them?" Steve asked. It wasn't a large bowl, but it was half-full.

Joe grinned. "What, you think I'm trying to throw a monkey wrench into the romance?"

"Why would you need to?" said Steve. "We've monkeys enough already."

Cara and Melody had created their own little corner of gloom behind the table. Steve gave them a long, considering look.

"Actually," he said, more to himself than Joe. "The real problem is that we seem to have forgotten who the parents are here."

Melody and Cara snapped their heads around and glared at him.

"I want the two of you to go watch TV. We'll call you when dinner's ready. Now," he turned to Joe. "How small on this garlic, and how do I peel the damned things?"

Both girls scraped their chairs across the floor in an individual mutiny and let them thud against the wall.

Steve was acting like a father—to both girls, and both had responded immediately to the confidence in his voice. Elizabeth, remembering who was Mommy, said, "Please put those chairs back under the table and straighten the rug."

Impassive compliance. They then left the room. Cara slapped the swinging door with the flat of her hand and disappeared. Melody let the door swing shut then opened it with the tip on one finger, as if it were something slimy, avoiding the area Cara had touched.

Elizabeth sagged against the wall. "God, they're horrible," she said. It was the first time she had admitted it to anyone but Steve.

"They certainly are," said Joe quietly. "I had no idea."

"Maybe we shouldn't eat this garlic," said Steve. "Maybe we should tie it around our necks, instead."

"I wish I thought that were funny," said Elizabeth dismally. She uncorked the wine and filled the glasses Steve handed her.

Joe took the bottle from her and let it glub-glub into the sauce. Then he grated Parmesan onto a small plate and poured olive oil over it.

"Here," he said, setting that and a loaf of Italian bread on the table. "You'll feel better if you eat something." He dipped a piece of the bread into the oil and cheese and went back to the stove, munching thoughtfully.

Elizabeth sat in the chair Cara had left. She felt absolutely exhausted. Apples in the cellar were looking better all the time. Steve took the chair beside her, broke off a piece of the bread and fed it to her.

Joe brought the spaghetti and sauce to the table and filled three plates.

"I have to call the girls," said Elizabeth wearily.

"I wouldn't," said Joe. "They'll give you dyspepsia. My mother always made anyone who was being obnoxious eat after everyone else did. Why should their temper ruin our dinner?"

"I should talk to your mother," said Elizabeth.

"You should," said Joe. "Having eight kids has given her some extraordinary insight into the art of raising children." He waited for Elizabeth to pick up her fork, then he twirled the spaghetti expertly and put a bite in his mouth. In a few minutes he said, "Not to change the subject, but do you still feel like showing me the Civil War stuff?"

"You don't think our own civil war is violent enough?" asked Elizabeth. "Do you want to know about somebody else's, too?" She pushed her plate away from her.

She hasn't eaten a thing, Steve thought. He squeezed her hand and patted it. She turned her palm into his and clung to him. "What Civil War stuff?"

"Things passed down in my family—sword, letters, et cetera. Want to see them?"

"Of course," said Steve, who was avid about history in any form. Unpublished letters were grist for his mill.

On her way to fetch the box, she looked over the stair rail at Melody and Cara. They sat with their arms folded, watching a situation comedy. Neither of them smiled.

Awful little creatures, she thought. And then, unexpectedly, she was filled with compassion for the two children. She went into the den and bent over the back of the couch.

"Don't you want some spaghetti?" she asked softly, laying a hand on each rigid back. "You can eat it in here. I'll even bring it to you."

A sniff from Cara and another from Melody. Tears welled up in their eyes and their chins quivered. Elizabeth put an arm around each skinny set of shoulders. "And then, as soon as you eat," she said, "we'll look at those old pictures. You can show Mr. Salvini the one of the baby, Cara." She got the spaghetti and put it in front of them.

"When you finish, Melody, you bring the plates into the kitchen, okay?"

Melody squeaked out a yes.

"Cara, after you're through, go get the box of pictures and letters. I want to show them to Mr. Salvini."

Cara sniffed again.

"Should I get the sword, too?" she asked, her voice quavering.

"And the sword," said Elizabeth. She gave each back an encouraging pat and returned to the kitchen. Well. That certainly hadn't been as hard as she'd thought. Cara and Melody seemed almost tractable for once. Maybe Steve had been right. Maybe all that was needed was for her and Steve to take firm control. It certainly seemed to have been effective so far.

Fifteen minutes later, Melody brought in the plates, and they could hear Cara going up the front stairs. She returned with the box of letters and the sword, and a faded Union jacket slung casually across her arm.

"I got this out of the cedar chest," she said to Elizabeth, indicating the uniform. She put the box and the sword on the table and held the coat up by its shoulders. "Is it okay?"

Joe and Steve were both on their feet, laying out the contents of the box and examining each piece eagerly.

"This stuff ought to be in a museum," said the historian, picking up a little envelope of pressed flowers and examining them with exquisite care.

"Have you ever thought about publishing these letters?" asked the writer, reading avidly. "What a gold mine of information on day-to-day living. Especially the letters from the wife. Amazing. No doctors, no medicine, the war raging practically outside her bedroom window, and if that weren't horror enough, having to go every day and read the casualty lists.''

"Why weren't there doctors?" asked Melody.

"All gone to war," said her father. "Not that they could do much good, for those old diseases. A cut could kill you then." He shook his head, imagining himself far away from Elizabeth and the children, worrying about their survival and not being able to help them if they needed it. He put his arm around Elizabeth's waist and pulled her close.

"But what did people do?" Melody persisted. "What if they needed help, like for the baby? And what's a casualty list?"

"The newspapers printed the names of men who had been killed or wounded.''

"That would be awful," said Melody. "To look in a paper and see your husband's name."

Unfortunately, Elizabeth could imagine that all too clearly. She could see that other Elizabeth standing in the street with her back to the cold December wind, clutching the baby and scanning frantically through the casualty lists. Could hear the wails and sobs around her as other women discovered, in that public place, that the men they loved were dead. Could see her giving the paper to someone else and walking her cold way home, still worried because she knew the battle count was not complete.

Elizabeth shuddered. What an incomprehensible horror.

Cara laid a picture on the table. "Here's the baby," she said. "It's a picture he asked her to send."

Melody examined the baby's face. "But he's got on a dress," she said.

"Boy babies wore dresses then," said Elizabeth. "Don't you think he looks sweet?"

Melody nodded. She looked up at Elizabeth. "Did his father get home?"

Steve had already scanned all the letters and was replacing them carefully. Melody removed them from the box as fast as he put them in and was busy arranging them in chronological order.

"The letters stop in January of 1865," she said. She looked up at her father with troubled eyes. "Nothing says what happened to him."

"I wish I knew," said Cara wistfully. "The baby's so sweet. And see? Here's a picture of his mother."

The young woman in the picture looked so much like his own love that the sight of her put a lump in Steve's throat. He leaned his head against Elizabeth's.

"War's such a tragedy," he said. "I wonder what did happen to all of them."

"Why don't you find out, Cara?" asked Joe. "That can be the surprise ending to your report. Did you know that the Department of Defense will have his records?"

"Really?" said Cara. "I can find out what happened to him?"

"Really," said Joe. He twinkled at her. "It's worth some extra credit."

Cara grinned. She'd forgotten her feud and her embarrassment for the moment, Elizabeth noted gratefully.

"I suppose I need it," Cara said.

"I suppose you do," said Joe. He picked up his suit jacket off the back of the chair where he'd left it. "Well, folks, it's been real, but tomorrow's a working day."

The yellow foyer light made Elizabeth look pale, and slight dark shadows gathered under her eyes. Steve leaned against the door and opened his arms to Elizabeth. She looked toward the kitchen with a shrug and a smile and put her head on his shoulder.

"What a night," she said.

"Pretty stressful," he agreed, stroking her hair as she rested against him. "You're tired, honey."

"Battle fatigue," she told him. "Like you said. I'm sorry Cara was so rude."

A little amused sound, almost a laugh, clucked in the back of his throat. "I don't know what you said to her, but it seems to have had some effect."

"I demanded good manners," she said, yawning. "In Miss Westcott's voice."

He did laugh, then. "God knows that would scare anyone into obedience."

"I know it can't possibly work all the time as well as it did tonight," she said. "She's just too adolescent. But," she looked up at him, with her first easy smile in some time, "I think I can see the light at the end of the tunnel, and I no longer feel as if I'm going to be run over by the train."

"You don't know how glad I am to hear you say that," he told her. "I've been worried about you. You've been feeling awfully hopeless lately."

She laid her hand on his thick blond hair and kissed him.

"You've been awfully patient lately," she said. "I appreciate that."

"Let's have another kiss," he said, wrapping her in his arms. "A really good one, sufficient to last me through the night. I'll call you soon as I get home, just to say goodnight, and then I want you to snuggle under the covers and get a good night's sleep."

"You know," she said, with wonderment, "I just might be able to manage that, for a change."

She gave him the kiss he wanted.

"I love you, Elizabeth," he said quietly.

"I love you, too," she said, and felt, deep in her peaceful heart, how wonderful that was and how rare.

He kissed her again and she clung to him happily, feeling more hopeful than she had since October. Steve loved her and was willing to face down even their bumptious offspring for her. Cara was showing a little manageability, and the girls hadn't exchanged a cross word all evening. And look how instantly, if not cheerfully, they had obeyed when Steve had told them to leave the room—that was certainly progress. And they'd eaten their dinner, and Melody had brought in the plates, and Cara had quietly fetched the pictures and the letters and had participated in an actual discussion, with Steve and Melody at the table.

A miracle, nothing less.

Then she turned around. Both girls stood woodenly, with their hands at their sides and their faces set.

Chapter Eleven

Steve hadn't called. Elizabeth, waiting, took a bath and curled up in bed with Steve's fifth *Fireman* book, *Fields of Gomorrah*. It began:

> A hot red dawn broke across a new world. Jord Varic fell to his back on the warm earth, exhausted. The children curled asleep beside him, safe for the moment from pursuit.

Jord Varic, relaxed and able to sleep? Elizabeth looked at the back cover: Steve's face, so haunted and worn in the *Kalik* picture, was still grim, but determined and alert.

Varic and the children were still in trouble, but the outlook was less threatening. Kalik's forces had been misled, and Jord had a little time to plan. There was none of the horrible, hopeless discomfort of the previous book.

Elizabeth read, but couldn't concentrate. Why hadn't Steve called? Had something happened to them on the way home? Worried, she picked up the phone to call him. There was no dial tone. She clicked the disconnect button several times.

Nothing. She looked at her watch. Only nine-thirty.

Frowning, she got out of bed to check the other phones in the house. She didn't see how any of them could be out of order—Cara's had been removed from her room, and all the other phones had worked fine when she'd gone upstairs. She knew, because she'd had to call the Time and Temperature number to set her alarm clock.

Must be a neighborhood outage, though she couldn't imagine why. The weather wasn't too awful, just cold, and the drizzle they'd had off and on for the past week would hardly disrupt the phone lines. First thing to do was check the rest of the connector boxes—a fool's errand, but always the first step before she called the phone company. She shrugged into her bathrobe and walked down the hall, flipping on lights as she went. Cara, petulant, reading in her room. Office phone, okay. Okay in the kitchen, okay in the den. She opened the basement door and stood there. Was there any point in going down? There couldn't be anything wrong with that phone. She hadn't been anywhere near it when she went to get the wine, and anyway, it hung on the wall and made a terrible noise if it fell.

Not willing to leave the job half-done, she turned on the basement lights and went to examine it, anyway.

The receiver was not only off the hook, it had been disconnected entirely from the body of the phone. She held it in her hand and stared at it, as if it could tell her what it had been doing and why it wasn't on the job. Finally she plugged it in, dialed Steve's number and leaned against the wall.

"Guess where I am," she said, when he answered.

"I can't imagine," he said. "What's going on at your house? I've been sitting here in my office with my phone on automatic redial for over an hour. I was about to come over and see what's wrong."

"I'm in the basement," she told him. "And this phone was off the hook."

He wasn't sure what she was telling him. "But why?"

"That's what I'd like to know," she said. "It was not only off the hook, the receiver was unplugged."

"But you were the only one down there," said Steve.

"This isn't the first time it's happened," she said. "It's become a pattern. Cara, I'm sure."

"Why would Cara unplug the basement phone?" asked Steve. "Oh. Of course. So we can't talk."

"Exactly," said Elizabeth grimly. "I'm going to have a little conference with her."

"Calm down first," said Steve.

Good advice, which she didn't want.

"And how should I do that?" asked Elizabeth, with some asperity. "Jog in place until the adrenaline dissipates?"

"She's in a lot of distress," said Steve. "Be compassionate."

She hated being forced to be reasonable.

"*I'm* in a lot of distress," said Elizabeth.

"I know," he said. "Sleep on it."

"I can't sleep," she said grimly. "I'm wide awake and probably will be for hours."

"Read a good book," he said. "One of mine."

"I started *Fields of Gomorrah,*" she told him, deciding she was glad to change the subject. Here was the opportunity to calm down. "While I was waiting in vain for you to call. It's much more comfortable than *Kalik.*"

"Did you finish *Kalik?*" he asked.

She hesitated. "Yes. It made me cry." The memory of the sadness and despair was like spiders on her skin. "This one—it's more comfortable." She searched for words. "*Kalik* seemed to mirror my own sadness so much," she said, "I thought I couldn't go on at first. But I wanted to, because it was so good, and it won that Nebula award, so I know it's famous. So I finished it, but I wish I hadn't."

"Don't be sorry," he said. "I understand. I couldn't read it myself, for several years after I wrote it."

"Was that when you were getting a divorce?" She remembered and bled for the hurt, hollow-eyed man pictured on the back cover of *Kalik the Destroyer.*

"Yeah. I was bitter and feeling helpless and couldn't understand why it was happening," he said. "What I'm thinking often shows up in my books, and *Kalik* got it in spades. It wasn't like your divorce from Robert. You knew why you were splitting up.''

"I certainly did," she said. Robert had not one, but two women on the side. And maybe more—she hadn't wanted to know. She had just wanted to get as far away from him as possible.

"Marian and I married too young," Steve continued. "And we grew up in different directions."

"Sometimes that happens," said Elizabeth.

"It's almost guaranteed, if you're just nineteen," he said.

There was a somber cast to his voice, which she couldn't quite identify.

"You still sound sad about it," she said.

"Not sad," said Steve. "Not anymore. A little melancholy, looking back at those two happy children. They never could have dreamed that what they were so sure about would cause them such grief."

She heard his office chair squeak as he leaned back in it.

"And when we did grow up, we wanted different lives, different things out of life, and we could never come to a compromise." The chair squeaked again, as if he were restless. "It was the worst possible ending, for both of us. A bloodless killing, sort of like a neutron bomb. All the wounds were internal. You left your marriage with a feeling of relief. We left ours with a feeling of failure. If one of us had been a real rat, it would have been easier, but we're both nice, well-meaning people."

"I'm glad Robert was a rat," Elizabeth said, with heartfelt sincerity. Then she realized what she said wasn't actually what she meant and tried to explain.

Steve laughed. "It's all right. I understand. I'm sort of glad he was a rat, too, except for Cara. It's opened up all kinds of new possibilities for me."

"Like me," she said.

"Exactly like you," he said. His voice was tender. "Darling, you ought to go back to bed. You're going to catch cold in that dank basement."

"I'd rather talk to you," she said. "I've waited all evening to do it."

"Tell you what, Sammy and I will come over for break-fast. We'll talk about going to Lin's."

"Will this be anything like the last time you came over in the morning?" she asked. "I can't say I'd mind, because I thought the entire event was spectacularly successful, but I promised McNulty that I'd see him at nine o'clock without fail."

"McNulty," said Steve, "is becoming an intolerable burden."

"McNulty," said Elizabeth, "is becoming the source of most of next year's income."

"McNulty," said Steve, "is perhaps a tolerable burden, after all. All right. I'll let you out of the house, fully dressed by seven forty-five."

"Actually, I don't have to leave until eight-fifteen, if you'll drop me at the station so I won't have to park."

"I can manage that," said Steve. "I'll be over as soon as I put Melody on the train."

"Okay." Elizabeth wished she could look forward to the time when they could have breakfast—and whatever else they wanted—every morning. With a sigh she wondered if that would ever become possible.

"Good night, then, sweetheart." His voice was a caress. "Sleep well."

"I love you, Steve," she said. And after she discon-nected, she said it again. "I love you, damn it. How are we ever going to work this out, when absolutely everything is going wrong?"

Disabling those phones was sabotage—well planned, carefully conducted and, she had to admit, fairly success-ful. Denied that, what other schemes would the child in-vent?

She found this subterfuge difficult to believe. Cara was fiery and short-tempered, but she'd never in her life ever been sneaky. Elizabeth contemplated this gloomily. It wasn't merely spite, on Cara's part. It was desperation. She was fighting hard, and not just to get rid of Melody. Her dis-taste for Melody simply could not have provoked such sus-tained guerrilla action, particularly in view of Cara's pronounced disdain for anything underhanded. And she really didn't seem to dislike Steve.

So why did she do it?

Elizabeth lay back on the bed, with her hands tucked behind her head and thought.

After considerable worry over her approach, she got up and ambled wearily to Cara's room. Cara was still sitting cross-legged on her bed, reading a novel.

"That's awfully bad light, honey," Elizabeth said. "Doesn't it hurt your eyes?"

"No," Cara said. She didn't look up.

Elizabeth sat on the edge of the bed. "Cara, I have to talk to you."

"So talk," Cara said. She kept her head bent over her book.

"Trying for three weeks?" asked Elizabeth. There was a touch of unsheathed steel in her tone.

Cara paid attention to that. She closed her book and gave Elizabeth her sullen attention.

"Why have you been disconnecting the phones?" Elizabeth asked.

Cara shrugged her shoulders convulsively and looked away.

"Cara," said Elizabeth. "You have to talk to me about this."

"He's trying to be my father," said Cara. "I already have a father."

"Did you think keeping the phone off the hook would keep me from seeing Steve?"

Cara shrugged again. "Why'd you divorce my dad?" she asked.

Elizabeth took a deep breath and told her. "He was going out with other women, behind my back. Every time he did it, he'd promised to stop. But he was lying about that—he told me what I wanted to hear. So he had to leave, because he wouldn't stop."

Cara glared at her. "He would have, if you'd been nicer to him," she told Elizabeth. "He loves you. He told me."

"Cara," said Elizabeth, not knowing how to explain, yet knowing that she must. "Your father loves you, not me. He doesn't want you to be unhappy, so he says what you want to hear. He's very charming and convincing. I know that, because I loved him once myself. But he doesn't love me, and hasn't in a long time." She didn't add *if ever.*

"Well, he said he loves you on his card!" Cara whipped it out of the pages of the book, where it had been placed both as keepsake and bookmark. "He says so, right on this card. 'Give my love to mommy.' There."

"Darling," said Elizabeth helplessly. "That's just being polite. He doesn't love me. His only link to me is through you. That's not even his handwriting. It's typed."

"Well, Daddy typed it," said Cara stubbornly. "And he wouldn't say it if he didn't mean it. And I bet his feelings are hurt because you're going out with other people."

"Cara, we're not married anymore. Both of us go out with other people."

"You never did before," said Cara. Her eyes were full of misery. "And then Mr. Riker came along, and all of a sudden you've forgotten all about Daddy. And he *does* love you. I asked him and he said he did."

God help me! Elizabeth thought.

"He can't stand to have anyone mad at him, Cara," she said, repeating her earlier message in different words. "He's insecure that way. He knows you want us to get married again, and he doesn't want you to be unhappy. So he's let you believe something that just isn't true, sweetheart. We are never going to get together again. I want you to believe that."

Cara's eyes were as opaque as jade.

Elizabeth looked at her helplessly and took her by the shoulders. "I don't want you to be unhappy or disappointed either, darling, but disappointment and unhappiness are part of life. You just have to learn to overcome them."

Cara tried to twist away from her. Elizabeth took a firmer grip and massaged at the tight muscles around her thin neck.

"I have always told you the truth, and I will keep right on doing it, even if it makes you sad," Elizabeth said. "It makes me sad, too, because I want you to be happy, and I know this makes you sad. But your father and I don't love each other. We are not going to get back together. We can't, because I have to know the truth and he is not capable of telling it. You can't stop loving him because of that—he's your father. He doesn't tell lies because he's mean or dishonest. He tells lies because his lies make people happy for a little while.''

Cara's eyes were shut and her mouth was set. Elizabeth's stomach felt hollow with anxiety. ''I love you and I want to make you happy, but I won't lie to you to do it.''

She let Cara go, and the child moved away from her. Her eyes licked fire and her teeth were actually bared.

''Daddy loves you and I know it, and if you keep seeing Mr. Riker, I'm going to live in California and you can't stop me. Daddy said he'd send me the money anytime I wanted to come.''

Elizabeth reached out a trembling hand to brush the wild hair away from Cara's eyes. Cara flinched away from her.

''Do you know how unhappy that would make me?'' asked Elizabeth quietly. ''My arms would be so empty. You mustn't think of such a thing.''

She got up and left Cara's room. Even with all she had said, she couldn't bring herself to tell her precious, antagonistic, vulnerable, beloved daughter that Robert didn't want her, had never wanted her, and never would.

She went back to her room with a heavy heart and crawled beneath a wool blanket and a down comforter, where she lay staring at the ceiling for hours. A winter storm rose with the moon. Dark clouds slid frantically across a darker sky and an icy wind whistled underneath the eaves.

The clouds swept no faster and the sky was no darker than her thoughts.

In the morning, when she went to Cara's room, it was apparent that Cara hadn't slept much, either. She lay, hollow-eyed, staring at the ceiling, just as Elizabeth had done. Elizabeth smoothed her hand across Cara's forehead.

''Don't you feel well, honey?'' she asked. Cara did seem a little warm to her. She went for the thermometer and stuck it in Cara's mouth.

''You have a fever,'' she said, a minute later. ''Is your throat sore?'' She made Cara open her mouth. Her throat

was a bit red, but didn't show the distinctive little white
eruptions of a bacterial infection. Probably just a cold.

"I have to go to school," Cara croaked. "I have a test
tomorrow."

"If you feel better, you can go this afternoon," Elizabeth soothed. She went into the bathroom and poked
through the medicine cabinet for the aspirin substitute.
Couldn't give a kid aspirin, anymore, she remembered, because of Reye's Syndrome. There wasn't much she could do
about Cara's cold, but at least there was assurance that if a
secondary infection developed, something could be done
about it. How much more worrying these little illnesses must
have been one hundred and thirty years ago. When young
Elizabeth Thomas was caring for her baby, even a cold
could put a child in danger of death.

She gave Cara the tablets and tucked her back into bed.
It wasn't until she was on her way downstairs to make the
coffee that she remembered McNulty, at nine o'clock.

"Oh, damn," she muttered. "I'll just have to call and
cancel again." If Mr. McNulty wasn't getting impatient, he
ought to have been. She wouldn't have blamed him. If anything could have made her regret that ecstatic morning in
bed with Steve, neglecting McNulty could.

She made tea with lemon and honey in it and carried it up
the stairs to Cara. Cara took a few sips and went back to
sleep. Elizabeth pattered down to get her coffee and take the
paper off the front porch. She'd heard the door rattle as the
paperboy passed.

And Steve was coming. How could she have forgotten
that? She smiled. He was the one bright spot in what was
shaping up to be a pretty bad day. By the time he arrived,
she had donned her usual winter garb of sweaters, jeans and
loafers and had her curly hair pulled into a ponytail.

"You look sixteen," he said, when she opened the door
to him. "I love it, but are you sure McNulty will?" He had
a bag of fresh bagels in one hand and Sammy's leash in the
other.

"No McNulty today," she said, kissing him hello. She
freed Sammy and kissed him, too. "Mama loves you best,"

she told Sammy, grabbing his whiskers and touching her nose to his.

"At least I got the first kiss," Steve said. He set the bagels on the foyer table as he shed his coat. "Why no McNulty?"

"Cara's sick." She picked up the bagels and led Sammy into the kitchen by dangling them in front of him. He sat by the table and slavered.

"What's the matter with her?" Steve asked. "She looked a little wan last night, but I thought it was just because she was mad."

"A cold, I guess. She has fever and a sore throat and a headache and just feels generally bad. I can't go off and leave her." She gave Sammy a bagel. He carried it into the dining room, so he could dine in elegance on an antique oriental rug.

"You could if you left her with me. I've had lots of experience with tea and cookies and bringing sick little girls soup."

"She wouldn't like it."

He grinned. "She probably wouldn't, but it won't make her any sicker, and you won't have to leave poor McNulty in the lurch. Besides," he said, "I feel like I owe him something."

"That you do," Elizabeth told him. "Okay. It's a deal. I'll go dress. Can you make oatmeal?"

"No. I hate oatmeal. How about a nice bagel and some scrambled eggs? I can manage that."

She grabbed his ears as she had Sammy's whiskers and kissed him soundly. "I adore you, did you know that?"

"It's about time," he said. "God knows I've worked hard enough to get it. Are you sure I haven't lost out to Sammy?"

"Well, I wouldn't push my luck," she said, as she headed for the back stairs. "He's very appealing."

Elizabeth, as she dressed, smelled burning toast. "That would be the bagels," she thought, grinning. She took a winter white wool suit from her closet, thought of Sammy and put it back. She had, somewhere in all these cleaner's bags, a lovely heather brown tweed. Sammy ought to match that just fine, and she could pet him to her heart's content.

Finally she confined her curly hair into a bun, approved of her image in the mirror and left the room.

Now for the hard part. She crept into Cara's room and touched her cheek.

Cara, seeing her mother dressed, said with dismay, "Are you leaving?"

"Yes," said Elizabeth. "But Steve's here, if you need anything."

Cara's eyes flamed, and not with fever.

"And," said Elizabeth hastily. "He brought Sammy. Do you want me to bring him upstairs?"

Cara scowled and closed her eyes again. "Yes," she said.

"Want some more tea?"

"Yes," Cara said. Elizabeth bent to kiss her cheek, and Cara held up her arms for a hug. Elizabeth pulled the blankets up around Cara's shoulders and kissed her again.

Then she said, "Cara, mind what I said about being polite," and went downstairs to the eggs and burned bagels.

"How's she feeling?" Steve asked, when Elizabeth appeared in the kitchen. He was scraping the burned bits off the bagels into the sink.

"Feverish." She sat at the table.

"Too feverish to complain?"

"No. She objects to you but considers Sammy a sufficient compensation."

Steve smiled. "Sammy the Conciliator."

Sammy, sitting beside Elizabeth, heard his name. He laid his huge muzzle on the table and stared fixedly at her plate.

"Bad dog," she scolded. She gave him half a bagel.

"You're impossible," said Steve.

"He is not," Elizabeth retorted. "A bagel now and then won't hurt him."

"I wasn't talking about him," Steve told her. "Do you have any idea how his manners have deteriorated since he met you? It's scandalous."

"He has perfectly wonderful manners," Elizabeth said. "He never grabs and he never takes anything without asking."

"You call laying that fur ball of a head on the table *asking?*"

"You're just jealous because he's better looking than you are," said Elizabeth. Steve's bagel was loaded with cream cheese and raspberry jelly and ready to eat. Elizabeth lifted half of it and fed it to Sammy, bite by bite. "There. That's two whole bagels. That's enough for one big dog."

"I see I'm going to have to be faster if I'm going to get anything to eat while he's got you around to pilfer for him," said Steve. He moved his plate out of her reach.

"You don't have to do that," said Elizabeth, who had gulped her breakfast and was now preparing to leave. "I told him he couldn't have any more."

"*You can't have any more* are the only five words in English that he doesn't understand." Steve stood to walk her to her car.

The tea, he thought, as he brewed it, didn't have any nourishment in it. He rooted about in the pantry until he found some instant rice, which he cooked until it was soggy. Then he sprinkled it with sugar and cinnamon and poured a little milk on it. It looked awful, but Melody loved the stuff when she was sick. Maybe Cara would, too. He put the tea and the rice on a tray, added a couple of bagels as an afterthought, called Sammy and went upstairs.

Cara squinted up at him from her nest of blankets. "Where's Sammy?" she said.

Sammy put his big nose on the bed and licked her face.

"If you'll move your legs a little, he'll get up here with you," Steve said.

She moved her legs, and Steve patted the space she'd left. Sammy sprang up joyously, circled two or three times and flopped down so vigorously that the bed bounced like a trampoline. Cara looked pleased. She sat up so she could pat Sammy's head.

"If you try to make him get off," Steve told her, "he pretends to be in a coma."

She almost smiled at that. Her blue flannel pajamas were twisted and looked uncomfortable and her hair fuzzed messily around her face.

If I knew her a little better, Steve thought, *I'd offer to tie that hair back so it wouldn't bother her.*

"You ready for a little breakfast?" He produced the rice.

"I'm not hungry," said Cara, looking at it suspiciously.

"My mother used to make me this, when I was sick," said Steve, dipping the spoon into the mush and poking it at Cara, as if she were a baby. "It's got brown sugar and cinnamon in it."

She was feeling ill enough to want to be pampered, even if Steve was the pamperer. She opened her mouth.

"That's good," she said reluctantly. She opened her mouth again. After five or six bites she took a sip of the tea and lay down. "Can Sammy stay?"

"I don't know how I'd make him leave," Steve said, patting her legs.

Sammy slitted his eyes when Steve got up and collected the food but made no move to follow him, even when he walked out of Cara's room with the bagels in his hand. Steve decided to leave the door open so Sammy could get out if he wanted to. As he left, he glanced over his shoulder to see Sammy snuffle happily and snuggle against Cara's legs.

Cara's pajama sleeve fluttered as she reached down to scratch his ears.

"Aorrwr," he complained, when she withdrew her hand. She smiled as she burrowed into her pillows. Sammy inched his way up the bed so he could put his head on her hip. She patted him again and he subsided with a satisfied "Mrroph."

Steve got a pad and pencil from Elizabeth's office and looked in on Cara again as he passed her door. She was asleep with one hand on Sammy's big head.

He whistled as he went downstairs.

Elizabeth returned at noon.

"How'd it go?" she asked, as she came into the kitchen.

"Very well," said Steve, who was proud of his success. "I fixed her some breakfast, and she ate it. She and Sammy are still asleep."

"She wasn't rude?" said Elizabeth.

Steve grinned as he kissed her. "She didn't feel well enough to be rude."

"I don't know if that's good or bad," said Elizabeth ruefully.

"I think it's bad," said Steve. "I hate to see her sick. Go check on her, and I'll put some lunch together."

"What kind of lunch?" asked Elizabeth, remembering the primitive breakfast.

"Tuna salad," said Steve.

"And how do you make tuna salad?" Elizabeth wanted to know.

"Tuna and mayonnaise," Steve said. "Why?"

"Go back to what you were doing," Elizabeth said. "I'l put lunch together."

"You don't like my cooking," Steve said.

Elizabeth pinched his cheek. "What you do can hardly be called *cooking,* my heart, try though you may. I don't see how Melody managed to grow up without rickets or some thing."

"Does this mean we're invited to dinner?" he asked. He put his arms around her, and she leaned against them.

"Of course. Any night. Every night, if you want to. But only if Sammy comes, too."

"I'll buy the groceries," he offered.

"You can help pay for them," Elizabeth said, smiling at him. "But you all too obviously don't have any idea how to buy them. Your poor child."

"I'm an idiot savant," he agreed. "I'm only good at one thing."

"Two things," she said. "And that's sufficient to keep me happy forever. Go back to your plotting, or whatever that is you have spread all over the table. I'll be back in a min ute."

Cara was still asleep, and Sammy snoozed beside her. When Elizabeth kissed her, she woke up and said, "Sammy's taking a nap with me."

Sammy raised his head, but made no move to get off the bed.

"Grin, Sammy," said Elizabeth, scrubbing at his curly pate with her knuckles.

Sammy grinned.

Cara laughed. "I love that," she said.

"And how are you, pet?" Elizabeth asked. "Now that you've slept all morning?"

"Better," said Cara.

Elizabeth got a hairbrush and two red ribbons off the dresser and helped Cara sit up.

"You're a mess," said her doting mother. She straightened the pajamas and put Cara's hair into two near braids. "I understand Steve made you some breakfast. What was it?"

"Some goop with brown sugar and cinnamon," Cara said.

"And was it good?"

"Yeah," Cara said. "I guess. It was soft on my throat."

"And how is your throat?"

"Not sore anymore. Can I . . ." Backtrack. "*May* I go to school this afternoon?"

Elizabeth laughed. "In this case, your first instinct was correct. It's *can I.* No. You're still sick. So you're not able to go."

"I can't tell the difference," Cara grumbled.

"We'll talk about it later," said Elizabeth, tugging at a braid. "You want some lunch?"

"I guess," said Cara. "What?"

"How about some nice chicken noodle soup?" She got Cara's bathrobe and helped her into it, then searched for her slippers. One was under the bed, the other was nowhere to be seen. "Where's the other one of these?" she asked.

Cara didn't know.

Elizabeth tossed the lone slipper into the closet and got Cara into socks and sneakers.

"There," she said. "Wash your face and brush your teeth and come downstairs."

Cara came to the table carrying the book she was reading and set it beside her bowl. Steve noticed the title and author and asked, "How many of those have you read?"

"All of them," Cara told him. Sammy ambled over and put his head in her lap. She gave him her toast, and he lay down under her feet to eat it.

"I have some others I think you'd like," said Steve. "I could bring you some, if you want me to."

Cara slurped at her soup, torn between her desire for the books and her unwillingness to consort with the enemy. The books won.

"Okay," she said.

She left her bowl half-full on the table and went back up to bed. Elizabeth broke some toast into it and set it on the floor for Sammy, who ate much more enthusiastically than had Cara. When he'd licked it clean, he stood in front of the sink and barked.

Steve got up. "I need a bowl for water," he said.

"Is that how he lets you know he's thirsty?" Elizabeth asked, mightily impressed. "That's really smart of him, to know where the water comes from." She got a bowl and filled it and set it on the floor.

"He not only knows where water comes from," said Steve. "He wants the bowl cleaned out and refilled every time he wants a drink. It gets to be a nuisance. Day after tomorrow is Thanksgiving. Do you think Cara's going to be well enough to go to Lin's?"

"I expect so," Elizabeth said, whisking the soup bowls into the dishwasher. "I don't think she has any fever this afternoon, and her color looks better to me. I may send her back to school tomorrow."

Sammy finished his drink and wiped his chin across Steve's pants.

"Damn it, Sammy," he said. He got some paper towels and soaked up the water on Sammy's beard. "I hate it when you do that."

They sounded like parents, she thought, discussing the minutiae of kitchen and kids and dogs and daily life. And it was no illusion. Cara was thawing toward Steve, Steve treated Cara as tenderly and gently as he treated Melody— he was a good father, and Cara, Elizabeth thought, was beginning to respond to that, a little. A comfortable contentment filled her, hope and stability and Steve's committed presence combined to make her feel more secure than she had since they'd met.

Sammy climbed the stairs, presumably hunting for Cara.

"I've got to go back to work," said Steve. He got a paper towel and wiped up the water Sammy had dripped on the floor.

"So do I. Are you going home?"

"I can work here in the kitchen, if you don't mind," Steve said, "Plotting is a pencil and paper job for me. Give me a kiss and get out of here so I can concentrate."

Elizabeth went up to her office, floating on air. For the first time in weeks she worked without worry clouding the back of her mind. She'd have to call Lin later, she thought, and find out what to bring for Thanksgiving dinner. Cara and Melody hadn't exactly called a truce, but all those little boys were wonderful buffers, and Cara truly enjoyed the Vorklands. The day, which had started out so badly, had turned out very well. Even the prospect of the girls scowling at each other across the supper table didn't cause Elizabeth any discomfort. She'd had victory enough for one day.

On Thursday morning Steve drove away from Elizabeth's house with a carful of girls, dogs and pies. The pies were safely in the trunk, but Sammy could smell them and kept barking into the hole where the armrest went. Melody turned him around several times and said, "Sammy, sit!"

Sammy wouldn't.

"Is he going to bark all the way to Lin's?" asked Elizabeth.

"Looks like it," Steve told her.

Cara took hold of his collar. "Lie down, Sammy," she said.

Sammy wouldn't. He put his front legs on the hump in the floor and his fanny on the seat and hung his head over Steve's shoulder.

Steve elbowed him. "Don't slobber on me," he said.

Sammy moved.

"Don't slobber on me, either," said Elizabeth, but she put her arm around him. He put his nose into her neck and snuffled. She moved her arm. "I'm going to smell like dog," she complained.

"He just had a bath," said Melody. "He smells better than I do."

Elizabeth turned around and eyed Cara, who already had her mouth open. She subsided into her corner of the car. She and Melody still hadn't spoken to each other.

Steve turned into a convenience store.

"I told Lin I'd bring some soft drinks for the kids," he said. "You girls come in with me and pick some out."

Cara headed for the ginger ale.

"Oh, yuck," said Melody disdainfully. "That's so babyish." She herself had considered ginger ale the pinnacle of sophistication, until she'd discovered sparkling apple cider, put up in champagne bottles. She had a magnum of it in her hand.

Both girls were dressed in skirts and blazers, but Melody had recently begun a growth spurt, much to Cara's dismay. She actually had a waist and nascent bosoms, of which she was very proud. Cara remained unadorned by nature and considered Melody's surging development manifestly unfair. She was, she had told Elizabeth indignantly, the only girl in her class who didn't wear a bra.

The clerk, an older woman, smiled across the counter at Cara. "Never mind her, honey," she said. "When she grows up, she'll be glad to have a little sister."

"She's not my sister," said Cara, through her teeth. "And we're exactly the same age."

Which was almost true—their birthdays were a month apart.

Melody set the apple cider on the counter and preened.

"Great," Elizabeth muttered to Steve. "Just what we needed."

"Stiff upper lip," said Steve, whose hands were full of ginger ale and colas. "Let's go, everybody."

From the car, Sammy moaned pitifully.

Elizabeth felt like doing the same.

When they were back on the road, Cara stewed in silence, while Melody carried on a lengthy and obnoxious monologue about her prospects for skipping a grade.

At last Cara could stand it no longer.

"Why would they let you skip a form?" she asked, dripping scorn. "You can't even write an A paper in English."

Unfortunate, but true. Melody had a good head for math, but English didn't interest her. Cara had much better grades and never let anyone forget it. They traded insults for five minutes.

Finally Elizabeth turned around in her seat.

"Stop that," she said. "I'm tired of listening to it. And don't you dare upset Lin's house with it. Those little boys try to copy what you do, and this mean-spirited sniping is no example to set."

Neither miscreant looked contrite, but each did, at least, be quiet. Elizabeth, facing forward, could feel hostility like a blanket of doom emanating from the back seat. As Steve pulled into the Vorklands' drive, she turned around again.

"Be pleasant, even to each other, if it kills you," she instructed. "The boys think you're adults, and children feel very insecure if the adults they depend on fight."

They filed in silence to the house. Johnny met them at the door. Elizabeth happened to enter first, and Johnny flung himself at her legs, yelling, "Me up! Me up!"

Elizabeth picked him up and hugged him. He had on a turtleneck with red dogs printed on it, and denim overalls and little red hightops. He looked adorable.

Sandy followed, with two fingers in his mouth. He had on jeans instead of overalls, and they had slipped down over his little round belly. He looked solemnly at Elizabeth and Johnny, then said to the assemblage at large, "He gots to wear diapers and sleep in a crib."

By then the rest of the family had appeared to say hello. Daniel and Zach compelled the girls up to the playroom to inspect a fort they'd built of blocks, and Elizabeth, glad to be rid of them for a few minutes, carried Johnny into the kitchen. She looked around her wistfully.

Lin said gently, "The girls giving you two a hard time today?"

"I'm beginning to consider a boarding school," said Elizabeth. "A convent, with walls twelve feet high."

Lin grinned. "You find one yet?"

"No," Elizabeth said. "I don't think they have 'em anymore. I keep searching the back pages of women's magazines, but all I find are country clubs for underachievers."

"Which Cara and Melody definitely are not," said Lin. She dipped her hands in flour and patted at a mound of risen dough.

"Parker House rolls?" asked Elizabeth, seeing the muffin tins sitting on the cabinet. She let John slide off her lap and offered to help.

Lin waved her over to a stack of raw vegetables that needed to be cut for salad. "Steve looked a little tight-lipped."

Elizabeth related the activities of the past few days as she chopped carrots. "I really thought we were making some progress," she said mournfully. "And today they sounded worse than ever."

Lin considered. "Leave them here for the weekend," she said. "I've got some nonpregnant clothes they can wear. Even for Cara, in the attic. I used to be almost that skinny, when I married Tom."

"You think they'd go for that?" asked Elizabeth hopefully.

"I don't see why not. God knows I could use the help. I'm sleepy all the time." Lin poured the salad into a wooden bowl. "I'll ask them myself." She went off to the playroom and returned a few minutes later. "All set. You're a free woman until Sunday afternoon."

Thanksgiving was an unqualified success.

Chapter Twelve

Steve pulled the car over as soon as they were out of sight of the house.

"Come here," he said, turning in his seat and holding out his arms.

Elizabeth came. "I hate bucket seats," she said, leaning across his lap.

"We could move to the back." He pulled the chignon pin from her hair and let it flow across his arm. Her green eyes glittered wildly as she slipped her arms around his neck.

"We'd get arrested," she murmured against his lips.

He kissed her slowly, savoring the taste of her, the soft pressure of her breasts against his chest, the feel of her securely in his arms. They hardly ever had the opportunity to be alone, and he was going to make the most of it. He slipped his right hand under her sweater and scraped lightly at the lace over her nipple. He got an immediate response.

"I really ought to get you home," he said huskily.

"Yes," said Elizabeth. "And hurry. We can get arrested from the front seat."

Elizabeth unlocked her front door.

"Last one in bed's a Puritan prig," she said, racing for the stairs. Steve slammed the door and locked it and took the stairs three at a time until he caught her.

They exploded through the bedroom door, laughing and shoving. Steve collapsed on the old bed and pulled Elizabeth down on top of him.

He gathered her skirt in his hands and rubbed at her bottom. "I hate panty hose, did you know that?"

"Less conversation," growled Elizabeth. "More action."

"I love you," he said. He hooked his thumbs in the hated hose and pulled them partially down.

She pushed up, straight-armed and leaned over him.

"If you really love me, why don't you do something about Cara and Melody?" she said.

"What would you suggest?"

Elizabeth grinned. She got up and took care of the panty hose herself. "Exorcism?"

Steve began to laugh. "Come here," he said.

"I want another kiss," she announced.

"I think I can manage that," he said. "Anything else you want?"

"How about a little loving?"

"I think I can manage that, too."

"I'm sure you can," she said approvingly. She put her hands to the buttons of his shirt.

"It's our pants we have to take off," said Steve.

"First things first."

"Okay. Marry me."

"Oh, Steve, how can I? Those two would destroy us. We'll have to wait until they're grown up."

"They're never going to grow up, and it's five years till they're in college. Never mind growing up. I am not going to wait five years to marry you because we have the two worst children on the East Coast."

"Are you sure they're the worst?"

"Damned near it," he said grimly. "Maybe exorcism isn't a bad idea at that. Or hypnotism. Now, hypnotism—that's a good idea."

"Like this." She swung his boxer shorts rhythmically in front of his eyes. "You will be reasonable. You will be reasonable."

"Marry me," he said again. "We have to take control sometime, Elizabeth. Now's the time."

"You call this control?" she asked, grinning.

His clothes were in a heap on the floor, and he was rapidly stripping off the last of hers.

"Marry me," he said. "Or I stop right here."

"Oh, no, don't do that. We'll get married. We'll get married."

"You mean it?"

"Let's talk about it later," she said, eagerly running the flat of her hands down his body.

He started to refasten her bra.

"What are you doing?" she asked, alarmed.

"A little judicious blackmail. No marriage, no sex."

"That's supposed to be my line."

"Talk about it now."

"Okay. I'll marry you. I have to. I love you too much not to."

"Will you still mean it in the morning?"

"I'll still mean it in a century, if I'm still alive to say it."

"When?" he demanded.

"Christmas," she said. Christmas, with its anticipation, joy and pleasure. Definitely sometime around Christmas.

"Christmas?" He beetled his brows. "When, Christmas?"

"New Year's Eve," she said, with certainty. A time of hope and renewal and looking to the future. Her heart rose inside her like a helium balloon.

He smiled into her shining eyes. "New Year's Eve it is." He unfastened the bra again and cast it away from them. "There," he said, lifting her breasts in his hands. "It's nice to come to an agreement."

Elizabeth sat on the edge of the bed and held out her hands. "You come here," she said. She spread her knees so that he could stand between them and bent her head to bite at his thigh.

"Ow!" he said. But he didn't move.

"Crybaby." She bit again.

Steve considered it, later, as one of the best afternoons of his life, even though three more very satisfying days followed.

Sammy climbed into the car on Sunday with the air of an exhausted playboy and responded to all attentions with a grunt. He had snatched and run with so many toys that he was worn out with the hilarity of being chased. He sprawled across the back seat and snored, with his head in Cara's lap.

"Miggy's going to have pups," said Cara. She arranged Sammy's head so he'd be more comfortable. "The name of the father is Pierre's Pappy's Pass the Buck. Isn't that silly?"

"They're going to be born on Christmas," said Melody, who interrupted and took over the story Cara was telling. "Aunt Lin has them all sold, already, because Pappy is really famous. And, Daddy, you know what I did? I took Aunt Lin's horse, and Uncle Tom's teaching me how to jump. I didn't even fall off. I can be in a show next year, if I practice."

Elizabeth turned around in time to catch the look on Cara's face: complete disgust, as if she'd stepped in something nasty and had nowhere to scrape her shoe.

So much for détente.

Cara didn't speak the rest of the way. She kept her head turned away from Melody, staring at the passing landscape. She played idly with the buttons of her shirt or twisted her hair around her index finger or rubbed at Sammy's wiry coat. Melody, oblivious, talked nonstop about horses, about the prizes she was going to win, about the neat clothes you wore at horse shows, about boys.

Meanwhile Cara seethed with a quiet, furious energy that filled the car like a miasma rising from a swamp.

Steve had taken Elizabeth's hand as soon as they'd pulled away from the house. She was accustomed now to holding hands with him, and the physical connection with him was strengthening. All the way to Lin's they had discussed when and how to tell Cara and Melody that they were getting married, and had come to no conclusion as to the proper time. But to announce their intentions now, felt Elizabeth, in this hostile atmosphere, would be disastrous.

During Melody's monologue, Steve looked across the seat and questioned her with his eyes. She glanced at the girls and shook her head. She just couldn't stand the thought of any more emotion in the confined space of the car; it seemed about to explode at the moment.

His eyebrows snapped together and his lips tightened. He didn't say anything but withdrew his hand from hers and put it back on the steering wheel.

Elizabeth leaned her head back and closed her eyes. It seemed a long way home. She thought of the pot roast she'd left simmering, and a wave of nausea swept through her.

When they walked into the house, with Melody and Cara trailing like a couple of Cassandras, Steve said to Elizabeth, "No more waffling. It's time."

He herded the bunch of them into the den, looking as grim as if he were about to announce an execution.

No smile, no conciliation, no preamble. Elizabeth held her breath.

"Elizabeth and I," said Steve, standing before them like a litigator, with his hands behind his back and a scowl on his face, "are going to get married on New Year's Eve."

There was dead silence.

Après moi, thought Elizabeth fearfully. It seemed as if his words hung in the charged air for minutes, during which they flamed and curled and writhed like dragons.

But it was only a nanosecond before Melody shot to her feet. "I won't live in the same house with her!" she shouted.

"Sit down and be quiet, Melody," said Steve. His voice was rock hard and cold as death.

Cara rose like a ghost from the couch, wavering and unsteady on her feet, and said to Elizabeth, "I always knew you didn't love me."

This was the last straw for Steve. "Your mother does love you," he told Cara. "We love you both. We also love each other. This silly feud has gone on long enough. We are not going to be blackmailed by a couple of thirteen-year-old extortionists. You'll live together—'' this to Melody ''—and you'll learn to like it.''

Elizabeth, looking at their two intractable faces, foresaw disaster.

''It's time for dinner,'' said Steve. ''Come and eat.'' He went into the kitchen.

Melody slammed out the front door. Cara fled to her room. Elizabeth lay on the couch and put a pillow over her face.

In a few minutes Steve came to sit beside her. He rubbed gently at her stomach.

''Is it safe to come out?'' she asked. The pillow muffled her speech.

''I think so,'' he said. He lifted the pillow and laid it aside.

''That was horrible,'' she said.

''They'll come around,'' said Steve. The tears in her voice made him heartsick. ''We'll keep coming for dinner, we'll carry on a normal life, and they'll get used to it.''

She struggled to sit up and leaned into his arms. ''I hope you're right, but it looks pretty grim to me.''

He brushed the hair away from her face and kissed her temple. ''Everything will be okay. You'll see.'' She snuggled against his chest, and his voice rumbled comfortingly in her ear. ''They're just children, Elizabeth. If we lead, they'll follow. Do you want something to eat?''

She shook her head. ''I'm not hungry.''

''Sammy was,'' said Steve. ''I put some of the gravy out of the pot roast on his kibble.''

Just the thought of eating made Elizabeth sick. ''You should have given it all to him,'' she said.

''How about a glass of wine, then?'' said Steve.

''I'd agree,'' Elizabeth said. ''But I'm afraid Melody is going to freeze out there in the car. It's awfully cold.''

Steve didn't answer this. Instead, he rose and built a fire, then got the wine and a small bowl of mashed potatoes with gravy and set them on the coffee table in front of her.

''I know you don't want the roast,'' he told her, ''but I hate for you not to eat.'' He bent to kiss her. ''I'm going to take Melody home and talk some sense into her. We are going on as we planned, Libby. We'll be here for dinner to-morrow."

After he left, she put the pillow over her face again. The potatoes got cold and the wine breathed its efflorescence sweetly into the air, and she didn't care what became of either of them.

The next morning Cara came down to breakfast calm and dry-eyed and looking determined.

Elizabeth braced herself.

"Are you really going to marry Mr. Riker?" said Cara.

"Yes," Elizabeth said. "New Year's Eve."

Cara went to school without further comment. She showed up right after sports—no detention, the first day without one in a long, long time. Melody and Steve came for dinner every night. Cara ate quietly and retired to her room; Melody went into the den to read and do her homework. Cara and Melody didn't speak. They incurred no detention on Tuesday nor on Wednesday nor for the rest of the week. On Saturday, when they were at last able to sleep in, Elizabeth woke at six and lay in bed, staring into the dark. This poisonous, silent truce was almost worse than open battle.

Steve disagreed. In his opinion the girls had moved to a new stage along the road to understanding.

At nine-thirty Elizabeth got up and dressed. Cara was still asleep, which was unusual. She still liked her Saturday-morning cartoons, and she hadn't been able to watch any in quite some time. The coffeepot burbled and hummed, the kitchen was warm, the sun was out, for once, and it streamed through the new yellow curtains and splashed on the bright colors in the rug.

Elizabeth sat with her hands wrapped around her coffee mug and considered the future. She and Steve usually had breakfast on Saturday morning at Humpty Dumpty's. They'd have to establish a new routine if the detentions ceased. She picked up the phone and dialed his number to invite him and Melody for pancakes.

No answer. Probably on his way over, she thought, and began to mix batter. She stood over the bowl with the eggs in her hands and considered Sammy. She made a double recipe.

When Steve appeared a few minutes later, he had neither Sammy nor Melody with him. He punched the bell fifteen times before she could get to the door, and when she opened it, he burst through without even a hello.

"They think I owe them $17,852.64!" he said, wild-eyed. He waved a white piece of paper at her.

"Who, darling?" she asked, divesting him of his coat.

"The IRS, that's who." He gave her an absentminded, perfunctory kiss. "Who did you think?"

"Do you owe them the seventeen K?" She took the paper from his hand and began to read it.

"Libby!" he said. "Of course not! What am I going to do?"

"I told you not to throw those letters away unopened," she said. She shook her head. "Honey, you really are in trouble here."

"This is no time for recriminations," said Steve. "What do I do now? This is from five years ago. How can they do that? Isn't there a statute of limitations?"

"It's seven years for taxes," said Elizabeth. "You did keep your records, didn't you?"

"Of course," he said indignantly. "I just don't know where they are."

"Oh, Steve."

"I know. I need a keeper. Maybe my accountant has them."

"Check. Call him now."

"It's Saturday."

"This time next Saturday you could be doing time. Call him now. Tell him to fax everything he has for the last seven years."

"He's in Maine," said Steve, but he was already at the phone. A short conversation sufficed to determine that the accountant had no idea where Steve's records were, but that he'd fax copies of the tax returns.

"Go home and get them," said Elizabeth. "And find your records—all of your records—and come back over here. And bring Melody and Sammy, because this is going to take all day and into the night. We'll try to get this in some sort of order by Sunday night." She held his coat for him and headed him toward the door. "On Monday I'll call the IRS and see what I can work out. And Steve, do it fast. This is serious."

"You don't need to tell me it's serious," he said. He kissed her, as absentmindedly as before. "Seventeen thousand dollars. That's a whole year of college."

Elizabeth went to the kitchen and started turning out pancakes. She had an army to feed. Two armies, if she counted Sammy.

She woke Cara and bullied her into her clothes.

"Eat now," she said, "or don't eat. Steve and I have to work on his taxes all day."

When Steve and Melody returned, she stuffed them with pancakes, fed the leftovers to Sammy and cleared the table quickly. She didn't notice what the girls were doing, except to say to Melody, "Make yourself at home. You can have any book, any food and any bed I've got. If you feel the need to cloister yourself away from the noise and take a nap, there's a bedroom upstairs across from Cara's and you're welcome to it." To Cara she said, "Honey, I want you to rinse these dishes for me and put them in the dishwasher."

Then she turned to Steve.

"Okay. You separate your receipts and proofs of purchase and things like that into piles. Let me look at your tax returns."

"How can anything be boring and terrifying at the same time?" Steve complained.

Elizabeth looked up from the papers in her hand. "You're a madman, did you know that?"

She worked in silence for a while.

Then she said, "Who did these for you? No wonder you're being audited. Didn't this guy ever hear of income averaging?"

"It's not my job to know what's happening with my taxes," said Steve, somewhat defensively. "It's his."

"For God's sake, Steve, what an attitude. It's your money—you have to know what's going on with it. I'll bet all your investments are in a mutual funds, aren't they?"

"So what?" he said.

She rolled her eyes. "You do need a keeper," she said.

He grinned. "You can have the job," he said. "If you want it."

"I'm going to have to take the job," she said, shaking a handful of receipts at him. "If I want to keep you out of jail. Don't you know you can't deduct car repairs?"

Sammy snuffled in to hunt for more pancakes. Steve called for Melody to take care of him. Noon came and went. Cara complained of being hungry. Elizabeth pointed at the peanut butter. Suppertime appeared. Steve had a pizza delivered, ate his in two bites and told Melody to help Cara clear away the debris. Night came. Elizabeth stood and stretched and told the girls to do their homework. Steve took Melody home at nine so he could put her to bed.

Sunday was a repeat of Saturday. On Monday Elizabeth sent Cara off to school and ordered her not to get another detention—it was too dark after detention for the girls to walk to the train station, and neither she nor Steve could spare the time to pick them up.

Elizabeth planned her day as she headed for her office. The first order of business was to call all her customers to tell them she had an emergency. Then she rang up the IRS, got an appointment for Friday to review Steve's file and delved into his mountain of records.

Steve showed up at nine-thirty with Sammy and a bag of bagels.

The only difference between Sunday and Monday for Elizabeth was that on Monday the school fed the girls lunch. Every night they ordered out—Chinese, pizza, Mexican, until even Cara was sick of restaurant food. The girls did the dishes, Sammy snuffled for food, Steve and Elizabeth worked until nine, Steve went home with Melody, and they repeated the entire process the next day.

On Thursday, Elizabeth told Steve they were ready, and on Friday, when they left for the IRS office, she felt confident that the problem could be resolved easily.

Steve himself was grim. "What if they still want the seventeen thousand?" he said.

"They won't," Elizabeth encouraged. She took his hand as they walked up the steps of the IRS building.

The door was one of those big, steel things with chicken wire between the glass.

"Looks like a minimum security facility," said Steve.

"Don't worry," Elizabeth said, for the twelfth time.

The process took four hours and was conducted in a room without windows. Elizabeth was absorbed in the work; she didn't notice. But to Steve, who was preternaturally aware of his environment, it was like being trapped in a well. Just as he thought he couldn't stand any more, Elizabeth and the IRS agent stood and shook hands, and Elizabeth led Steve into the open air.

"Four thousand dollars," Steve said.

"Could have been worse," said Elizabeth. "Just write the check and forget it."

"Four thousand dollars?" he said. "That's food and clothes and two house payments."

"Don't fret," said Elizabeth, sounding sympathetic. She'd piloted many clients over the tax shoals, and not one of them was ever satisfied. "I'll buy you lunch."

She had hardly thought about the girls all week.

On Saturday Cara came down the stairs at ten-thirty, still in her pajamas.

Elizabeth met her with a smile.

"Feels good to sleep late, huh?" she asked, as Cara sat cross-legged in a chair.

"Yeah."

"No detentions this week," said Elizabeth, setting out cornflakes and milk. "Congratulations."

Cara ate quietly, and all the while she eyed her mother with definite intention. What now? Elizabeth thought, sighing to herself. She sat across from Cara, waiting.

Finally Cara said, "Are Mr. Riker and Melody coming for supper again tonight?"

Elizabeth said they were.

"I hate Melody," said Cara. "It makes me sick to watch her eat."

"I'll put you on the same side of the table, then," said Elizabeth. "Give it up, Cara. It won't work."

"I really tried this week not to fight with Melody," she said. "Just so I could show you. I won't ever fight with her again, if you'll just quit seeing Mr. Riker."

"What?" said Elizabeth, startled. Whatever she'd expected, it wasn't this.

"I hate her," said Cara. "She's horrible."

"She's no more horrible than you are," said Elizabeth, with perfect truth.

Cara's chin trembled and her big green eyes filled with tears. "I'm your own daughter," she said. "I'd think you'd be on my side."

"There's only one side here, Cara," said Elizabeth, who was thoroughly out of patience. "Our side. Yours and mine and Steve's and Melody's."

"But I don't want them here," Cara said, weeping. "They're over here all the time, and all we eat is pizza, and we have to do the dishes. I want to go back to the way we were before. Just tell them to stay away from us."

"Cara, I don't want them to stay away from us," Elizabeth said. "I love Steve."

"I hate him," Cara sobbed.

"Why do you hate him, Cara? He's always been so nice to you."

"He doesn't care anything about me," said Cara, "and besides, I have a father. Daddy says he loves you. I told you that. I don't know why you don't want him."

"I tried to explain, Cara," said Elizabeth. "I know it's hard for you to understand. But try."

"I understand!" said Cara, wildly leaping from her chair. "You don't love me! You only love Melody and Mr. Riker! Well, I'm going to live with Daddy. He said I could come anytime I want to, and I'm going!"

Elizabeth took Cara's shoulders and set her back down in the chair. "You may not do any such thing," she said fiercely. "I want you to understand that. You are not going to live with your father. In the first place, even if he says he wants you, he does not have time to raise a child. In the second place, I will not let you go. In the third place, you are being extremely selfish, and I want it to stop right now. I don't want to hear another word about it. Do you hear me?

Now go and put on your clothes and get yourself back down here. We have work to do."

The detentions started again, in earnest. Miss Westcott called on Thursday, distressed. Melody was a willing participant, but Cara had instigated every incident. And fist fights had resumed on the Lower School fields.

Elizabeth was furious. Cara was obdurate. Steve and Melody continued to come for dinner. Cara was made to sit at the table, but she stared at her plate and wouldn't eat and wouldn't speak. When she was excused, she went to her room.

"It's driving me crazy," Elizabeth told Steve, when they were alone.

"I can tell," he said. It was driving him crazy, too, and breaking his heart to see Elizabeth so distraught.

She clung to him. "I love you so dearly," she said. She sounded forlorn. "How could I live without you?"

Steve raised her chin and looked into the unhappy green eyes.

"Are you thinking about living without me?" he asked quietly, though there was a thick web of fear inside him that blackened his vision and blocked his throat.

"I'm thinking about how I can manage to live with a life full of hostility," she said. Her eyes filled and overflowed and she couldn't stop the tears. "Steve, be honest. Do you still think we can work this out?"

And honestly, he said, "I don't know, darling. I wish I did."

"It's Robert," she said, beginning to cry. "I've tried to explain to Cara. I really have, Steve. I told her he was unfaithful, that he had girlfriends, even when we were married, that he lies to me and to her. She doesn't believe any of it. I don't know what else to do."

He pulled his handkerchief out of his back pocket and wiped her face. She stood passively, like a child, while he attended to her.

"And the worst part—" Elizabeth gulped as he wiped the tears away "—is that Cara's so unhappy. She's not doing this just to be unreasonable."

"I know," said Steve.

"And Steve, she's losing weight, and she's so skinny, anyway," said Elizabeth, sobbing into his shirt. "She can't afford to lose weight. I have to do something about it."

Steve gathered her close and buried his face in her fragrant hair. He knew as he faced his Armageddon, that when he let her go, he would be letting her go forever. The only thing he could do to help her was to make the separation easier for her.

"Maybe we ought to quit seeing each other until things settle down a bit," he said gently. "We'll give it a few weeks and see what happens."

Kalik at work. A world destroyed.

She clutched at him. "I can't bear it," she said.

His face was pale under his tan. He fought his silent struggle with great courage, to control his face and his voice, to protect her from his grief and longing.

"Kiss me now, darling," he said, as sorrow consumed him. "Because the sooner I go, the sooner we can begin to mend."

Walking away from her was the hardest thing he'd ever done.

Elizabeth took enough soup for two up to Cara's room.

"Mr. Riker and Melody have gone," she said.

Cara had been sleeping. She sat up on her bed.

"They're not staying for dinner?"

"No," said Elizabeth. "We thought it was better not to do that anymore."

Cara sipped at the soup. "Oh," was all she said.

Long days and long nights followed. Steve didn't call, nor did Elizabeth call him. But she thought about him all the time. She ached with missing him. His absence was a wound to her heart that would never be healed. She could taste him on her lips, feel his body under her hands, hear his voice in her ears when she woke and when she slept. By day she longed for his companionship. By night she wondered how she could possibly endure a lifetime of sexual deprivation. With Cara she was able to maintain a cheerful face. When she was alone she wept.

The week before Christmas vacation, she sat in her office, unable to work.

I have to pull myself together, she thought anxiously, as tears formed relentlessly and washed down her cheeks. *If I don't, we'll starve.* She hadn't been able to accomplish anything except the most repetitive and uncomplicated of tasks in almost three weeks. And Christmas was coming. She had bought no presents, hadn't sent her mother's box yet, hadn't even considered where she and Cara were going or what they were going to do. Perhaps they should fly to France. She didn't think she could stand to be in Philadelphia. Yes. France. She buried her face in her hands and sagged against her desk.

A rustling made her look up. Cara stood in the door. Elizabeth hastily brushed the tears away and tried to smile.

"Mommy?" said Cara uncertainly.

Cara seldom ever called her Mommy anymore. It was a little girl's habit.

"You're home awfully soon," said Elizabeth, getting out of her chair.

"Just the usual time." Cara went to the window and looked out and didn't speak for several minutes.

"Is something bothering you, cherub?" asked Elizabeth.

Cara turned her big green eyes up to her mother. They were full of trouble.

"Do you love Mr. Riker?" she asked.

Oh, God. How could she talk about Steve without crying? Elizabeth leaned against the door frame to steady herself. "Yes."

"Are you still getting married?"

"No, Cara," said Elizabeth. "We talked about this, remember?"

"Why not?"

"Because, darling, all four of us have to agree," Elizabeth said. "It's a four-person decision."

Cara leaned her palms on the sash and gazed out at the bare trees.

"But you're not happy."

"Do you remember when I told you that unhappiness and disappointment are part of life?"

Cara nodded.

"It's true of grown-ups as well as children. There are some things you can't have, no matter how bad you want them. You have to live with it. It happens to everyone. Now..." she said briskly. "Let's go out and get some dinner. What would you like, pizza?"

They had eaten out every night. Elizabeth couldn't face the memories in the kitchen.

Another sleepless night gave way to another weary morning. Elizabeth intended to go to McNulty's plant, just to get herself out of the house. Seeing McNulty, all pleased with his box works and his software application would lift her spirits. She dropped Cara off at the train on the way.

"That backpack is going to split its seams," she said to Cara, seeing how stuffed it was.

"No, it's not," said Cara. She leaned over the seat and hugged her mother fiercely. "I love you, Mommy," she said. "I love you a really lots."

"I love you a really lots, too, pet," said Elizabeth, smiling. "Have a nice day."

Cara stood among the milling students, waving, until Elizabeth drove away.

Edward McNulty was in buoyant spirits. His expanded company was acquiring new customers at an unprecedented rate—he could see his way to riches and an early retirement, and he felt he owed it all to Elizabeth and her brilliant software. He introduced her to his lawyer, to his wife and to his oldest son, and took them all to lunch at a small Italian restaurant with waiters in tuxedos and three-figure prices.

"You'll never retire early, if you spend money like this," Elizabeth said, laughing at him.

His wife grinned. "If I'd known he could afford a three-hundred-dollar lunch, I'd have bought the shoes I wanted, instead of the ones on sale."

Edward McNulty merely looked smug. He beckoned to the waiter. "Let's talk about grappa," he said expansively. He was having a wonderful time.

"Heaven help us!" said his lawyer, knowing grappa was almost one hundred percent alcohol.

"It's lethal," agreed McNulty, reaching for the bottle. "Have some."

Elizabeth left the celebration feeling much better for the day out. Perhaps she would even cook dinner at home for a change and get a movie for her and Cara to watch.

She went into the house and switched on all the lights. No more work today, she told herself. She built a fire and curled up on the couch with a volume of P.G. Wodehouse and giggled at the antics of Bertie Wooster while she waited for Cara to come in from school.

Suddenly, it seemed, it was dark, and Cara wasn't home yet. Elizabeth got up to look out the windows. It was after five—she had been out of school for over an hour. And there hadn't been a detention—the school always called. Frowning, but telling herself that she wasn't really worried yet, she dialed the Fanes' number.

There was nobody home. Perhaps Cara had made plans to go to Megan's after school, and Elizabeth had just forgotten. Cara was a compulsive record keeper, so the calendar on her desk would have any appointment written down. Elizabeth bolted up the stairs, still insisting to herself that she wasn't concerned. But she was.

On top of Cara's calendar was a sheet of white notebook paper, with Cara's careful schoolgirl script:

Dear Mommy, I have gone to California to live with Daddy so you can be happy.

Love, Cara

Elizabeth's heart stopped in her chest. For a second she

was seized with such panic that she couldn't think. Then with trembling hands she called Steve.

"Cara's gone," she said when he answered. Her voice shook. "She's run away from home."

"I'll be right there," he told her. In fewer than five minutes he was at her house, with Melody and Sammy trailing behind him. Melody was crying.

"Melody helped her get her money out of the bank," said Steve grimly. "They've been planning this for several days. She left as soon as school was out, on a bus, but Melody doesn't know which one."

Elizabeth collapsed white-faced into a kitchen chair.

"Something will happen to her," she whispered wretchedly. "There's so much meanness in the world today. Something will happen to her." All the air seemed sucked out of her. There was a vast, sickening vacuum where her heart and lungs were supposed to be.

Steve had his cellular phone to his ear. He called the central bus station and charted every bus leaving toward the West for the last hour and a half.

"I need to know the scheduled stops," he said, and apparently the employee on the other end gave him a hard time. "Damn it!" he exploded. "I have a child on one of those buses, and I intend to find her in one piece before the night is over!"

Capitulation from the bus company. Steve began to write.

"We have to call the police," said Elizabeth.

"I already have," Steve said. "But we can't just sit here and do nothing. It will kill us. Here's the list of phone numbers for the scheduled stops. Do you have call-waiting?"

Elizabeth nodded.

"Then Cara can call in, if she needs us. You start calling the stop list. I'm going to get the dispatcher to radio every bus. We'll find her, darling. Don't worry." He spoke rapidly into the phone. "I'll wait," he said to the dispatcher, when he had explained what he wanted. "Get moving on this."

Every number Elizabeth dialed had the same answer: they hadn't seen Cara. In the middle of the fifth call, the call-waiting signal beeped. She connected with it, mad with hope.

Robert. Complaining that Cara had called.

"Don't you ever care what's happening to her, Robert?" asked Elizabeth. "She's alone and in trouble and we don't know where she is."

"Of course I care," said Robert, sounding very annoyed. "Why do you think I called? I didn't realize at first that she wasn't at home, and she hung up on me before I could find out where she is. Why'd you tell her she could come here, Elizabeth? You know I can't take care of her. I'm too busy."

Elizabeth paused for only a second, to keep herself from crying. "I despise you, Robert, did you know that? I really, really do. I never realized how much before tonight. A plague-infested gutter rat is a better father than you are. I would list in detail the horrible things that I hope will happen to you, but I have to hang up now so Cara can call me and I can find her before she's raped or murdered."

And she hung up, trembling with rage and terror and physically sick with a horrible, stomach-wrenching fear.

Steve put his arms around her and gave her a brief, hard hug. "Keep calling," he said. He put his phone back to his ear.

He listened intently, then disconnected.

"One of the drivers headed down Lancaster Pike thinks she was on his bus. He's checked, and she's not there now. He doesn't know where she got off."

Elizabeth covered her eyes with her hands and said a prayer. "What shall we do?"

"You know my phone number?" he asked, and waited for affirmation. "I'm going down Lancaster Pike, and I'll stop at every station. You stay here. If you hear from her, call me and tell me where she is."

He hadn't taken off his coat since he'd walked into the house. Now he dropped the phone in his pocket and buttoned it tight.

The phone rang again, and this time it was Cara, calling collect. She was hysterical with terror.

"Cara!" said Elizabeth. "Where are you? Are you all right?"

Cara sobbed into the phone. "Daddy doesn't want me. I called him, and he says he doesn't want me. Can you come get me?"

"Darling, darling, where are you? Tell Mommy."

"I don't know," she wailed.

Steve spoke into the den extension. "Cara, did you take a bus?"

"Yes."

"Do you know what road you're on?"

"No." Sobbing. "I was going to California."

"Did the bus stop lots of times, or are you on a freeway? Stop crying, honey, and help me."

"It stopped." She tried to think. "I think it's going to York."

"Do you know the name of the place where you are?"

"Roadagent's Tavern."

That's appropriate, thought Steve, grimly. "Do you know what town it's in?"

"No," said Cara. "I mean, it's not in a town, it's just on the road, with neon. I got off to go to the bathroom, and the bus left without me." She began to cry again. "And this place is so dark and it scares me, and there was a woman here, but she went upstairs with a man. And all the men when I went to the bathroom said come here, cutie, you're new, and whistled and said really disgusting things, but I had to go, because somebody threw up in the bathroom on the bus and it was disgusting, and then the bus left without me."

Oh, God help us, Steve thought, with panic rising in his throat. *She's in a whorehouse.*

"Stay in the phone booth, honey," Steve said. "Keep the door shut and put your foot against the hinge. Your mom is going to keep talking to you. I'll be right there."

"Keep her on the phone, Libby," he said to Elizabeth. "I'll call the Highway Patrol from the car and get some help."

"I'm sorry, Mommy," said Cara. "I'm really, really sorry."

"Hush, baby," Elizabeth soothed. "Just keep your foot on the hinge, like Steve said, and talk to me about normal things. That'll help make you feel safer."

Cara's voice shuddered over the line. "What, normal?"

"Well, tell me what you packed," suggested Elizabeth, willing herself to sound calm.

"I packed my teddy bear," Cara said, her voice quavering.

"So that was why your backpack was bursting at the seams," said Elizabeth. "Poor Teddy must be squashed by now. You'll have to poke him back into shape when you get home."

As they talked, loud music pulsed over the line, mingled with the clink of dishes and rough voices.

Then Elizabeth heard the crash of glass, and Cara screamed.

"No! Leave me alone! Mommy! Mommy!"

"Come on out of there, sweetheart," said a drunken voice. "You know what you're here for."

"No!" Cara was sobbing. "Let go of me! Let go of me!"

"Let her go!" screamed Elizabeth into the phone. Horror. Terror. "Let her alone! Cara! Cara!"

A slammed door, the pound of running feet and blessedly, Steve's roar. "Leave that child alone! You son of a bitch, I'll break every bone in your body!" And then what sounded like a thunderclap.

"Don't you dare hit him!" Cara shouted. The receiver hit the side of the phone booth with a clank, and Cara's receding voice yelled, "I'll help you, Mr. Riker!"

Then Elizabeth heard the drunk say, "Ow! You little bitch! You bit me!"

"Get back, Cara, out of the way. You turn around here, you bastard! I'm not through with you yet!" growled Steve.

Then another thunderclap and a stranger's awed voice saying, "God, mister, I think you broke his jaw."

"He's damned lucky I didn't kill him for manhandling my daughter. Cara, come here, baby. Are you all right?"

Sirens and police and Cara's sobs came clearly over the wire. Then Steve picked up the dangling receiver and said into Elizabeth's ear, "She's okay, darling. We're on our way home."

Melody threw herself into Elizabeth's arms.

"It's all my fault she left." She wept, full of remorse. "If she gets hurt it's all my fault."

Elizabeth held her tightly and stroked at the shiny hair. "No, honey. You might have helped her, but it's Cara who made the decision."

"It doesn't matter. It's my fault. I was horrible, and it's my fault."

Elizabeth pulled the sobbing child closer to her chest and rocked her back and forth. "Hush, Mel," she said, in an automatic, crooning, maternal sing-song. Everything's all right. You mustn't cry anymore."

"I didn't know Cara could get hurt," she said. "And I didn't know Cara's father didn't want her. How could he not want her? Everybody's parents want them."

"That's not anything you could ever imagine, sweetheart," said Elizabeth, rocking her back and forth. "Quit crying now. She's all right, and so is your dad, and they'll be home here in just a few minutes. Hush, now."

Gradually Melody's tears slowed, and she went to the window to watch anxiously for her father's car.

Steve's headlights were swallowed by the night. Cara sat silently beside him as he drove. Finally she said, "You came after me."

"Of course. And I have never been as glad to see anybody in my life." He reached across the seat and massaged at the back of her neck. "You scared me to death, Cara, do you know that?"

"Daddy didn't care," said Cara in a hard little voice. "He told me I was stupid, and he couldn't send me money, and I couldn't live with him, and hung up."

Steve was silent for a minute. "That would hurt my feelings really bad."

"It hurt mine," Cara said. "And besides, I was scared, and all he could say to do was call Mom."

Steve tugged at the black ponytail. "Well, Cara, realistically, what could he do from three thousand miles away?"

"I don't know. Worried, anyway, instead of sounding mad."

"He is worried. He called as soon as you hung up."

"Ha," said Cara, somewhat mollified.

Steve had a violent inclination to find Robert and pound him into a slimy mass of raw DNA.

"Cara," he said. "About your father."

"I don't ever want to talk about him again," Cara said.

"Honey, he does love you," said Steve.

"Right," said Cara scathingly.

"But some people, Cara, though they love you, can't take responsibility for anyone else. Sometimes they can't even take responsibility for themselves. Your father is one of those people."

"So?" said Cara, and not insolently. She was actually interested.

"Well, you have to love people for what they are, not for what you wish they were. Do you understand that?"

"I guess," she said reluctantly. "I don't know if I can do it, though."

"If you can, you should try," said Steve. "It's not good for you to hate somebody."

There was a silence, while Cara digested this.

"I don't hate you or Melody," she volunteered. "I just don't like Melody very much."

"I think you could learn to like us," he said, smiling to himself in the dark. "If you gave us a chance."

"Oh, I like you, all right," said Cara. "I suppose I could probably like Melody. I've been mean to her."

"She's been mean to you," said Steve. "You two could stop that, couldn't you, if you made up your minds?"

"I guess," said Cara.

"That's a step in the right direction," Steve told her. "I'll do just about anything I can to help you—with that, and with anything else you ever want to do."

"Just about?"

"Yeah. I don't want you to leave home anymore. Your mother and I would be brokenhearted if anything happened to you."

"How can you love me?" mumbled Cara. "You're not my father."

Steve squeezed the back of her neck. "Your mother loves you," he said.

"So?"

"She's not your father."

Cara giggled. It was a little tentative and shaky, but it was definitely a giggle.

Steve squeezed her neck again. "Sammy loves you, and he's not your father."

"You know how to tell if a dog loves you?" asked Cara, after a minute.

"No, how?"

"If you have a piece of bacon and you show it to the dog, and then you wave it in the air, if the dog looks at you and not at the bacon, he loves you."

"He hates me," said Steve. "I just realized."

Cara giggled again. "Mr. Riker?"

"Miss Fairchild, don't you think people who are allies in a bar fight ought to be on a first-name basis?"

Cara giggled nervously. Then she said shyly, "Steve."

"Cara." He tugged at her hair again.

"Are you going to marry my mom?"

"With your permission, madam. You know that we can't have a happy marriage if you and Melody aren't happy."

"Melody doesn't mind," said Cara. "Only me. And I don't guess I mind anymore."

As soon as they pulled into the driveway, both Melody and Elizabeth burst from the house. Melody hugged Cara fiercely, sobbing, and Elizabeth wrapped her arms around them both.

Steve herded his wounded little band into the kitchen. Cara sat on her mother's lap while Steve made hot chocolate. Melody stayed close, as if she were afraid Cara would disappear again, and clung to Elizabeth's hand.

He got hot chocolate down the whole bunch of them, and together, he and Elizabeth put the exhausted children to bed.

Once they were safely tucked in and out of sight, Steve put his arms around Elizabeth and kissed her gently. Her muscles, under his hands, felt like coiled steel.

"All the trouble's over," he said. "You look pretty wrung out, baby. Don't you want to go to bed?"

She inclined her head towards the girls' rooms.

"Oh, not with me, I'm sorry to say," Steve told her. "You can sleep with Sammy. I'll take the couch downstairs."

"I hate setting a good example," said Elizabeth, feeling happy for the first time in weeks.

"Still got a date for New Year's Eve?"

"I think we'd better move that up to this weekend," she said. "Just to make sure it doesn't get away from me again."

"Sounds good," he said, gathering her in closer. "The girls can be bridesmaids and Sammy can carry the ring."

"We can tie it to his collar," said Elizabeth. "And Melody can walk him down the aisle."

"This is very silly, you know," he said.

"I hope it works. The girls can't go from despising each other to—" she grinned "—the Bobbsey Twins in one night."

"Well, no, we can't expect that," Steve agreed, kissing her over and over. "But I did see an olive branch or two being offered. Let's see how it goes. After the wedding, of course.

Go put your nightgown on, sugar. You need to go to bed yourself.''

''It'll be a long night,'' she said. She wanted to stay there until the sun came up, wrapped in his arms.

He smiled. ''Just like the night before Christmas.''

And indeed it was. The kiss he gave her before she went to bed called up vast, remembered pleasures and a joyous, wakeful anticipation of delights yet to come: his hands at her breasts, his legs at her thighs, his mouth heavy on hers, and the long solid feel of him, cuddling her against his naked warmth.

She lay happily wide-eyed until dawn.

Epilogue

On Christmas Eve, as Steve loaded the car with presents, cakes and pies to take to Lin's, Cara received a letter from the Department of Defense.

She ripped into it eagerly, while Melody hovered. Elijah Thomas's picture of his wife and baby were framed and sitting on Cara's desk. She'd been waiting anxiously to discover what had happened to him.

Steve heard both girls shriek and turned to see them caper across the frozen grass.

"He made it! He made it!" shouted Cara. "I knew he would!"

It was as if a personal friend had gotten home from war.

Steve shut the trunk and put Sammy in the car.

"Time to leave," he said. "If you want to see the boys before Lin puts them to bed."

All the way to the farm, the only topic of conversation was Elijah Thomas and what had happened to him next. Steve grinned to himself. Cara would learn more about

American history by digging into Elijah Thomas's life than she'd ever learn in school, and she'd remember every bit of it. No doubt she'd put it in a book someday. She was at the moment writing a novel, having been inspired by the science fiction she'd read. And it was Steve's unbiased opinion that she had the talent to be pretty good. Pretty damned good, in fact, he thought with satisfaction and considerable fatherly pride. A daughter to follow in his footsteps.

Lin's house smelled of Christmas, and the scent of bay and evergreen, roasting turkeys and Virginia ham enveloped them as they went through the door.

The boys bounced wildly from wall to wall.

"Miggy's having puppies!" shouted Sandy. "On the couch."

All six children rocketed into the living room, where Miggy reclined on a Chinoiserie couch that was obviously an antique.

"Geez, Lin," said Steve, as his sister got up to kiss them hello. "What's that dog doing up there?"

"Do not call her 'that dog,'" said Lin. "Not if you want to sleep here."

Steve wasn't intimidated. "Tom and I spent two weeks rebuilding that couch. And I know the fabric was forty dollars a yard."

"Only thirty-eight," said Lin, resuming her position beside Miggy. "Don't exaggerate."

"Can't she sleep in your bed?" said Steve. "It's not worth as much."

"You guys didn't actually think you were restoring this thing for me, did you?" asked Lin. "I thought I told you it was for Miggy to litter on."

"What does Tom say about this?" said Steve, who seemed to think that his brother-in-law had some say in how the zoo was managed.

"Nothing," said Lin. "*He* wants to sleep in my bed."

"I decided I'd rather have Lin than the couch," said Tom. "It came down to that. At least she let me put a tarp under all the activity."

"Poor little Miggy," Lin crooned. "These nasty horrible men just don't understand. Love 'em and leave 'em, that's all they do."

"Demonstrably untrue, my darling," said Tom.

Lin grinned up at him. "I wasn't talking about you."

Miggy gave another yip.

"Cara told me you have all these pups sold," said Elizabeth, laughing at the circus. Steve came up behind her and put his arms around her waist, and she leaned comfortably against him.

Tom tugged at Lin's blond mop. "Yeah. If she has six it will just about pay the vet bill."

"You wait," said Lin, with relish. "Miggy will get her championship at the National this year, and people will be standing in line for her babies."

The first pup emerged.

"Eeuw!" chorused Melody and Cara. "Yuck." They disappeared with the boys in tow.

Miggy finished with the first pup and turned to the second.

They were both sturdy, huge, black infants who bore no resemblance whatsoever to dogdom's prime aristocrat, Champion Pierre's Pappy Pass the Buck. The only evident trace of their poodle ancestry was a tiny spot of white at the end of each tail.

Lin scooped up the first baby and looked him over carefully.

"I thought you had Sammy cut," she said to Steve.

"Well, I meant to," said Steve, looking at Miggy and the two black pups. "Aw, gee, Lin, I'm sorry. Nuts." But he was grinning broadly, along with the rest of the company.

"Yes. Nuts," said Lin. "First I am going to cut off Sammy's, and then I am going after yours."

"Don't do that!" said the new Mrs. Riker. "I'm not tired of him yet."

"Looks like Pappy passed the buck, all right," said Tom with a shocking lack of diplomacy.

"For a man whose wife is so focused on surgical deconstruction," said Elizabeth to Tom, "you're being awfully indiscreet."

"I don't have to worry," said Tom, who had by then begun to laugh. "I'm one of her hobbies."

"Don't count on it," said Lin, examining the second pup with dismay. "Damn. How am I going to explain this disaster to Pappy's poppa and all the other expectant parents?"

Cara came back into the room. "How come they're black?"

"Because Sammy's their daddy," said Lin with a sigh. "Want a puppy?"

"Two Sammys," said Cara, thrilled. "Is there a girl?"

Tom let each of the boys pet the puppies, then he said, "Okay. All the excitement's over." He picked up Johnny, who had been rocking sleepily back and forth. "Come on, boys, it's time for bed."

He and Lin ushered their brood up the stairs. Steve and Elizabeth relaxed on the couch in the family room, enjoying a big fire and listening to the girls clanking around in the kitchen, looking for snacks.

"It would be really fun if you had a dog, too," said Melody, offering peace.

"We could walk them together," said Cara, grabbing the end of the olive branch.

"And you know what? Tomorrow, we could ride..." She stopped. "Do you hate all horses, or only some?"

"Just some," said Cara cautiously. "The ones that bite."

"Oh!" said Melody. "Aunt Lin's horses never bite. They're really well trained." She hesitated. "There's one named Caesar, who's really black. He'd look good with your hair. You could ride him, if you want to. He doesn't ever run if you don't want him to."

"I could let him run," said Cara, unable to admit inexperience.

"It makes your legs strong," Melody said. "Good for lacrosse. I've been practicing running for the game against the Linwoody guys."

Cara giggled. "Did you know the boys have to wear our uniforms?"

"Our *kilts?*" said Melody, agape at the prospect of all those gangly male legs. "*Really*, they wear our *kilts?*"

Elizabeth, hearing all this, smiled and snuggled contentedly against Steve. He was warm and solid against her. His arms were tight and strong around her, and they were hers. Their days were filled with joy and laughter; their nights were filled with love; their future was filled with possibilities wonderful to contemplate.

The girls weren't babies anymore, thought Elizabeth, listening to Johnny's infant jabber wafting down the stairs. But there were babies yet to be.

* * * * *

COMING NEXT MONTH

#973 THE BRIDE PRICE—Ginna Gray
That Special Woman!
Wyatt Sommersby couldn't help but be attracted to the passionate
Maggie Muldoon. When her free-spirited nature resisted Wyatt's
tempting proposal of marriage, it left Wyatt wondering—what
would be the price of this bride?

#974 NOBODY'S CHILD—Pat Warren
Man, Woman and Child
Feeling like nobody's child compelled Lisa Parker to search out her
true parents. It brought her face-to-face with J. D. Kincaid, a
man whose emotional past mirrored her own, and whose tough exterior
hid a tender heart....

#975 SCARLET WOMAN—Barbara Faith
Years ago, Clint Van Arsdale watched as his brother eloped with
Holly Moran, a girl from the wrong side of the tracks. Now Holly
was a widow—yet despite the pain of a shared past, Clint could
no longer escape their undeniable attraction.

**#976 WHAT SHE DID ON HER SUMMER VACATION—
Tracy Sinclair**
Melanie Warren's vacation jaunt unexpectedly landed her in an
English country manor. When the very proper and very sexy
David Crandall invited her to become nanny to his adorable
twins, she just couldn't turn him down....

#977 THE LAST CHANCE RANCH—Ruth Wind
Life's hard knocks forced Tanya Bishop to leave her son in the
care of strong and sensible Ramon Quezada. Returning home to
reclaim her lost child, she didn't count on falling under Ramon's
seductive spell.

#978 A FAMILY OF HER OWN—Ellen Tanner Marsh
Jussy Waring's lonely heart longed for that special kind of family
she'd only heard about. When Sam Baker came into her and her
young niece's life, would she dare hope that her dream could
finally come true?

MILLION DOLLAR SWEEPSTAKES (III)

No purchase necessary. To enter, follow the directions published. Method of entry may vary. For eligibility, entries must be received no later than March 31, 1996. No liability is assumed for printing errors, lost, late or misdirected entries. Odds of winning are determined by the number of eligible entries distributed and received. Prizewinners will be determined no later than June 30, 1996.

Sweepstakes open to residents of the U.S. (except Puerto Rico), Canada, Europe and Taiwan who are 18 years of age or older. All applicable laws and regulations apply. Sweepstakes offer void wherever prohibited by law. Values of all prizes are in U.S. currency. This sweepstakes is presented by Torstar Corp., its subsidiaries and affiliates, in conjunction with book, merchandise and/or offerings. For a copy of the Official Rules send a self-addressed, stamped envelope (WA residents need not affix return postage) to: MILLION DOLLAR SWEEPSTAKES (III) Rules, P.O. Box 4573, Blair, NE 68009, USA.

EXTRA BONUS PRIZE DRAWING

No purchase necessary. The Extra Bonus Prize will be awarded in a random drawing to be conducted no later than 5/30/96 from among all entries received. To qualify, entries must be received by 3/31/96 and comply with published directions. Drawing open to residents of the U.S. (except Puerto Rico), Canada, Europe and Taiwan who are 18 years of age or older. All applicable laws and regulations apply; offer void wherever prohibited by law. Odds of winning are dependent upon number of eligible entries received. Prize is valued in U.S. currency. The offer is presented by Torstar Corp., its subsidiaries and affiliates in conjunction with book, merchandise and/or product offering. For a copy of the Official Rules governing this sweepstakes, send a self-addressed, stamped envelope (WA residents need not affix return postage) to: Extra Bonus Prize Drawing Rules, P.O. Box 4590, Blair, NE 68009, USA.

SWP-S795

As a Privileged Woman, you'll be entitled to all these Free Benefits. And Free Gifts, too.

To thank you for buying our books, we've designed an exclusive FREE program called *PAGES & PRIVILEGES™*. You can enroll with just one Proof of Purchase, and get the kind of luxuries that, until now, you could only read about.

BIG HOTEL DISCOUNTS

A privileged woman stays in the finest hotels. And so can you—at up to 60% off! Imagine standing in a hotel check-in line and watching as the guest in front of you pays $150 for the same room that's only costing you $60. Your *Pages & Privileges* discounts are good at Sheraton, Marriott, Best Western, Hyatt and thousands of other fine hotels all over the U.S., Canada and Europe.

FREE DISCOUNT TRAVEL SERVICE

A privileged woman is always jetting to romantic places. When you fly, just make one phone call for the lowest published airfare at time of booking—or double the difference back! PLUS— you'll get a $25 voucher to use the first time you book a flight AND 5% cash back on every ticket you buy thereafter through the travel service!

SSE-PP3A

𝓕REE GIFTS!

A privileged woman is always getting wonderful gifts.
Luxuriate in rich fragrances that will stir your senses (and his). This gift-boxed assortment of fine perfumes includes three popular scents, each in a beautiful designer bottle. <u>Truly Lace</u>...This luxurious fragrance unveils your sensuous side. L'Effleur...discover the romance of the Victorian era with this soft floral. <u>Muguet des bois</u>...a single note floral of singular beauty.

YOURS FREE!

$50 VALUE

𝓕REE INSIDER TIPS LETTER

A privileged woman is always informed. And you'll be, too, with our free letter full of fascinating information and sneak previews of upcoming books.

𝓜ORE GREAT GIFTS & BENEFITS TO COME

A privileged woman always has a lot to look forward to. And so will you. You get all these wonderful FREE gifts and benefits now with only one purchase...and there are no additional purchases required. However, each additional retail purchase of Harlequin and Silhouette books brings you a step closer to even more great FREE benefits like half-price movie tickets... and even more FREE gifts.

L'Effleur...This basketful of romance lets you discover L'Effleur from head to toe, heart to home.

Truly Lace... A basket spun with the sensuous luxuries of Truly Lace, including Dusting Powder in a reusable satin and lace covered box.

𝓒omplete the 𝓔nrollment 𝓕orm in the front of this book and mail it with this Proof of Purchase.

PROOF OF PURCHASE
Offer expires October 31, 1996

SSE-PP3